T0005765

MERCY MERCY

a novel

Marlene Stanton

The Acorn Press
Charlottetown
2019

ACORNPRESS

P.O. Box 22024
Charlottetown, Prince Edward Island
C1A 9J2
acornpresscanada.com

Edited by Marianne Ward
Designed by Matt Reid
Cover illustration by Krista Wells
Printed in Canada

Library and Archives Canada Cataloguing in Publication

Title: Mercy, mercy / Marlene Stanton.
Names: Stanton, Marlene, author.
Identifiers: Canadiana (print) 20190154195 | Canadiana (ebook)
20190154209 | ISBN 9781773660202
(softcover) | ISBN 9781773660455 (HTML)
Classification: LCC PS8637.T354 M47 2019 | DDC C813/.6—dc23

The publisher acknowledges the support of the
Government of Canada, the Canada Council of the Arts
and The Province of Prince Edward Island.

For Tony and Krista

Chapter One

"Christ, that took long enough. I just about ran out of tape." Danny jerked the camera off its stand. The woman Mercy had just interviewed was barely out of earshot.

"She was nervous. Give her a break." Mercy bent down and put the microphone in the kit bag. Danny was already collapsing the tripod, the halls of the court-house amplifying the tortured sigh of metal sliding against metal.

"I heard lawyers are supposed to be smart. Guess I heard wrong." He unbuckled the battery belt and dropped it at his feet.

"Well, this one happens to be more thoughtful than most," Mercy said. "Legal aid lawyers can be like that." With an effort she kept her voice light, reasonable.

"Two minutes of tape's plenty for that type. Me, I'd get a clip, just the basics, then get us out of here. Efficient, that's me. Bim, bam, thank you, ma'am. But you...you think you got to stand there listening to all that crap about *on the one hand* and *on the other hand,* blah, blah, blah. If you ask me—"

"Well, I won't. Okay?"

They had worked together only a few times, but somehow Danny always found an occasion to trumpet his favourite slogan: *A picture's worth a thousand reporters.* Then he would wait, chin thrust forward, for her to react. Did he ever try it on Chaz, his regular partner? Not likely. So, why her? Just trying to prove himself the alpha dog?

In the van now, Mercy looked out the side window as they came to a small park, hoping for something to distract her from the irritation she felt. Danny was driving slowly, maybe preparing another jab. She watched a couple of toddlers in bright red sweaters wrestle on the grass in a play area. Bigger children dangled from monkey bars. On nearby swings, legs pumped and pumped, as if trying to soar beyond what the rusted chains could possibly deliver. Moms were exhorting kids to leave the fun, come and help a little brother or sister back into the stroller because it looked like rain.

Danny was quiet as he navigated the one-way streets that surrounded the park. Mercy let her mind wander until it arrived at an image, an engraving she had once seen of this very square as it was a century-and-a-half ago, with formally dressed Victorian ladies and gentlemen strolling through manicured gardens, posing, examining flowers, all very civilized. It was a scene that might have greeted Sir John A. and his band of merry tipplers, the Fathers of Confederation, as they arrived for the historic meeting in this tiny perfect city, an unlikely venue for the creation of an enormous unwieldy country.

As Mercy got out of the van behind the television station she heard what sounded like a muffled boom. One of the old cannons mounted at the harbour? Some special occasion? A one-gun salute to mark the visit of a minor head of state?

But by the time she and Danny were at the back door, a horn at the downtown fire hall was blaring five long notes, and within seconds the first siren whooped, immediately overtaken by another siren, and another, until it sounded like every piece of equipment in the department was on its way to the party, wailing in anticipation.

Mercy got her cellphone out as they ran back to the van. Before they were out of the parking lot she had the location and told the assignment desk they were on their way.

Danny parked as close as they could get, a block away, and got out the gear. A light misty rain was starting. Mercy took their yellow rain slickers from the back seat and passed one to Danny.

Fire trucks jammed the street in front of an old wooden two-storey building on the fringes of Charlottetown's business area. The storefronts were occupied by a flower shop and an insurance agent. Despite the rain, gawkers had already gathered. The police gently shooed them away and helped drivers manoeuvre around the scene.

Black smoke seeped from around the window frames of the flower shop. Three firefighters went through the front door. But something behind the building was producing a thick cloud that pushed skyward. No flames so far. It didn't look like much. Whatever story she got here would likely be kicked off the lineup before the six o'clock newscast.

She spotted Danny moving quickly to get the basic shots: hoses snaking from the trucks, lights flashing, the faces of watchers, details of the building. He knew the drill.

A middle-aged man in a suit stood near her, a huge stack of files under his arm.

"We heard an explosion," Mercy said. "Do you know what that was?"

"Something in the basement, I think. Everybody got out, thank God." Papers slid from a file to the ground. Mercy picked them up. His hand shook as he took them.

A team of cops now carried saw-horse barriers, herding people ahead of them, away from the site of the smoke. Within thirty seconds Mercy was aware that this was more than routine. She looked for the fire chief, normally watching from the sidelines, and spotted him at the ladder truck, hunched over a cellphone, in what looked like a tense conversation. Not the time to ask for an interview. Another crew arrived to haul more hoses to the back of the building, and more cops appeared, now actually pushing people, impatient. But still no flames.

Danny came toward her, the camera still on his shoulder.

"I've got lots of cover shots," he said. "What've you got? Interviews lined up?"

"Not yet." Over his shoulder she saw two firefighters heading down the driveway carrying a piece of equipment that looked like a rack.

"See if you can get some shots behind the building before they kick us out."

He looked toward the laneway. "You could get a couple more batteries out of the truck while you're waiting," he said. "Make yourself useful, like?"

"Batteries are your job, Danny. Mine is to find out

what's going on."

He tried the familiar smirk. "Could be tricky back there, smoke and stuff. Might need you for a guide dog. But in my opinion, it's nothing much. Don't think you'll need those shots."

"Goddamn it, Danny, just get the shots, will you? And cut the attitude. I'll call your cell when the chief's ready for an interview."

His smile told her he was enjoying her anger. He handed over the full tape, pulled a fresh one from the pocket of his rain jacket, loaded it, and walked off. At the driveway he started down slowly, camera on his shoulder, tape rolling, one eye against the viewfinder, his feet feeling for the hoses as he moved. She knew he was right about the smoke. And it wasn't unusual for a reporter to act as a guide when the shooter couldn't see what was underfoot. She turned away.

There were now twice the number of firefighters usually found at a small fire, their yellow jackets, like Danny's, giving an odd cheerfulness to the scene. The fire chief was still on the phone, now with the police chief beside him. She tried to stop a cop going by. He kept moving but shouted over his shoulder, "Get out of here!"

No way was she leaving this scene. The excitement around her was palpable now. She felt as alert as a deer but at the same time inexplicably safe. She had experienced it a couple of times before. Other reporters had described it, too: heightened reflexes, a sharper eye, and a feeling of invulnerability, a burst of energy impossible to dampen.

Her cellphone rang. She thought of ignoring it, then scrambled to get it out and open. Jinxy, the assignment editor, more stressed than usual.

"Emergency Measures is evacuating. Evacuating! Got that? All the blocks around the fire. Something serious going on. Won't say what. We're getting a bulletin to air in two minutes."

"I'm right in front here. No flames. Chemicals maybe? No one has time to talk. Danny's shooting around the back."

"Find him. Get away from the building. Look for shots of people leaving their homes. Clips, too, if you can. I've already sent Chaz and a cameraman to the top of the parking garage. They can pick it up from there. Close enough. You got the basics?"

"Action and smoke. No interviews."

"Be careful." He hung up.

She punched in Danny's cell number and got his voice mail. Deliberately ignoring her?

"Get out of there, Danny. Now. EMO's evacuating. Meet me at the van."

Only cops and firefighters were left. But lots of them. And they weren't bothering Mercy. Must be her yellow rain jacket. Ironically, it made her as good as invisible. Down the block in both directions police blared at stragglers through megaphones, their voices loud but muffled.

The first blast of energy had now become a thumping excitement. She moved quickly to get out of the danger zone, passing the chief, still with a phone to his ear. In the next block where they had left the van, people streamed past, away from the scene. But no Danny. Along the street a few cops knocked on doors. An elderly woman came out holding a white cat. She went back in. The cop paced on the porch.

Mercy looked at her watch. She would give Danny five minutes, then go looking. But she couldn't wait and within two minutes she was heading back, against the flow of people.

The cop at the corner barrier stopped her. "No way, lady. Leave now. This is an emergency."

"My cameraman's still in there. Behind the building. I need to look."

"Somebody'll get him. Not you." He turned away and shouted something to the cop on the next barrier. It sounded like "friggin' morons."

Another uniform arrived at the corner and gave fresh orders. The two cops nearest Mercy picked up the barrier and advanced toward her. She retreated, but sideways. They passed and headed for the next corner, expanding the area of the danger zone. She imagined cops following the same orders on streets all around the smoking building.

No one was watching her now. Black smoke still hung above the building halfway down the block. Was she only imagining that it looked less intense than when they'd arrived?

She started along the block to the left. By the third house she was in a direct line with the source of the smoke but still had no clear view. At a narrow driveway she squeezed past a car. The backyards were deep. She tried pushing through a scrawny hedge, tore her hand on a thorn, only to be faced by a wire fence and forced to detour until she found a route across three more lots behind buildings on the same street as the flower shop. Then the side wall of a three-storey brick apartment building stopped her, the last obstacle between her and the smoke. She followed the wall to the rear, crossed a half empty parking area below a confusion of outdoor stairways, and stepped around the last corner.

Behind the smoking building sat a big silver tanker truck. Large white letters on its side—MILK—nothing else. It was parked parallel to the back wall, less than a metre away. Black smoke poured through a nearby opening that had once been a basement window. A set of concrete steps disappeared down to what must be a cellar door. It was hard to see. She could understand why the yellow jackets were important. But there were no firefighters anywhere here. All that was left was the rack she had seen them carrying earlier, now with hoses inserted, trained on the tanker. A steady hiss came from the truck as hot metal turned the water to steam. She was about ten metres away, and the heat was intense but not unbearable. Still, there was no way she wanted to go any closer. And where in hell was Danny?

She moved back around the corner and dialed the newsroom. Jinxy hadn't heard from Danny. And he was sending a third camera to cover the evacuation.

"Come on in, Mercy. You've done enough. He knows how to look after himself."

Okay. One last look and she would leave. But something had changed. There were now only two hoses aimed at the truck, and the smoke coming from the basement was a wispy grey. It struck her that the scene was pretty bizarre. All this effort to protect a truck full of milk? Somebody would have to explain.

At that moment the cellar door opened from inside. She could see only the heads and shoulders of a couple of firefighters. But their shouts drew her closer, to a full view down the outside stairwell, where Danny lay in a loose fetal curl at their feet.

The camera was on top of him, covering his head. A firefighter lifted it away. Danny's skull was crushed, his neck twisted at a grotesque angle, the only sign of life the moving worm of an almost black liquid feeding into the small pool on the bottom step. The rain suddenly came on in a rush and, as she watched, the blood became gradually lighter, more red, as it mixed with the rain and puddles of water gathered in the folds of Danny's yellow jacket.

Chapter Two

The small waiting room reeked of cheap aftershave, either left behind by the last patient or reaching her from the man who slouched opposite, a magazine hiding his face. Mercy's next glance caught him peeking at her, like a timid hunter using *Maclean's* for a duck blind. Should she lean over and say that she, too, was embarrassed to find herself here, apparently unable to cope?

"Mercy Pepper?" The assistant smiled from the doorway and led her in. Mercy shook Dr. Novak's hand for the fourth time that week. The routine reminded her of an amateur play rehearsal. Trouble was, she hadn't been learning her lines.

Mercy had been assigned a therapist who must have skipped every other grade to get a PhD before his first shave and was still waiting for that teenage growth spurt. Maybe it was the blond curly hair, the guileless blue eyes, like a cherub in a Renaissance painting. She felt no more like confiding in him than she would in the paperboy.

"Glad you're here, Mercy. Ready for another chat?"

When she didn't answer right away he started talking again. "So, how's it going?" The body language said he sincerely wanted to know.

"Fine. Fine. Can't wait to get back to work."

"Well, sure. But let's give it a little more time."

He kept the smile, gestured to the upholstered chair, and took the one facing her, hitching it forward an inch.

"How are you sleeping?"

"Eight hours, at least. No change there."

"Just checking. You've done well."

Done *what* well? Sleeping was about it. And showing up here, of course. Dressed, fed, and watered and without detectable body odour. Looking very much like her old self.

But inside, in some newly formed hollow place in her chest, there was now a disturbing tremor, weak but constant, like the fluttering wings of a trapped and dying moth. The trembling was there waiting as soon as she was conscious in the morning, even though she slept soundly every night, had no dreams, her bed like a narcotic.

At their first session Dr. Novak explained that some people reacted that way to trauma, using sleep as a kind of escape. He offered sedatives, just in case. She pocketed them without thinking.

Now he shifted in his chair, appeared to be settling in. "So what do you think we might sort out today?"

"Well, let's see." She put a finger to her lip and gazed out a window blazing with light. "We could work on controlling the Taliban. Then, um, maybe have a go at finding Osama bin Laden? A little therapy needed there, wouldn't you say?"

But when she turned back to him his smile was gone, his face closed, disappointed.

"Sorry," she offered. And she meant it, aware that

she had turned into a nasty person almost overnight. No, not overnight. She'd been headed in this direction for a while.

The day the twin towers came down in New York, eight months ago now, she'd had to watch hours of video fed in by satellite from the scene. Her assignment was to choose the shots for a montage to run to the evening newscast. People at home had been learning the details all day. More facts were not needed. The pictures said it all. Her editor's hands shook as he worked at the monitor. Instead of the usual voice-over, she asked him to add only the strains of Samuel Barber's moving *Serenade for Strings*.

That was the day she became conscious that the world was entering a new and monstrous decade, when fear would never be far away. She tried to bury her anger. But now she saw Danny's death as a direct result of that anger. She had been impatient with him and now she was being rude to this sincere counsellor.

"Sorry," she said again. "That was unfair. I don't really see why I'm here."

"No need to apologize." He got the smile going again, then a little furrow in the brow. "You've had a stressful event this week. You don't seem ready to talk about it, at least not here. Maybe you have a good friend who's willing to listen?"

"The thing is," she began, "I want to get my life back to normal. My job's a big part of that life. And you probably have clients who need your time more than I do. I could go back to work tomorrow."

But he didn't appear to have heard. "Have you tried writing it all down?" he asked, leaning a little closer. "A kind of journal of what happened and how you feel about it? I think I suggested that."

"I did try, yes. It came out like a news report. The only kind of writing I know how to do. Where I'm the observer, not the participant."

"Yes, I see."

Does he?

"We've only had a few sessions, Mercy." He glanced at the file on his knee. "Three before today." He sounded as if she was returning his product, found to be faulty.

Therapy was mandatory for anyone involved in an accidental, work-related death. She knew that much. Touted by her union rep as a hard-won job benefit. The minimum number of sessions was four. And she had opted to complete them on consecutive days, the last one today.

"Look, Dr. Novak. Please don't think you haven't helped me. You have. And I feel quite all right." She hoped it sounded sincere.

"Yes, I understand what you're saying. But Mr., uh, your executive producer..."

"Arthur."

"Yes. He's very concerned. On top of the events of last week, I understand that your daily job can be stressful, too."

"It's a good kind of stress. It suits me."

He peered at her. "So you're sure you don't want any more sessions here?"

"I'll take it slowly," she promised. "And you'll be the first person I'll call if there's a problem."

Friday morning now, like any old workday, but a new start, just what she wanted. And behind her, another night of perfectly blank sleep. The plan was to be at her desk when the rest arrived. Better yet, on the phone, busy, like nothing had changed. But the usual morning routine at home seemed to take longer than normal and she didn't manage to leave earlier after all.

The TV station was less than twenty minutes away, a drive that took her from the bucolic farmland that surrounded the old schoolhouse where she lived, to the very heart of Charlottetown. Most mornings Mercy welcomed those minutes, time enough to sort out details of whatever story she was working on, the interviews she should get, what shots were needed. But she had nothing in the works now, and after only four days off she already felt out of touch, limp.

Today the sun was too bright, bouncing off every piece of metal in the car, like a stage light on some giddy song and dance number from *Anne of Green Gables—The Musical.* New leaves seemed to have exploded on bare branches overnight. Fresh grass thrust itself through last year's dead sod, all too green. Coming down the road to the bridge over the Hillsborough River, the old Toyota sped toward her goal without effort. A few blocks farther, through a modest suburb, and the car pulled in behind the station. As she got out, the smell of bacon frying at the nearby fast-food outlet made her stomach zig.

Not a chance now of being first into the newsroom. At least half of them would be there already. Walk briskly, not too fast, climb the ramp to the door. Hold the security card up to the thingamajig. Wait for the click. Get in, right turn, down a few steps and along the hall. No buzz of voices from inside. Just the familiar shabby door with *Newsroom* painted black on white, to which some long-departed joker had added red paint dripping like blood from the letters.

Instead of walking straight in she turned left toward the washroom, locked herself in a cubicle, and stood with her back against the cool metal of the door. She had been so eager to be back that it hadn't occurred to her until this minute that with a week to talk about what had happened to Danny, her colleagues might now have placed some of the blame squarely on her shoulders. She would see it in their eyes. Just as they would see the guilt in hers.

Her thoughts were interrupted by a voice in the hallway humming the theme from *Hockey Night in Canada.* She took a couple of deep breaths and ventured out. The only person in the newsroom was Jinxy Doyle, the assignment editor, phone to his ear, thick white hair hanging over his eyes. He raised a hand in greeting, grinned at her, said a few more words into the receiver, and hung up.

"Hey, thought you'd forgotten us." He gestured for her to join him at the large meeting table and passed over a copy from the stack of local newspapers. She took it, relieved to have something to do, and sat down beside him.

"Where is everybody? Thought I was late."

"Waiting for Arthur. His Friday fitness class."

"Ah, yes. How could I forget? Vital stuff, fitness."

Jinxy would have been here since seven, organizing the next few hours, matching assignments to reporters and camera techs, checking national stories on the wires, getting a sense of how the day might unfold.

Three years ago when Mercy had arrived at his desk, newly hired from the Ottawa city bureau, she was feeling ready for a fresh start. But her enthusiasm didn't impress Jinxy. He'd taken a faded newspaper clipping from his drawer. It showed a brown-eyed toddler wearing a tiny gold crown.

"Cute. Yours?" she'd asked, to be polite.

He'd pointed to the date: July 12, 1949. The *Peterborough Examiner*. She read the cutline. "Fourteen-month-old Jamie Doyle. This year's Golden Corn Syrup Baby."

"'Twas I, my dear. It's been downhill ever since." His attempt at an Irish accent made her laugh. "And look at me now. Just another middle-aged journalist gone to seed. And what's your story? What brought you to our little backwater?"

"Oh, you know, a change of pace."

"Most traffic goes the other way. Reporters want to move up, not down." He pulled a chair over and pointed her into it.

"Listen," he said. "I'm not trying to embarrass you. I'm a good listener. So feel free to let loose your life story any time. Otherwise your new colleagues here will make it up for you. And it'll be too late for damage control." He took off his glasses and leaned closer. "Only one word about you has reached us from Ottawa. *Creative*. Not a desirable quality in someone paid to report the facts."

Then, without a pause, he laughed out loud. It was the moment she realized she had a new friend.

Now reporters and producers began to straggle in, nobody making a fuss at seeing Mercy, saying *hi* or *good to see you back*, a greeting for someone returning from vacation. But the usual relaxed banter was missing. They looked serious, wary, as if a fragile package had arrived. Then, last to join them, Arthur, red-faced from the gym.

"Mercy!" He sped over, the thunderous voice arriving well in advance, his short legs moving so fast he might have been on wheels. For a heavy man he was amazingly graceful. She had once watched him dancing an old-fashioned waltz at a staff party with his wife, also short and plump. They moved as one, feather-light, two dolls on top of a music box.

"Hello, Arthur." She tried for serenity but sounded tense.

"Look!" he said, pointing at her. "Great!"

The meeting followed its familiar pattern. Jinxy listed the events that couldn't be ignored. There were groans. He reminded people about stories that were already in the works or needed follow-up. A couple of reporters made pitches for extra research time, promising a good story. But today, no one made the sale. Chaz, the political reporter, was deep into a phone conversation at his desk, his way of avoiding the morning meeting. A producer criticized a report from last night's newscast, pointing out that a couple of shots didn't match the script.

"Saw that," Arthur said, ever ready to jump aboard a passing bandwagon. "Sloppy. Loses viewers."

Somewhere on his way up the administrative career ladder Arthur had picked up the mannerisms of a reporter from a 1930s movie, the newsman wearing a porkpie hat with a press card stuck in the brim. Arthur rarely spoke in full sentences.

Feet shuffled under the table, eyes wandered. Normally Mercy would have been as twitchy as the rest, eager to get away to the phones before that full tank of early energy was sucked away by the numbing routine of the meeting. But today it worked on her like a tonic, as if she had come back from a long, dangerous voyage and was seeing the familiar scene with fresh eyes.

Arthur ended the meeting with the daily groaner. "Go out. Slay dragons. For Arthur." They had given him a toy sword last Christmas.

She started toward her desk, planning to call a crown prosecutor to ask about new cases in the works so she wouldn't go down to the courthouse cold.

"Mercy. My office. Little chat."

"Sure, Arthur."

She stopped at the assignment desk. "So if the docket sounds interesting, Jinxy, will you send a camera to meet me at court later?"

"No. He won't." Arthur threw the words over his shoulder as he walked away.

Mercy followed him into his office and he closed the door. In spite of its large corner window the room felt crowded. Almost every surface was overloaded with papers and files, even the windowsills. She took the hard chair, the only one for visitors. Arthur went to the big soft one behind his desk and began flicking the edges of a file, not looking at her.

"Something new," he said. "Opportunity."

"Oh, yes?"

"No court. No police. Julie's on it. For now. Learning."

Mercy sat motionless. He held up a hand. "Don't interrupt. Julie's okay. Short-term." Then he nodded, the usual signal that no more booming word clots were on the way.

"Arthur, I'd really like to go back to what I've been doing."

"Not yet. Slow down. Avoid setback." His gaze wandered to the ceiling.

"I'm fine, Arthur."

"Halls of government. Big decisions."

Was he talking to himself? Musing?

"Politics," he continued. "Fascinating."

Politics? What did politics have to do with her? Maybe she hadn't heard right.

"Change. Do you good."

"Oh, no. Please, Arthur. You can't." But of course he could. "I've never been interested in local politics. You know this. I find it boring and predictable."

"Think so?" He was looking at her now. "Bad attitude."

"And where does that leave Chaz?" she asked. "Are you saying we need *two* political reporters? For a legislature the size of a doll's house?" She had to make him see how ridiculous it was. "And a provincial budget that could fit into Bill Gates's change purse?"

Arthur's eyes drifted to the ratings graph above her head. "Chaz? Busy. Election coming. You? Daily stuff. Announcements. Committee reports. Press conferences—"

"In other words," she snapped, "all the tame, filler junk you'd give a kid right out of college, someone here for the summer. Someone..." She could hear the panic in her voice. The words were coming out too fast.

She had his attention now. His eyes registered alarm. He stood up in a rush and the chair bounced back against the window ledge. She heard herself as she must have sounded to him: close to hysteria.

She covered her mouth to cut off the next stream of words and waited.

"Trust me," he said, and picked up the phone and punched in four numbers. "Chaz. In here." Then he spun his chair to face the window until Chaz opened the door and Arthur waved him in. "Shut it."

Chaz moved his big, smartly dressed frame to the bookcase and parked himself against it, arms folded.

Arthur glared at him. "Election date? Hell! Asked you twice."

Chaz searched the corners of the room. "Jesus, Arthur. That isn't info you get on the recorded message from the weather office. Word is, the premier hasn't even decided himself yet."

"Not possible. Fixed date. Already agreed." Arthur pointed at the calendar on the wall above the bookcase.

Chaz turned and looked, as if there was new information there. Then he unfolded his arms, took a deep breath, and gave Mercy one of his knowing winks before turning back to Arthur.

"This delay isn't a crisis, Arthur. I explained it all last week. The government is looking at a computerized voting system. It would be a first. Special training. All that stuff. More prep time needed. And, anyway, that fixed election date was never written in stone. It was just to make planning easier."

"Damned right!" Arthur's face was flushed. "Clock's ticking. People talking." He sounded close to tears, stopped suddenly, and waved the air in front of him.

"Point is." His voice fell to a hiss. "Our role. My role. Vital. Election night. Live coverage. Preparation. Planning. Decisions. All on me!"

"I know, Arthur." Chaz held up his hands, a surrender. "Your job's enormous. *And* crucial. No one can pull an election broadcast together better than you. But we'll still have the four weeks of the campaign."

"Not enough. The date. Get it. Like last time. That leak."

"Well, sorry, Arthur. I believe this time the premier really hasn't picked the date."

"Unacceptable."

"Yes, of course, it's unfair to you, Arthur. All this on your shoulders. But you'll rise to it as you always do. You're amazing. Really, you are."

Arthur sat up a little straighter. "Keep at him. Get that date." His voice was calmer now. Not for the first time Mercy saw how Chaz could handle Arthur.

"Absolutely, I promise." Chaz put his right hand over his heart. "Soon as the premier decides, you'll have it."

Arthur looked at Mercy for the first time since Chaz had arrived.

"I've told her. She'll do it." His stare dared her to contradict him.

"Good decision." Chaz gave her a thumbs up and walked out, closing the door behind him.

It felt like a defeat. Did Chaz think she'd be his *assistant?* That she'd be following him around now like a puppy? But she had to be honest—this assignment wasn't his fault. However unappealing she found him these days, Chaz was good at his job. He understood all the weighty economic issues like transfer payments and federal/provincial cost sharing. He never faltered during live segments. And he did have fans. Some older viewers even wrote in to say he looked like a young Tom Selleck. Well, around the eyes anyway.

"All right, Arthur," she said. His eyebrows lifted. "Just don't expect me to win any more of those." She jerked a thumb toward his "Wall of Excellence" then walked out the door. Two of the citations bore her name.

Chapter Three

Mercy stood in the hallway outside Arthur's office with her fists clenched. Little Dr. Novak could have a field day analyzing the last ten minutes. Back in the newsroom Jinxy was standing at her desk, lion-tamer pose, her chair in front of him.

"You knew about this?" she asked.

"Arthur wanted *me* to tell you. Typical. I said he'd have to do his own dirty work." He moved away from the chair and bowed her into it. "Listen, you know him. Still believes in chivalry, all that. Last Friday was probably the roughest day you'll ever have. Rougher than any of us have had."

"Except Danny."

"Well, sure..." His hand rubbed the back of his neck. "It's... Arthur expected you to react more like, I don't know, that you'd burst into tears, need a man to console you."

No, there had been no tears. But as she had looked down at Danny's body, dark threads had crowded into her line of vision. She'd turned away and groped for the edge of the concrete stairs, sat and put her head down. When the gloom cleared, the gravel at her feet appeared magnified. An ant scurrying past pebbles was enormous, shiny. A wet earth smell almost choked her with its intensity. She looked up and the focus had changed. She was viewing it all from a great distance, the scene alien, voices coming from far away.

"Actually, I'm not sure how I reacted right after I saw Danny's body. I just remember coming back here, then going home," she said. "But not the details."

Jinxy was watching her now. "Do you want to hear the version I got? Could be way off-base."

"Tell me." It might do her good to hear it.

"They say you wouldn't take any help. Just asked somebody to get the keys from Danny's pocket, then walked to the mobile, drove it back here, and started viewing a tape of the street shots. We didn't even know about the accident yet." He paused. "Sure you want to hear this?"

"Yes."

"When the word got through to us, Arthur had to wrestle the tape away from you. Then you started to shake. Julie took you to Outpatients. Then you insisted on driving home alone in your own car. She followed. Said you drove very slowly and didn't want her to come in once you were there. She was worried."

Walking into her little house, it had seemed years since she'd last seen the place. And that first evening, the day of the explosion, she couldn't help watching the newscast, to see the story *she* should be telling, recounted instead by Chaz, first assigned to get shots from the top of the parking garage but later taking on the whole report because Mercy was sent home. And he did it well, just the right attention to "the death of one of our own" without becoming maudlin. Then his report moved to the fire chief who explained the enormity of the crisis: a space heater that warmed plants in the basement of the flower shop had ignited rags and paper. The flames reached one of several propane tanks stored there. It exploded, blasting out the cellar window. Inside, firefighters fought flames that threatened two more propane tanks. The crew outside saw that the vehicle near the window was built to carry gasoline, not milk. And it would have been extremely dangerous to try to move it. The fire-fighters succeeded in keeping the tank cool enough to avoid a devastating explosion, while the flames inside were put out. The chief, normally a man of few words, couldn't say enough about how his men had saved the city.

When the news was over she'd made the weekly call to her parents in Ottawa, wanting to tell them what had happened but losing courage at the sound of her father's voice, fearing that if she began to talk about Danny, she might not be able to stop. But it didn't keep her from *thinking* about Danny, that it was her impatience, maybe her dislike for him that had sent him stumbling alone through the smoke behind that building. The knowledge felt like a wound that she expected would never heal.

"Everybody understands you were in shock," Jinxy was saying now. "But you look pretty good today."

"Yeah, I'm fine. I just didn't expect...well, an assignment to the fringes of politics. Feels like a demotion."

"Sure. But play along for now. Once the election's called Arthur will be so strung out you'll be the last thing on his mind."

"So," she said. "Guess I'll be sent to cover antigovernment demos where fewer than six whiners show up." God, *she* sounded like a whiner. "Sorry, Jinx. I shouldn't be ranting at you."

"Just apply your famous sense of fun." He tapped her shoulder. "Think of that guy who held up the bank with the butter knife. You imagine politicians are smarter? Chaz sees stuff every day that'd keep you and me laughing for a month. He just doesn't get it."

That made her smile.

"Why not get on the phone," he said. "Acquaint yourself with a few of the powerful bureaucrats who spend our hard-earned bucks. Nothing too taxing. Pardon the pun."

"You know, actually, I'm glad just to be back here," she said, aware for the first time that morning that Danny would *not* be back, ever. Jinxy gave her another tap on the shoulder, like a check mark. Then he walked off.

Her desk looked no different. Some field tapes to sort out and release for reuse. Not much else. Except that one of her colleagues had left a couple of clippings for her growing collection of newspaper typos and inane headlines. Both were missing the crucial letter *I*. One was an ad for a church concert: "St. Andrew's Rectal Planned." The other was a headline: "Illteracy: A Growing Problem."

The hours dragged, not the kind of workday Mercy had ever known. People around her moved at a gallop. Last week she had been galloping with them, full of purpose, racing toward that six o'clock finish line. She tried to look busy, culled files, organized videotapes, but couldn't bring herself to pick up the phone. Anyway, who did she need to call? Assignments would now be dictated. She'd have to show up at "news" conferences and stand around with the rest of the sheep waiting to be fed stories from a platter. The image brought thoughts of lunch, but she wasn't hungry.

Others fetched food on the run, between interviews. Reporters typed and munched, crumbs falling unnoticed onto keyboards, to be flicked away later, or not at all.

By five thirty the hum of noise was closing in on high *C*. No time for courtesy at this stage. If information was needed it was shouted across the room, every minute precious from now to deadline. Three reporters waited to be vetted, pacing behind chairs where producers attacked their scripts with red pencils. Another reporter's crabbed fingers still searched for words on their keyboard. Monitors blared, offering the latest version of stories from sundry locations. The lineup editor barked into the phone that, *goddamn it,* syndication *was* told the pollution story got dropped at noon.

Mercy picked up her bag and made for the door. No one seemed to care. Once in the parking lot she was overtaken by a sense of relief, as if she had just served the first day of a long sentence, but one that might yet be shortened for good behaviour.

Before leaving town she headed to the nearest supermarket. In the produce section colours jumped out at her: scarlet tomatoes, brilliant purple grapes, oranges and carrots, grapefruit, apples, all shining with health. She felt her spirits lift at the sight and filled a basket with whatever caught her eye. It reminded her of putting together a food hamper for a sick friend.

A little early for the season, but as easy to spot as the first robins, a pair of overweight middle-aged tourists in matching red golf shirts hovered at the checkout ahead of her. "This store is exactly like the one at home in Welland," the woman chirped, her partner nodding and smiling at the cashier. "The very same. Even the bread. So we know where everything is. It's wonderful."

What passed for rush hour in Charlottetown was now in full swing as Mercy began driving. It might last a half-hour. But in the next few weeks the place would be transformed as workers cleared away the dregs left by successive layers of snow, a winter's accumulation of plastic cartons, cups, and bags that now nestled in gutters and against fences. What the locals put up with for months could not be left for guests to see. Tourists by the hundreds of thousands would spend millions, line up bumper-to-bumper along the city's fast-food alley, and choke the country roads like an army convoy headed for manoeuvres on the beachhead.

The cleanup had already started. As Mercy drove past Rochford Square, she slowed to watch city workers wake a sleeping man and help him up from the fresh new grass and onto an iron bench they had just installed.

Waiting for a light at Grafton and Queen she watched a large man atop a ladder outside Confederation Centre of the Arts. He was replacing two provincial flags. Manitoba's and Alberta's hadn't survived the March storm. Not far from the ladder, a couple of street people sat on the Centre's concrete steps, legs akimbo and jackets open, letting the sun warm their fronts. Pedestrians didn't give them a second glance. Generally taken for granted by Mercy, too, fixtures in the familiar cityscape. Probably resting up, she thought, for the serious job of panhandling that would begin once the summer crowds arrived, when the opening night of *Anne of Green Gables—The Musical*, would get more local media attention than the opening of the legislature.

The light changed and two cars shot past, windows open, duelling stereos challenging her eardrums, the air now filled with the smell of burning rubber.

She glanced down the block toward the waterfront. Sign laws had done a pretty good job of rescuing the city's centre from ugly commercialism. Merchants were gradually replacing neon with small tasteful script. But none of this impressed Jinxy. He had raved for a year about the seafood at an unadorned little joint called Moe's.

"Get this, Mercy. Moe calls himself *Maurice* now. And he only serves crêpes. Caters to *real* writers these days. Not hacks like us."

Few people could match Jinxy for cynicism. But she felt herself headed in that direction. On the day of her job interview three years ago she had rented a car and driven into the countryside. As she rounded a bend in the road a whole magnificent bay came into view, so perfectly composed an artist might have arranged it. Neat fishing shacks stood at attention along a tidy wharf. Lobster boats rocked gently beside the pilings. The scene brought tears to her eyes. That magical impression was difficult to recapture now. Other pictures had begun to crowd it out. The sight of a certain village now reminded her of what had gone on behind the doors of a farmhouse where two generations of kids were sexually abused. Maybe it was time to leave, try somewhere else. She was free to make her future anywhere. But not without that last image of Danny. It was part of her now.

By the time she crossed the bridge, heading out of town, it was past six. Traffic was sparse. On an impulse she pulled into a liquor store and bought two bottles of red wine. Never drink alone, she remembered. *Unless, of course, you're by yourself.*

At her door she missed the little jab of pleasure that had always come with the turning of the key. Inside, the modesty of her possessions was usually a comfort, a world apart from the high-tech frenzy of a TV newsroom. Now her few pieces of second-hand furniture, the small Franklin fireplace, and her music collection appeared dwarfed by the dimensions of a room that had once held fifty pupils and a teacher. It did not welcome her, as if today she hadn't done the kind of work that would earn her the deserved respite.

She put away the groceries with no desire to eat any of it. But halfway through a glass of wine, with the same Herbie Hancock CD playing that had filled her waking hours for the past week, some unstoppable sense of duty made her cook and eat an omelet. That act seemed to justify another glass of wine. She didn't want to think about the day behind her, or Arthur. Or how underwhelming next week's work was likely to be.

The phone rang.

"Is this Mercy Pepper?" a woman's voice asked, but didn't wait for an answer. "It's Janice Brewer, Danny's mother. I didn't meet you when we came to...to take his...uh...take him back home to Moncton."

Mercy's heart was trying to slam its way out of her chest.

"Mrs. Brewer. Yes. I'm... I wasn't there when you—"

The voice cut in, the deep, harsh voice of a heavy smoker, or someone who had been crying a lot.

"I wanted to...sorry to bother you...wanted to ask what I should do with some things we found in Danny's bags. And...about the fellow who phoned."

"Oh. I'm a little out of touch..."

"It was just after we got back from cleaning out Danny's apartment over there. The place looked like he never had a minute to clean up. At his job all hours, likely. And for what? This?" The words caught in her throat. "Sorry... I didn't mean to get started."

"Yes, he worked very hard, Mrs. Brewer. And he was a real professional. He—"

"We put everything down in the rec room." The voice was stronger again. "I couldn't face looking through it that day. Then this man phoned. From your human-something department. Didn't say his name. Asked if we found anything belonged to the station, said a courier would pick it up. How could some old piece of equipment be important when our son... I hung up on him. I shouldn't have, but I did."

"I'm sure it wasn't important, Mrs. Brewer. Just put it out of your mind."

"I almost had. Except today I finally looked through Danny's duffel bag. Just junk, really, an old thermos, and mitts, but there was a tape, too. In some plastic bubble pack, caught inside the lining. We thought it might be of his birthday party, something nice for us to keep. But it wouldn't even fit in our machine."

"No. It's probably a news tape, Mrs. Brewer. Only meant for broadcasting. Not the same as a home video. He likely kept it to show a technician some camera problem."

"What should we do with it, then?"

"There's no reason to keep it. You can just throw it out."

"Oh." Her voice was fading now, hope gone. "All right, if you think…"

"I'll miss him, Mrs. Brewer. We'll all miss Danny." She tried to think of something specific she would miss. All she could come up with was his energy.

"We were proud of him," the woman said, sounding more bitter than proud. "He never said his job was dangerous. His dad still doesn't understand. Wanted me to find out more. Not for me, you know. It's his dad. I couldn't… I wasn't at the inquest. But his dad says it was full of that doctor and lawyer talk, couldn't understand the half of it."

"It was a freak accident, Mrs. Brewer. He was doing his best to get pictures at the scene. But he couldn't see because of the smoke and…and fell. I'm so sorry. I know it must be a great loss to you." She heard herself saying the trite words, felt ashamed she couldn't do better.

Chapter Four

"Does it ever strike you as strange," Pat said, "that a city girl like you is living out here among the cows and chickens, and I'm sitting in a fourth-floor condo in town with a dog? I'd be more comfortable here among the pig farmers. Maybe we should switch."

They were in Pat Sukata's car, looking for a place to park on a narrow dirt road already lined with dozens of vehicles.

"If I'd known you a couple of years ago I might have agreed," Mercy said. "When I fell for the schoolhouse I was thinking coziness and history. But when the carpenter was finished with his saw and hammer it was *really* quiet. Then there was the winter with seventy-five blizzards. God, how I wanted to hear the sound of heels clicking on pavement, to wake up to big buses huffing up and down the street. I got over that. The school is home now."

"Yeah, I've noticed. So I'll drop the idea. Anyway, you probably found the last salvageable one-room schoolhouse on the Island."

Mercy had met Pat last fall, when police appeared to be getting nowhere in the case of the midnight beating of a female student on the campus of the veterinary college where Pat taught. Even the victim had no clues to offer. And the dean was trying to minimize news coverage.

Then Dr. Patricia Sukata had challenged the college's public relations policy by calling Mercy. "Didn't want some guy arrested on my say-so. But I thought a journalist like you might give me some advice."

They got together at a coffee shop that afternoon. Pat had tried to explain. "There's a student who failed his first year and thinks it's a conspiracy. And that I'm in on it, that we favour female students." Mercy watched her become more agitated as she spoke.

"Did he threaten you?"

"Not in so many words. Shouted and ranted. It was a little frightening. He really has something against women."

"You *should* go to the cops," Mercy said. "Talk to Jon Tillerman. He's a detective sergeant. Explain you didn't want to come forward without real evidence. He's a good guy. He'll understand."

"Thanks for listening. I'll think about it." Pat seemed to relax then and joked that she and Mercy might carry out their own investigation.

"We could use the assistant dean as bait. Sit him on a bench outside the college at midnight, in drag. He's quite pretty. Although the spoiler might be the handlebar moustache."

But it turned out the cops had a couple of clues after all. And Pat's suspect was already undergoing a psychiatric exam to see whether he was fit to stand trial for assault causing bodily harm.

Now their destination was in sight: a very old white farmhouse set about thirty metres from the dirt road. Pat tucked her car neatly in a small space between two farm trucks.

Mercy had awakened an hour earlier to a barking dog. Her head felt thick and stupid but not too stupid to know she didn't have a dog. A fragment of her brain sped off and nabbed a clue. *Saturday.* She shielded her eyes and opened the door, letting a torrent of sun pour through. Pat came in. George, the border collie, stayed out to watch for sheep.

"Sorry. I forgot about the auction." Mercy snatched a stray piece of hair out of her eyes and tucked it behind her ear.

"It's okay. You've had things on your mind. Today might be fun. You remember *fun*, don't you?" Pat placed her neat frame on an arm of the couch, unaware as always that wherever she touched down a perfect life study was created.

"Are we late?" Mercy asked. "Sorry."

"Get dressed. I'll make coffee. And stop apologizing. Let it go."

Mercy considered Pat the record holder in letting go. Forgiveness was no small part of her family tree. Japanese grandparents interned for years in a camp in BC, but no place in Pat's heart for bitterness. When at last the government had expressed official remorse, she said all she felt was embarrassment, the shame of any Canadian.

As they walked into the farmyard now, Mercy took a closer look at the old house. It wasn't small, but it reminded her of the first sight of her schoolhouse. Abandoned and sagging. She wondered whether this derelict building would ever be a home again. She saw a thin grey cat slide silently through a window left open about ten centimetres. The garden in front might have been beautiful once, but today only a few perennials were left to struggle through the shrivelled relics of last season. No animals stood in the fields beyond the empty grey barns. The yard was filled with furniture. People strolled among cupboards and sofas and peered into crates of battered pots and dishes. Pat wandered off.

"You're not as tall as you look on the TV," said a voice behind Mercy. It sounded like an accusation. When she turned, it was an elderly couple.

"No. This is it. Sorry," Mercy said, forcing a smile. They remained grim.

"Tell Bill we don't like that tie he was wearing on the news. Last Thursday, wasn't it, Howard?"

"Wednesday," Howard said. "It was my Kiwanis night."

"The tie had cows on it," the woman said. "Strange. I was so busy looking at it I missed what he was reading to us about the deficit."

"I'll tell him," Mercy said. Their anchor, Bill Wordsworth—as far as a man could get from his namesake, the poet—liked to display his support for the dairy industry. Mercy waited for a question about the cameraman who had died. These people would know all about it, of course. But they didn't ask.

"You could use a little more meat on those bones," the man said, and patted her hand. Then they wandered off with a wave.

She retreated to a quiet spot under an old linden tree where she could watch the scene. It was likely that every person here knew about Danny, including details added by someone who had got them from a friend of a friend in the city fire department. And they would have watched the newscast as she had that first night, and again three days ago when Chaz reported on the coroner's inquest. His report had included clips with firefighters.

"Never saw that camera guy. Sure, he *could've* been there," the first witness said. "Could've come round the other corner. But there was a lotta smoke. And we weren't standing around."

"Another yellow jacket back there?" The next firefighter was adamant. "*No way* we had time to count heads. That damn truck was ready to blow." At the end of an hour's break, the coroner had brought in a verdict of accidental death.

Across the farmyard Mercy became aware of a very tall slim guy relaxing against a sideboard, eyes surveying the scene but stopping on her. More than the passing glance of recognition she was used to. Early twenties maybe, strong and wiry, his hair thin for his age, a little rough-looking.

He started moving in her direction but stopped every few feet to pick up some small object from a table, then put it down again. Not eager, or not wanting to look as if he was. She turned away.

"Hi there." He was grinning down at her. "Never saw you in real life before, just on the tube." He had a trace of an American accent. New England? Did tourists watch the local news?

"Name's Skim. Short for Skimmings. That's my last name. I know yours. Mercy Pepper, right? Not a name from around this place."

"No."

"Another one from away? Me, too. Boston. Grew up there. But my mom was from the Island. I'm living with my aunt in Charlottetown for now." He shrugged. "Well, for now's coming up to three years."

"Ah." She looked away, hoping he'd take the hint.

"How long *you* been here?"

"About the same." She avoided looking at him again, knowing now that he was the type who wouldn't leave her alone until he had more information. It wasn't the first time she'd been cornered by a TV groupie.

"So, we got something in common," he said. "Where you from?"

She hesitated. "Ottawa."

His grin became a chortle, as if she had just dropped a punch line. "Full of feds up there. Where the pogey cheques come from."

"That's one way to look at it." She examined the ground, didn't want him to think this little chat would continue.

"Sorry to hear about your sidekick there. Danny, wasn't it? Saw him a couple of times in town. Seemed like a sharp guy."

She felt her shoulders tighten and turned to watch the auctioneer testing his microphone, tapping it with a finger. People headed toward the platform like cows making for the barn at milking time.

"Man, he was sure proud of that camera, Danny was. Knew it inside out."

"That was his job," she said, still watching the auctioneer.

"Yeah. He showed it to me. One night we were all leaving the pool hall."

Now he had her full attention. And what he had just told her made no sense.

"What do you mean?" She looked directly into his face for the first time.

"What I said. We went by his car. *Boy.* That red Mustang. Pretty friggin' cool. Anyway, he got the camera out. Heavy as hell. Hoisted it on his shoulder, showed me and some of the guys how it worked. 'Course it was pretty dark. He didn't shoot anything. Just told us what all the buttons were for."

Mercy didn't feel capable of figuring this out right now. What was Danny doing with the camera in his car at night? It belonged back at the station in the techs' room with the other gear, unless he was on an assignment. But if he was working that night, he would have been using a station van, not his own car. She could imagine him outside the pool hall, though. Cocky. Showing off.

"Well, gotta get to work." The guy called Skim gave her a limp salute, turned, and walked away, then looked back and grinned. She didn't react. At the old farm wagon set up as a stage he stopped and turned the speaker a little to face the crowd. The auctioneer nodded to him.

Mercy filed away what he had said about Danny. No need to think about it now. Maybe not ever. *Let it go*, as Pat would say. Get interested in old furniture. Pat's dog brushed against her leg. She patted George's head and rubbed his ears. He looked so grateful she bent down and hugged him. Maybe a dog was just what she needed.

Pat waved from her spot on the edge of the crowd. The auctioneer was beginning his spiel, about how everything for sale was in perfect condition. But, if not, then he wasn't responsible. He picked up a delicate glass bowl.

"Look at this, folks. At least a hundred years old. All kinds of valuable goods here today. So bid high and bid fast. Who'll start it at thirty? Thirty anywhere?"

It began slowly, as if people were suspicious of the patter. But gradually he got a rhythm going, once or twice surprising them by selling an item to the first bidder.

"See folks? Gotta stay on your toes."

Mercy moved to where Pat had installed herself in a big wingback chair.

"See that gorgeous pine cradle over there?" Pat pointed across the yard.

"A cradle? You don't even have a boyfriend. Something you're not telling me?"

"I was thinking more like a litter of pups. Get a wife for George first, of course. See anything you like?"

"Haven't really looked. I got cornered by that tall guy with the ratty moustache."

"I saw that. Another fan?"

"More like one of Danny's drinking buddies."

The auctioneer droned on. From somewhere off to her left a man's voice was delivering gossip about the son of the family who owned the farm, back briefly from his life in Calgary to convert the empty homestead into cash.

"Should have waited for July," the man said. "Some tourist'll get this idea to fix it up, move down here away from the rat race. Then after the first winter he can't get back to Ontario fast enough."

Pat decided not to bid and they left just as the food

truck arrived to cater to the appetites of those who hadn't brought lunch.

Back at the house they gave George some water and sat at the table, eating cheese and bread and apples. When the food was put away Pat raised an old issue.

"Catch any mice yet?"

"I got rid of the droppings. Rubber gloves and bleach. Just what you said."

"And the traps? Where did you set them?"

"I didn't. Strangulation? Isn't there another choice?"

"A cat, maybe. But most of them have lost the skill. They play with their victim until it dies of fright."

"And that's it?"

"A couple of others. You can arrange for their tiny mice feet to get stuck in glue and let them starve to death. Or they can decompose behind your walls from a dose of lethal poison. You won't see it, but you might smell it."

"I can't understand it. Have inventors been on holiday for the last hundred years?"

"Quit stalling. You live in the country. It's country mice that carry the hantavirus. And it can be fatal to humans. You've heard all this. I'm turning into a nag. Look, I'll set the traps. So you won't be the actual first-degree murderer, only an accomplice. I'll even come and remove the carcasses."

Mercy pushed the image away. "All right. I surrender. There's probably some old cheddar in the fridge."

"For a last meal? What, no Camembert?"

"We just ate it. The traps are in a box in the closet under the stairs, clearly marked *Weapons of Mass Destruction*."

"Ah. That's more like it." Pat headed for the closet.

The phone rang. Mercy picked it up, her mind still on tiny horrors.

"I've been trying all morning to get some goddamn person to answer over there."

Stay calm. "Who is this?" Mercy said.

"Brewer. It's *Brewer.* Danny's father. Called your station. Nobody there. Typical. What? News never happens on a Saturday?"

"The message should have given you the number of the senior producer." Mercy concentrated on keeping her voice level.

"Yeah, well, you think people want to hear a bunch of recorded garbage? So I'm calling you. The wife has your number, lady."

"Yes."

"And this is what I'm gonna tell your boss. I'm talking to a lawyer. No real information from you people. And that inquest? A joke."

"I know you're upset, Mr. Brewer. We *all* are. But when I talked to your wife—"

"Useless. That's her. Always worried about saying the wrong thing."

"I'll find my boss, Mr. Brewer. I'll have him call you. Right away."

"No. Get me his cellphone number," he shouted. "See how he likes it when I interrupt his golf game."

When she had provided Arthur's number and put the phone down, Mercy was shaking. Not a nice man. Well, not this week anyway. Grief wasn't always about tears.

Chapter Five

Another Sunday morning now and the same old question in Skim's head. What the hell was he doing lying here in a field beside the village idiot, both of them staring at a farmhouse? Didn't help that this time he was beating back the hangover from a few beers at the pool hall with the guys, then a couple more at that new club on Grafton. But it was the waiting drove Skim nuts.

He looked over at Cab. Quiet, maybe thinking, maybe not, thinking not being one of Cab's big talents. Didn't mind waiting, though.

Other days of the week, if Skim thought about it, he knew this was something he had to do. He was taking care of business. A business he was kinda proud of. His own boss. Well, almost, anyway. Today it felt more like grunt work. But probably better than what he'd be doing if he was still in Boston.

Man, his folks were real surprised when he said okay, he'd get out of the city. Jeezus, leave the country, even. Then they could relax, quit worrying about who he was running with, about the kid next door, Skim's pal since kindergarten, waiting for his trial date on sixteen B and E's. And cops at Skim's house asking questions. After an hour alone with one cop who acted friendly but maybe had his mind on baseball, Skim saw his future. Might charge him, the guy said. Like it didn't depend on evidence, more on whether the Red Sox won that day. Either way, from now on they'd be watching him.

That was when he figured his mom had the first bright idea of her life. Could still see her face. Stunned when he didn't argue and happy as hell that he didn't change his mind. Said sure, he'd go stay a while with the aunt on that island in Canada where his mom was from. Quiet and safe, she said, something like Nantucket only without the rich people. And far away from the types that might turn him wrong. A smart move.

Except now he was living in a place where his big-city skills didn't count for shit. And fucking *nature* everywhere you looked. Trees growing out of control in big bunches. Who knew what went on in those dark woods? Not just little humping bunny rabbits for sure. And then these spaces, bigger than football fields with heavy mushes of animal turd hiding in the long grass just waiting to plaster his shoes. And the cows looking stupid, maybe savage, and no dumpsters anywhere to give you cover. He couldn't believe there were groups got money to protect all this.

A different world from Boston. There he could sniff out danger on any street twenty blocks around his house. He knew what noise belonged and what didn't, knew the stinks and shadows of every vacant lot, every dark doorway. Felt alive, sharp.

Now he looked over at Cab again. The kid'd never survive in a real city. Skim almost laughed out loud, lying right there in the field. The guy'd walk into a blind alley after a kitten and no clue until a knife was on his throat.

43

Beside him, Cab was humming, lying on his stomach, his chin on his fists, chewing gum in that lazy way he had, his brain on slow time same as his jaw. And his nose and eyes all crowded together under a round turnip forehead. A small brain in a big head. So what was filling up the rest of the space? Made you wonder. Yeah. About himself, too. About his own future.

But things were looking up lately. Met a TV reporter yesterday, didn't he? When would he ever have a chance to do that in Boston? Never, that's when. Wasn't hard, either. First he noticed her walking down the farm lane with the other chick, Chinese or something. He kept watching when she turned and gabbed to the older folks, the sad look covered by a presto smile that stayed only for the talk and no more. And then she was walking over to the furniture, stepping on the grass sort of gentle, like it was alive or something. She was easy on the eyes. Good body, small but round in the right places. A few years older than him, past thirty even, but no way was she over the hill. Face was kind of pale, but he saw how the dark hair curled behind her ears, as if it liked being there, close to her. And her pal, the Chinese chick. She had lots of hair, too, long and black and heavy-looking.

He looked at people's hair a lot. Maybe because his wasn't great. Light and thin. Every time the wind blew seemed like a chance for it to get away on him, couldn't wait to go. More luck with the moustache. Looked real good. Felt older, too. Tougher even.

Funny to think about her now, how she stood there so still under the tree, like she was hoping nobody could spot her. And when she saw him looking he just kept staring. Why not? Free country. So go over for a little talk. Why not? Show he wasn't some hick impressed that she was on TV. Turned out he was right. She tried not to show it, but she was surprised at a few things he knew.

Sure, today it might look like he was only some guy shivering in a field with a dimwit for company, waiting for the folks in the farmhouse to go to church so he could get at their stuff. But his ideas were what you called *long-term*. Sharp people worked that way.

"My cousin might get some money. Got this grant lady goin' to see her all the time," Cab said out of the blue.

"One of those Grants from Kings County?"

"Nuh. Somebody works for the government, kind of. Findin' people to give grants to. Says my cousin is a *folk* artist."

"An artist?" News to Skim.

"Makes these pictures with leffover paint from the house. Folks like it. Why it's called folk art."

"Oh, yeah?"

"She puts in Elvis Presley. Sittin' in a dory, or lookin' out from behind a tree. But the grant lady says Elvis is not Canadian, so my cousin might not get the money. And she needs it to get a new truck."

Now Cab was frowning, like something else was trying to get out.

"I'm scared about the truck, Skim."

"You sayin' her old truck's dangerous, Cab? Think it's gonna bite you?" Skim had to laugh. One reason he took him along on these Sunday trips. Entertainment.

"They found it, Skim. Don't know what's gonna happen to me."

"Jeezus, will you fill in the blanks for me, Cab? What the hell you talkin' about?"

"My uncle's truck. The big one. The one was behind the building where the 'splosion was. Police took it away."

"So what's it to you?"

"I was drivin' it."

"You were *what?*"

"Just the one time. Uncle Herb give me a new job deliverin' gas for him. And I went to the first place, that garage out on the road to St. Peters. And the man paid me cash like he was s'posed to. But then I couldn't find the next place. It wasn't where he said. So then I thought about havin' a beer because my uncle said he'd pay me five dollars for every delivery. So I just sort of went to the Legion and—"

"Whoa. Stop right there. You were driving *that* truck?"

"Yeah. But I walked home from the Legion. See, I didn't remember that I left it back of that building, out of the way, like, dark. And now my uncle's mad at me."

It made some kind of sense to Skim, Cab's uncle into a scheme like that. Had that place out on the highway to Summerside. Worked on engines and some salvaging. Now Skim remembered the pictures from the TV news. And he could see how easy the uncle could do it. Get hold of an old milk truck cheap, change the hoses and stuff. Fill it up with gas. Make a deal to get the gas wholesale? No, a wholesaler wouldn't go for that kind of two-bit operation. Had to be somebody stealing it for him. Somebody who *worked* for the wholesaler. And customers ready to pay cash to cut out the middleman and the government tax. *Shit.* He almost wished he'd thought of it himself. Just the idea, not doing it. Because it wasn't that smart when you considered. Too many people involved. And real stupid to give Cab the job of delivery. Real stupid. You couldn't let the kid out of your sight.

Then Skim had another thought. That fire was more than a week ago. How come the cops didn't have it all figured out by now? Like what that truck was doing there. Not that hard. But he never heard a word. And Cab right there in it. That was something to worry about. How would the kid act if the cops leaned on him? Tell his whole life story and maybe Skim's, too?

"What did your uncle say, Cab? Any visits from the cops?"

"Dunno. Won't talk to me. Says stay away from him."

A screen door whacked shut and Skim lifted his head enough to see the farmhouse. And there they were, the whole damn family, getting into the old Escort and heading for the church, right on schedule. Research. It paid off. But this better be the last Sunday job till he found out what was going on with that milk truck.

Once the sound of the car faded, he stood up, Cab following like a shadow. The house was off by itself, not a neighbour in sight. And no dog. Always the first thing he checked out. Skim rubbed his arms, feeling the cold. Not as bad as when they did the Catholics, though. Should be a law against getting up that early. Even though it was May, sometimes there was frost on the ground. *Fuckin' hell.* Keep this up he'd catch arthritis. Be hobbling around like an old geezer. As they walked to the house he started to feel better. Really, come right down to it, he was kind of an artist himself, and he heard artists had to suffer.

Getting in was easy. Some people didn't even lock up. These did, but Skim had the back door open in thirty seconds. Always the back door. Nobody on a farm ever used the front except for funerals. So that lock was stiff and cranky.

Inside he did a quick survey and headed up the stairs with Cab right behind. Good pickings here by the look of it. Modern furniture, the latest appliances. That meant they'd have Granny's stuff stored away. Upstairs. Skim pointed at the opening to the attic.

He saw a table and chair at the end of the hall and they moved them into place without any talk. The usual routine. Skim put down his backpack, opened it and took out the newspapers, spread a thick layer on the table, and climbed aboard. He pushed back the panel, hoisted himself up and he was in like Flynn. Took out his small flashlight and looked around. Loads of boxes and a couple of small trunks. All neat, but enough dust to show nobody'd been up here for years. And sitting in the middle of the floor like it was just waiting for him was a real old mantle clock with gold-coloured pillars like on some fancy building. Worth at least a hundred and fifty to a tourist and gone from the Island long before it was missed. He walked over and picked it up, careful not to disturb anything. Heavy. Behind it was a big round wooden bowl somebody'd carved out of one piece of wood. He'd only seen a couple before. Worth a hundred for sure.

Times like this Skim knew he was smarter than most people. There was guys'd smash windows before they'd even try the door, cart off everything that wasn't nailed down: computers, TVs, stereos, lamps, cameras, even old toasters. But he knew not to upset a family's every-day life. He'd be out of there in five minutes tops, with only the clock and the bowl. And it'd be years before anybody wondered where they went. No harm done. He never took cash, even if it was lying there begging to go. Saw the connection between that money and the work somebody did. Never got violent either. Wouldn't carry a knife. Some he knew carried a knife *and* a fork, so if a cop did a pat down, the answer'd be, *Headed for the soup kitchen, officer. Like to use my own utensils.* He had to laugh to himself, thinking about that.

"Somethin' funny up there, Skim?" The voice came through the open hatch.

Skim shook himself. What the hell was he doing, letting his mind wander off like that in the middle of a job? He had to use his head for business, or what future did he have, right? Like his name said. *Skim.* It was what he did. Took the cream off the top, not good for you anyway, and recycled it for profit. Kept his ears open. Heard from his aunt about families with "old money." Those types always had a shitload of stuff, called heirlooms. They'd hang onto them forever but would never look at them again.

He passed the bowl and the clock through the opening, and Cab set them on the floor. Then he let himself down again onto the table. Almost went over when he landed, it was so small. But caught himself in time. Wrapped the clock in the paper and put it in his bag, wiped off the table with his sleeve, and they put the table and chair back in place.

With the bag heavy on his shoulder and the bowl under his arm, Skim stopped to take a quick look into the bedrooms. All real tidy. Modern furniture there, too. Looked pretty stupid in an old house. Going down the stairs he heard Cab clumping behind him. Looked around and there he was, arms full of an electric blanket, the cord dragging.

"What the hell you doing?"

"It'll be good for keepin' us warm next time when we're out there waitin'."

"Smarten up, Cab. We're lying in a field. Where we gonna plug it in?"

Silence. Skim counted to three.

"Yeah. Some cold out there, though." Cab dropped the blanket on the nearest chair.

"Put it back where you got it. Exactly where you got it. Folded and everything. Or they'll know right off somebody was here."

Cab started back upstairs. Skim waited, but something else wasn't right. He thought harder but nothing came.

Then he heard it. A car. He moved to the edge of the kitchen window, saw the little Ford coming up the lane, slowly.

"Cab," he shouted. "Get down here. Now! We gotta get out."

Above, he heard a jumble of noise, then Cab was stumbling down, missing every second step, almost falling, but getting there fast. Skim made a sign for him to keep quiet. He handed over the bag and shoved the bowl under Cab's arm. Then he led the way through the living room and tried turning the front door lock. It scraped, but not too loud, and he opened it, getting ready. He flipped the tab on the storm door, held up a hand for Cab not to move, and took a step over to a side window. The car was just rolling up to its spot beside the house, right where it was when the family piled in. Then Skim saw what he'd missed. The guy getting out of the car, the father. He was wearing overalls, not dressed for church at all.

Skim still had his hand up to Cab, like you'd tell a dog to stay. When the man disappeared behind the house, Skim slipped out and held the door for Cab, who was looking terrified, sweating, but moving smooth as a tiger. Once Cab was out, leaning against the wall, panting, Skim closed the doors carefully and took the heavy bag from him, then motioned to put the bowl up under his jacket. Inside a minute they were in a side field, walking toward the road, Skim hunched over so he wouldn't look so tall. If the man happened to see them out his window they'd be two guys just heading out of the woods, in no hurry. It'd be months before anybody noticed the front door was unlocked.

Ten minutes walking and they were in the truck, gravel kicking up and dust following them for five kilometres to the main highway. Skim didn't relax till they were on the pavement, thinking about how he'd just dodged a real big screw-up. Almost started yelling at Cab but didn't. Knew it was his own fault.

Dropped Cab off at his place, then headed straight home, drove the old half-ton into the garage, what his aunt called her "carriage house." Climbed up the crooked stairs to the loft. Stashed today's take with what was already there. Then he locked up and went through the gate into the back garden. Everything neat. His aunt made sure of that. He could live with green stuff if it was under control, not trying to strangle the house. Grass just starting to grow. Anyway, not his worry. His aunt liked paying somebody to do it, like she was a boss. He opened the door, careful as usual. Good practice. Amazing how many people just barged into a place.

Chapter Six

Raining Monday morning but that was okay. Once inside the car and on her way to town Mercy even found it cozy, the gentle drumbeat on the roof calming.

Over the weekend she had convinced herself that only wounded pride kept her from accepting her new assignment to politics with an open mind. She resolved to go to those government-staged news conferences and find something interesting to report. Next to impossible, she figured. But it would be her latest challenge. She would impress Arthur with her maturity. And when the next big court case came along she could find herself back on the crime beat. But, in the meantime, let Julie get a taste of it. Only fair.

When Mercy walked into the station a teenager was standing inside the back door, skinny arms hanging like noodles out of the wide sleeves of a T-shirt with *SECURITY* printed across the narrow chest and on his belt a nightstick as thin as his arm. She rewound her brain tape and began the scene again. If she'd been forewarned she could have opened the door and thrown in a small cabbage, see if he caught it, then shouted, "Grenade drill! We do it all the time here." But those lighthearted days when small practical jokes were an almost daily occurrence seemed far in the past now, never to return. She nodded at the boy and moved along the hallway where the familiar plastic buckets sat, strategically placed to catch the leaks. Next rainy day they would be in new spots. Nobody bothered to comment anymore.

In the newsroom they settled in around the big table, exchanging post-weekend anecdotes about blind dates gone wrong and minor domestic disasters. Was the old camaraderie creeping back? Jinxy passed the outlook sheets around. That day's court docket was assigned to Julie who offered Mercy an apologetic shrug. Mercy found her own name opposite an eleven o'clock news conference at the government media centre.

She looked up to see Arthur watching her. He was wearing what they all referred to as his PR-ing suit. So he must be headed for a Rotary luncheon, or worse.

"Election date!" He peered at Chaz.

"Give me a break, Arthur. It's not even nine o'clock."

"Get it. Today."

"I explained last week, Arthur. The premier hasn't decided."

"Tough. Him? Set our agenda? No way."

Notions like this had earned Arthur the title "His Royal Thickness." And it didn't refer only to his bum.

Jinxy leaned toward Arthur's ear and said gently, "He's the premier, Arthur. It's already his agenda."

"Move on." Arthur said, and tapped his watch.

"Hey, what's with the kid at the back door?" Chaz was smirking now. "High school role play again?"

This time Arthur took a few seconds to gather his thoughts. "Phone threat. Possible violence. Safety. My duty." He straightened his tie.

"A threat? What have we done now? Libelled some-body's cat?" Chaz looked around the table for reaction. Julie giggled.

"The accident. Danny Brewer. The father. Angry."

"Shouldn't we tell the police?" Julie asked.

Arthur folded his arms across his chest. "Done. Lives in Moncton. Cops will visit."

"The kid looks a little...well, underdeveloped," Jinxy said. "Karate genius?"

"Young. But confident. Very. From my church. Not corruptible."

Twelve pairs of eyes rolled to the ceiling.

Within fifteen minutes the meeting was over and chairs emptied quickly. Arthur intercepted Mercy before she got to her desk.

"You, too. Election date. Get on it."

"It's at the top of my list," she said.

Mercy stopped at Jinxy's desk. "So what's this news conference I'm going to?"

"Some initiative for the tourism industry. No details." He lowered his voice. "Look, just show up and go through the motions. If it's a real snoozer, we'll drop it."

"Sure. Who am I going with?"

"Luc. Get your cameraman while the supply lasts!"

He must have seen the shock on her face.

"*Christ,* Mercy. Sorry." He slapped his forehead. "Don't know what I was thinking."

By ten thirty she had made enough calls to refresh her memory on details of the tourism industry and checked the computerized library for stock shots she might need. At least a dozen tapes held video to do with *Anne of Green Gables*: performances of the musical, Japanese tourists visiting favourite sites of the fictional heroine, cottage industries producing costumes, soap, perfume, cookbooks, and trinkets. There were Anne motels, Anne cottages, Anne campgrounds. Somewhere, she figured, someone was selling Anne frozen pizza.

When Luc showed up at her desk she grabbed a notebook and followed him to the van, the same one Danny used to drive, but neater now. No gum wrappers blowing around. No empty pop bottles rolling and smacking the door when the vehicle took a corner.

She had worked with Luc only once before, on a basic sit-down interview. He was small but strong, with short brown hair and tiny round granny glasses that made him look like a Parisian college student from her mother's time.

"Sorry, I have no background to give you on this one," she said as they left the station. "Tourism. That's all I know. You might have to show me the ropes."

"The hard thing is to keep yourself awake. *On ne doit pas dormir.*"

She laughed. "Okay. Give me an elbow if you see me nodding off."

"*D'accord.*"

He parked behind the government building and opened the hatch. She carried the tapes and the small sound bag with the wireless mics and the hand-held. Luc loaded himself down with everything else: camera, tripod, lighting kit, and battery belt. And, unlike Danny, without complaint. Like a good soldier, Luc was prepared for anything. Except maybe a high-speed chase.

They found the media room already lit, with more candlepower than an arena. At the front was a long table with microphones strategically placed and chairs ranged behind. A huge colourful map of the Island hung overhead with the provincial flag drooping beside it. Every available wall space was taken up with big bright posters. In dozens of photos happy kids romped in the surf, dads sank perfect putts on breathtakingly beautiful golf courses, and moms bought souvenirs from charming salespeople in sleepy fishing villages. The tourism department had never met a cliché it didn't like.

Chairs were set out for a small audience. Half a dozen were already taken by local radio and newspaper reporters. Luc set up the tripod and camera to one side and Mercy sat at the end of the nearest row. Others began filing in, men in well-cut suits and ties and a few women in stylish office garb. There was no mistaking a flock of bureaucrats in full plumage. They took seats in the front row. She recognized a couple of officials from the justice department.

And, dashing here and there was Fred Fredericks, the trim energetic whippet, head of public relations. He'd shown up at the station a couple of times to prep some politician for a studio interview. She watched him scurry over to whisper something to a civil servant. Just as Mercy was wishing she had brought along a good novel, heck, even a bad one, Fredericks raced to the back of the room to escort the mayor, the police chief, and two officers to the table.

She caught the chief's eye as he passed her seat and he nodded. Not his usual relaxed greeting. Maybe he didn't want to be here any more than she did. Both of them out of their element. And seated beside the chief was Det. Sgt. Jon Tillerman, looking right at her, grinning.

Tillerman had always been Mercy's best source. More helpful than most and with a dry sense of humour that she liked. Not tall but fit-looking. He didn't stand out in a crowd, probably a good quality in a cop. A couple of months ago the whole police department, even the women, had shaved their heads for a big charity fundraiser. And Mercy's next sight of Tillerman stopped her in her tracks. He was suddenly the best-looking guy she had ever seen. What was happening? Had she developed a bald fetish? She had never seen such a perfectly shaped head. And somehow it made his other features compellingly attractive. A wonderful strong jawline, fascinating mouth, good ears, an appealing nose, thick eyebrows, and striking, dark brown eyes. Details that had failed to get her attention before. And from that day she couldn't keep her eyes off him. When all his colleagues grew their hair back, she was happy to see he had kept his to a shadow.

Now she tore her gaze away from him to take out her notebook and hold a sheet of white paper to the lens so Luc could get a colour balance on the camera.

"This is all there is to it," Luc said. "You hurry, hurry, hurry for to set up. Then you wait, wait, wait. Exciting, *non?*"

Next thing she knew a heavily built man was striding to take the seat at the centre of the table. Charlie "Puck" Overton, recently named minister of tourism. Mid-forties, Mercy figured, and a physique made for weightlifting, not the pole vault. She remembered Chaz talking about him. A local hockey hero in his younger days, later snatched from an exciting career in vinyl siding to win a landslide election victory on his first try. Today he was nodding and smiling, bestowing special waves on a couple of reporters. The man did not look comfortable in a suit. Yet she shuddered to think what lay beneath: heavy muscle and hair everywhere. The bristly moustache was plenty. His thick neck looked desperate to get out of his shirt collar, and the round face was slick with perspiration. But the most notice-able feature was a deep red scar that connected his eyebrows and gave him a permanent frown, the source, she remembered, of his nickname. Puck Overton was best known for having mistaken a fan's noisemaker for the game-ending buzzer. He'd torn off his helmet just a couple of seconds too soon and taken a puck right between the eyes.

Now he pulled the microphone closer and got instant silence. Beside her, Mercy heard Luc start to record without having to be told.

"Welcome, everybody," Puck began. "You're invited here today to learn about important steps we've taken to make this city of Charlottetown a destination even more irresistible to visitors than it is now." His smile panned the room. "Ah. How can that possibly be done? Well, I'm going to tell you." He reached for a sheaf of pages in front of him. "But first, a little background."

Mercy turned on her brain filter and looked around. Civil servants listened politely. Some reporters ap-peared to be scribbling down every word, turning pages quickly in their notebooks. Puck droned on. Then a metaphor caught her attention.

"Think of a tripod," he said. "A tripod that holds up the economy of our province. Those three supporting legs have always been fishing, farming, and, well, to be honest, federal transfer payments. But now we have tourism. The fourth leg of that tripod."

Had she heard right? She looked over at the suits. Only one was smiling behind his hand, looking down.

Maybe Jinxy was right. He would enjoy hearing about a four-legged tripod. There were laughs to be had here. She started to listen, hoping for more.

"Let me remind you of our record," Puck continued. "Through a supreme effort and at no small expense, we've kept our capital city spotless. We sweep our streets, we wash our streets, and we repave our streets." To go with the words, his arms tried to mimic the action of sweeping, washing, and repaving. There was a titter from the reporters' row.

"But still." He looked down at his notes. "There's a blot on our streetscape. And most of you realize what it is. Yes, the most shameful sight is…? Right, our street people. True, only a couple of dozen. But if just *one* tourist is confronted by a panhandler then we've spoiled that visitor's day and left a bad impression." The index finger he'd used to represent the tourist was still pointing to the ceiling and he now shook it at the audience.

"No one can say we aren't sensitive to the plight of the homeless and the, well, let's be honest, the *drunks*. They deserve sympathy and help. And we've thought long and hard about this. I'll ask my deputy minister to explain our plan. Mr. Kelly?"

A suit further along the table jolted to standing attention as if responding to an electrical shock under his chair. "Thank you…um… Minister. I'll get right to it." A sheet of paper shook in his hands. Remembering the microphone, he sat down again.

"One." He juggled the paper and stuck up a thumb. "Your government has bought a small farm twenty kilometres west of the city." He dropped the thumb and raised his index finger. "Two! This farm will be the new summer home for Charlottetown's street people."

Just as Mercy was concluding that this man and Puck had gone to the same kindergarten, Mr. Kelly lowered the index and raised the middle one. "Three!" He looked at it, blushed, and abandoned the finger count.

"These needy people will be housed, fed, and clothed at government expense all summer. Four! They'll do chores, grow vegetables, um...etcetera. Five! They'll be in the fresh air. Six! They'll have no worries about where to sleep at night. Seven! They'll take life-skills courses." He was well over the speed limit now. "Eight!" He turned the page over, but found nothing there. "Well, that's it." He leaned back in the chair, out of gas.

Puck didn't miss a beat. "So that's our good news today, folks. And you, the members of the media, will carry it directly to the public, to the people we work for. You'll explain that their government has come up with a truly humane and generous way to solve a serious problem by taking some very, yes, *very* proactive, um, action. The result? Visitors to the city will enjoy a carefree and beautiful experience. Guaranteed. Not to mention providing a summer home for the otherwise hopeless, er, homeless. Let's face it. At times these individuals have been found fighting on our streets."

"That was the college soccer team," one of the radio reporters called.

Puck ignored the remark and looked along the table. "Ah, here's Chief Matthews. Maybe you'd like to add a few words, sir."

The chief stood, towering over the table like an indoor tree. Next to him, Sgt. Tillerman looked way up but pointed down to the microphone, now too far away. The chief sat down.

"Safety is always our goal," he said. "That's our job. I'd like to make this city so safe my ninety-year-old grandmother could go for a stroll in Victoria Park at midnight." He pushed the microphone away and folded his arms.

"I've seen your granny, chief." It was the radio reporter again. "No worries there. She's built like you." He got a big laugh.

Mercy got up. Beside her she could hear that Luc was still rolling tape.

"Mr. Minister. May I ask a question?"

"Certainly, Miss...uh...Pepper, isn't it?" He surveyed the room. "Yes, as a crime reporter you must be very interested in this."

"Of course. And since you raise it, what crime do you expect to charge the homeless with? Before you take them off to their new home in the country."

"Aw now, wait. No one's saying it's a crime to be homeless." He faced her and squared his shoulders, ready for a body check.

"So," she continued, "if they haven't been convicted of anything, can the government tell them where to live?"

Puck looked at the bureaucrats in the front row and chuckled. The one next to him at the table was slipping down in his chair, like a kid who can't face the broccoli on his plate.

"We have no intention," Puck said, "of telling them where to live. But can you imagine anyone refusing an offer like this? Is there a person anywhere who doesn't dream of living in the countryside?" His gaze moved to the window, heading for distant hills and valleys. "This is Prince Edward Island! People from Ontario gladly pay thousands of dollars just to spend a week here."

"Did you ask any of the homeless *before* you bought this farm?" she said. "The phrase *internment camp* comes to mind." She looked along her row. Didn't other reporters have questions? Most were still scribbling in their notebooks. A couple of them watched her, interested.

"Just hold on there, Miss...or *Ms*, probably..." Puck chuckled, then began again. "Why do you people always try to turn good news into bad? Here we are, with the best of intentions, thinking ahead, for the sake of *all* our citizens, and already you're looking to criticize. There may still be a few details to work out, but the plan is sound. The people of this island will thank us for it, if you'd just do your jobs and put the news out there."

"Could I say something?" It was the chief, on his feet again, never mind the microphone. "We've had some questions, too. And I've raised them privately with the minister. He's assured me that the police will have no involvement except to help identify those people who might...qualify. But no one will be forced to go anywhere." He sat.

"Right on, chief," Puck said. "They'll be lining up to get on the list. Granted, there may be a couple of, uh, candidates, who, through no fault of their own, have lost the ability to think straight. So we'll work to help them see the benefits."

Mercy was aware that Sgt. Tillerman was watching her, as if it was now her turn.

"I'm a little confused here," she said. *That's it. Plead stupidity*. "Are you saying, Mr. Minister, that you'll offer *incentives* to make the homeless leave the city? And what might they be?"

"As I just said, details. We'll have that announcement within a week." Several civil servants were nodding.

Puck nodded back. "Absolutely. Within a week. So, stay tuned." He stood up, game over, and headed for the dressing room. Mercy saw Fred, the little PR guy, heading her way.

"Hi." He stuck out his hand and made solid eye contact. "Fred Fredericks. Here to help." He was wearing a stylish charcoal suit and what looked to her to be the latest in designer glasses. But the haircut was right out of the fifties, a high brown pompadour that added a couple of inches to his height.

He held on to her hand, shaking it gently as he spoke. "And I know who you are, Mercy. Great to meet you. Covering politics now? Want more background info? To talk to the minister? I can get you a one-on-one." She understood now why reporters called him Fred the Flack.

"No, thanks. I've got what I need."

"Give him a try. He's pretty excited about this project."

"I noticed." She started to move away.

"I'll get him," he said, and scuttled off.

Mercy looked around for Luc. There he was, already moving the camera to a quiet spot in case she needed more clips. Go through the motions, Jinxy had said. She moved closer to Luc, then glanced over to where a group hovered near the table set with coffee and something orange on crackers—cheese slices beginning to curl at the edges. No sign of Jon Tillerman.

But when she sensed someone behind her and turned, there he was. Same guarded look, with only the dark brown eyes showing his interest.

"So. Haven't seen you since the explosion," he said.

"I took the week off."

He frowned. "Feeling okay?"

"Oh, sure. Needed to get some stuff done at home. Spring cleaning. The garden."

"But no bouquets for the minister's plan, I notice. Maybe you could have been a little more gentle. He's not used to your...style." He waited, still serious. "I like it, myself. But then, I've had time to get used to it." Then a smile broke through and they both laughed.

"I'll have to be more careful," she said. "Politicians are such sensitive blossoms. Not like you guys, hardened from dealing with all those vicious street people." She could feel herself relaxing.

"The chief isn't thrilled with this plan. And you didn't hear that from me, by the way. He thinks we've been doing okay with them. A couple of complaints, we take the offending party to the slammer for a good night's sleep. Drop him off next day at the treatment centre of his choice, or back to his buddies." Jon's eyes stayed on her face as he talked. She had noticed it before. Whomever he spoke to got his full attention, even a thug waiting to be booked.

"I've heard in the old days they hung out down around the waterfront," he said, "where the rail yard was. Lots of shelter, didn't bother anybody. Now the harbour's been tarted up for the cruise ships and we're getting more calls."

This wasn't their usual rushed talk at the courthouse or at his office when she needed a few facts. It was more like a real conversation.

"The minister really thinks street people are danger-ous?" she asked.

"Yeah, well. Politicians. They like to crank up the fear factor. Makes their solution all the more terrific." He shook his head.

"Sounds like a roundup to me," she said.

"Street people likely don't vote. So what do the politicians have to lose?"

She didn't figure he wanted an answer so she just stood looking at him, her favourite work of art.

"I offered my own solution," he said. "Hardly cost a thing. Give the homeless tambourines and a pile of those orange robes like the Asian monks. They could walk around and talk to anybody they wanted. Collect donations even. Religious tolerance. Nobody'd bat an eye."

They laughed again. It felt good.

Then he said, "We were waiting for your follow-up call after the fire."

"What follow-up? Didn't the fire inspector's report wrap it up pretty well?" she said.

"A few threads still hanging,"

"Like what?"

"I'm surprised at you, Mercy. The milk truck?"

"Oh, right." The whole episode seemed remote now, like a horror movie, the plot long forgotten, only the horror left.

"Drop by the station. I'll tell you what we've got."

"Or you could just tell me now."

He hesitated, his eyes leaving her for the first time to glance toward the chief, standing with a cup in his hand, talking to two reporters.

"Thought we might have a talk," Jon said.

"Okay. Sure. But I'm off the police beat. For now."

"Come in anyway." He left her standing there, already feeling his absence.

Chapter Seven

"Here we are." Fred the Flack stepped into the void, but didn't fill it. "One cabinet minister," he announced, "delivered as required." Without waiting for a reaction he led Puck over to Luc and posed him in front of the camera.

Too late now, she thought, and followed.

"Now, don't be too hard on me, ma'am," said Puck. "Just a guy working for the public, doing my best." She could imagine him on the election trail, stickhandling his way to voters' hearts.

Mercy faced him, her back to the camera but keeping out of frame. Luc handed her the hand-held microphone.

"First, Mr. Overton, can you tell me where this idea came from, to move the street people out of the city?" she said.

"Well, back about fifty years ago the problem never even..."

Damn. The historical answer. We could be here all day. She looked back at Luc. The tape was rolling. When she returned her attention to Puck she saw that her arm holding the microphone near his chin was now a little lower, and Puck's mouth was following it like a kid after a lollipop. Maybe he watched too many pop singers. He talked on. She gradually let the mic lower a little more. Still his head followed. She lowered it again. Now he was beginning to bend from the waist, still yapping. She hadn't listened to a word, fascinated by what was happening. She looked at Luc again. His eye was still glued to the viewfinder as he followed Puck's head. But Luc's shoulders were shaking.

"And then, ten years ago, you mustn't forget, the feds started cutting transfer payments by..."

"Thank you, Mr. Minister." He blinked like a man awakened from a dream. She put her free hand gently under his elbow and helped him straighten up.

"That should explain how we arrived at our decision," Puck said. "And the results will soon speak for themselves. Forward planning, it's called. Progress." He got his shoulders moving, as if he couldn't wait to get started.

"Before I forget," she said, "When will your government call the election?"

"Well, I believe...that's up to the premier himself... and I'm not privy..."

"Sure. Never mind."

As soon as Puck was out of the way Fred Fredericks was at her side. "Could I have a word?"

Luc said he'd meet her at the van. Fred steered her away from the traffic of people leaving.

"I realize you have a job to do, but what was that stunt with the microphone?" He was trying to maintain a smile, but his nostrils flared.

"No stunt. He did it all by himself."

"I'm asking you to please not use that interview."

"It'll be tough, but I'll try to get along without it," she said.

Relief spread over his face like sunshine. "Thanks. I owe you one. Hey, how about a coffee later. Talk about how I can make your job a little easier."

"Sorry. Busy day, Fred. Another time?"

Before she was back at her desk she had the report organized in her head. Tempting to use that line about the four-legged tripod, but maybe not fair, off topic. Focus the story where it belonged, on the street people. She expected that half the viewers would complain about the use of taxpayers' money to turn drunks into gentlemen farmers. A few might bring up the issue of civil rights, and the rest just wouldn't get it.

At her desk a hunger pang shot her a message. She'd wait a while, see if it was sincere. She saw Arthur stroll out of his office, take a casual roundabout route and end up beside her, as if the idea had just occurred to him.

"Went okay?" he said.

"Sure. It was interesting. But that minister of tourism, Puck Overton? He's something else. Might try hanging upside down for a few hours to improve the blood flow to his brain."

"Cut the ridicule."

"Ah. Sorry, Arthur."

"Problems? Stressful?"

"No, Arthur. Not at all."

"Good story?"

"Yes. Want to rush it to air right now with a bulletin?"

He heaved the sigh of the long-sufferer. "Just tell me."

"In a nutshell, if you'll pardon the expression, the government plans to rid the city streets of various panhandlers and layabouts by taking them off to a farm retreat. I'll take Luc downtown now and find some of them, get reaction, see what they think of the project."

"No. Facts today. Reaction?" A pause. "*Not* today." He started to move off.

"Hey, wait." She got up and followed. "They're street people, Arthur. You think they'll be sitting watching my report in the comfort of their living rooms? Everybody will get the facts tonight except them."

"Tomorrow." He stopped and faced her. "Did you...?"

"Yes, Arthur. I did ask about the election date but the minister wouldn't go there. He even got a little flustered."

Arthur threw himself into a nearby chair and peered at the floor.

She hated to see him like this. What followed was often one of his sudden wild outbursts in which heads could roll, or at least begin to ache. The staff used to call them Arthur's unpredictable rants. But they were becoming more and more predictable, which at least gave the targets a chance to dive for cover.

"Don't worry, Arthur. Chaz might have some hint by now."

"No. He called. Nothing. Nothing. Nothing." He banged his fist against his forehead three times for emphasis.

It was painful to watch. Mercy looked away, hoping he wouldn't hang around the newsroom much longer. When she looked back he was posed like Rodin's *Thinker*.

"I should start viewing my tapes now, Arthur."

"Impossible."

"What?"

"Election night. Not prepared. Need time."

So this was now his overwhelming preoccupation, was it? She had some sympathy. Normally, even without anything official, they'd be able to figure out a couple of likely dates and get the plan started. Venues had to be booked early, special phone and fibre-optic lines ordered, live remotes placed in half a dozen towns across the province. And other networks would be sending crews to PEI for election night coverage. Arthur would want to book the best spots ahead of the competition. No use reminding him that the competition was working with the same lack of information. Well, good luck to him. She might start pining for an election date herself soon. Anything to get him out of her hair.

When her phone rang it was a welcome interruption, and she left Arthur sitting there.

"Hi. It's Tillerman. You coming by?"

She laughed, surprised to hear from him so soon. "Does the information have an expiry date?"

"Are you busy?"

"Just thinking about how to tell this homeless story without sounding outraged."

"What about this afternoon? I'm stuck here for a few hours," he said.

She looked at the clock. "Sure."

"Before four?"

"Okay."

Once she'd hung up she sat for a moment with her hand still on the receiver. Something to look forward to, something else she hadn't felt for a week.

Her report was easier to write than she expected. Lots of good cover shots, thanks to Luc, who had gone downtown for some careful footage of street people, out-of-focus or from behind. She had clips from Puck at the table and from the police chief, too. But it would have to be stock shots of the countryside, until they could get pictures of the actual farmhouse, the location under wraps until next week. A search of recent farm sales at the deeds office might find it, but was it worth the effort? Arthur wouldn't think so. She was in an edit suite by two o'clock and finished by two thirty, but not happy with the result, knowing the report was incomplete without reaction from street people. She handed the edit pack to Jinxy.

"I'm going out for a sandwich," she said. But he insisted she take half of his, that he had too much. She got a can of juice from the machine in the hall and ate at her desk.

It felt good to be walking into the police station again.

The desk sergeant told Mercy to go on up. In the hall she met a couple of constables and got a friendly greeting. One of them was just back from maternity leave. They talked for a minute about the new baby and the problems of shift work. It reminded Mercy that she was an insider here. Someone brought in for questioning would have a very different impression.

Jon Tillerman's door was open, and he got up when she came in. She remembered her first visit to the station, when the officer she spoke to kept his feet on the desk the whole time, flipping through the *Sports Illustrated* swimsuit edition.

She took the only free chair in the cramped office. Stacks of files and notebooks were as high as ever. Red binding on the *Criminal Code of Canada* caught her eye, the only hardcover book in sight.

The brown eyes were on her.

"Noticed you didn't show up at the inquest," he said.

"They didn't need me. I didn't actually see—"

"As I mentioned, there are some loose ends, and I thought you'd be interested."

"Sure. But Julie's the one who should get it. She's doing my beat for the next... I don't know how long."

"Well, she hasn't called so I'm giving it to you," he said.

"I'll pass it on."

Jon opened a file and glanced over a couple of pages. She watched his face. The expression she saw most often was stern and a little tense. He looked up.

"We traced the owner of that milk truck. Some bozo getting into the discount gas business by cutting out all the government tax. Dumb idea. He was sure to get caught."

"Where did he get the gas?"

"Paid a worker at the wholesaler's to siphon off a few hundred litres at a time from those big tanks on the waterfront."

"The company didn't notice? Don't leaks have to be reported to the environment people?"

"Sure. But those tanks hold millions of litres, and this was penny-ante stuff. They put it down to evaporation. The guy behind the scheme wasn't even clearing a hundred dollars a week. Hired some kid to make the deliveries at night, to country customers, where a milk-collecting truck wouldn't attract attention."

"Brilliant. Free enterprise can be so creative." It was a good, quirky little story. Julie would enjoy writing it. And now Mercy had a fresh image of the milk truck, no longer connected to the place where Danny's body was found. She wrote a few lines in her notebook.

"When does this guy appear in court?"

"Not for a while. We've had our little talk with him. He's terrified. Had no idea the charge would be more than minor theft. But you know what happens when tax fraud's involved. Government gets into the case. And not just the feds, the province, too. This file," he tapped the thin folder in front of him, "this is just our stuff. Half an hour's work. The main file's the size of a dictionary by now, bureaucrats shunting it back and forth between departments. They'll be at it for months. Hard to believe when you've seen this little creep that it's considered white-collar crime."

This was drifting toward small talk. Pleasant, but not something they usually had time for. He picked up a pencil and glanced at the room's only window, as if there was more to see than the dull grey paint of the fire hall. But his eyes came back to her again before he spoke.

"There's something I want to tell you," he said. "It's not official, just wanted you to know. And if it ever comes up outside of here, you didn't get it from me."

"Sure." He had her full attention now, even though she was feeling it might be something she didn't want to hear.

"We were watching Danny Brewer for a while before the accident."

"Watching him? What for?"

"Not heavy surveillance. Just...you know what it's like here."

He put the pencil down carefully and picked up a pen, placed it beside the pencil, not looking at her now. "Not like Toronto. They get a serious incident they have to get a whole team together, start pretty much from zero:

witness statements, forensics, lineups. But our guys here notice what's happening on the street every day. Then, when something goes down we usually have a good idea who's involved." He looked up. "You know what I mean. You've seen them. The same perps turn up in court over and over for breaking and entering and worse. Always the same guys, except maybe for a few who're away serving time. So we get an armed robbery and it's almost certain to be one of the dirty dozen."

She had no idea where all this was going.

"Some of our night patrols saw Danny cruising. All hours." He paused.

"So?"

"That car of his, the old red Mustang. Attracts attention. Anyway, our guys saw it, thought it was cool. Then, when it kept showing up, they got curious about who owned it. Sometimes they'd see him parked outside that restaurant on Richmond where a lot of gay guys hang out."

"Now, wait a minute. If Danny was gay it was nobody's business, Jon." She wasn't thinking of Danny now but about this man in front of her. If he was interested in this kind of gossip, she'd been wrong about him.

"No," Jon said. "It didn't look like he was interested for himself. More like he was taking in the scene. Two or three times he watched a couple of people leave, then followed them to a house and sat outside for a while."

"And that's it?"

"Yeah, nothing illegal. Suspicious, though."

"So why tell me this now?"

"He was your partner, right?"

"We only worked together a few times. Mostly he worked with Chaz."

"You don't need to get defensive. Just wanted you to know he was probably planning a little blackmail. Maybe still doing research but headed that way."

"That's ridiculous, Jon. You're making a huge leap. And he's not here to defend himself. So why even bring it up?"

"I noticed you were pretty shook up about what happened at the explosion."

"People have told me. I don't remember much. It's embarrassing. You were there?"

"Yeah."

It was her turn to look away.

"I'm only giving you this background about Danny because... Look, I've been in situations myself when I was on the street, working with a partner. You get into a bad situation together and later on you wonder if you let your partner down."

When she realized where he was heading, all the air seemed to leave her lungs. She dropped her pen. How had this man she hardly knew entered a space she'd thought was well locked? She wanted to tell him to back off. But more than that she wanted him to listen.

"Did you ever send a partner into danger alone just because you didn't like him?" she asked, but didn't wait for the answer. "That's what I did. Sent Danny behind that building, into the smoke, when I should have been with him, helping. I would have done it for anybody else. If I'd been there he wouldn't have fallen. If I hadn't been annoyed with him. If—"

"Whoa. Stop right there. You can drive yourself crazy with that 'if only' stuff." He leaned forward in his chair, as if he might reach out and touch her across the desk.

"I had the idea that knowing this stuff about Danny might make you feel not so guilty. He was bad news, Mercy. We start to recognize the type. People like him, I get the feeling they're incomplete without a set of bars between them and the rest of the world."

"And that's supposed to make me feel that what I did was okay?"

"No. But I figure Danny was pretty good at looking after number one."

"Not that good. He died, Jon. And you guys haven't got enough to do, you're out looking for *potential* criminals?"

"Didn't expect you'd get so upset." He was frowning now, even looked a little angry, as if he'd expected this to turn out some other way.

"If that's all," she said, "I'll be going." She couldn't keep the disappointment out of her voice.

When she was halfway out of her chair he said, "While I'm being so frank, I should tell you we had to keep an eye on you, too."

Was this some kind of joke? She sat down again and stared at him.

"Let me put it this way," he said. "We know you're a good person. But the job you do, there's a lot of power there. And it's possible Danny could have been taking advantage, maybe manipulating you. People like him work that way."

"I don't need a lecture in psychology, Jon. I can't believe this. Danny's into something shady so you assume I was involved, too?" Her voice was rising and she couldn't seem to stop it.

"I didn't say *involved*. He could have used you without your even knowing."

76

"Did you actually have people following me? Listening on my phone? What?"

"Of course not. You know we can't tap phones without a warrant. It was just a casual thing. They'd see you around, notice who you spent time with. You live a pretty quiet life." He offered a careful smile. "I'm sorry. Shouldn't have told you this much. It's done now. Forget it."

"Forget it? How?" The cops had watched her. That was bad enough. But Jon had been part of it. Weren't they on the same side? Didn't they respect each other? Maybe something a little more? She became aware of the details around her, knew that whenever she remembered this scene, she'd also see the sharp black edge of the framed citation on his wall, the gold lettering, the coffee ring on the light oak desk.

"All you need to know about me is this, Jon: it's my job to get information out of people like you so the public can find out how you're doing the job they pay you for." She was running out of breath and wanted to be far away from him. She got to her feet and slung her big leather bag over one shoulder with such force it almost knocked her off balance. She made for the door.

"Fine," he said. "So much for police–media relations. Why do we bother?"

She turned to glare at him. But he was standing now, looking out the window at that grey wall.

Chapter Eight

"What's this, Arthur?" The morning meeting had just finished when Arthur handed her a scrap of paper. On it was the name of a document file.

"Last election," he said. "Voting stats."

"And you want me to...?"

"Analyze. Make notes. Research. Got it?"

Yes, she got it. Of course. Arthur wanted to keep her on a short leash. He wanted to remind her that she was now expected to relieve Chaz of menial election prep. Arthur needn't have worried. Today she didn't have the energy to do more than follow orders. Soon the mechanics of extracting information from the database began to feel therapeutic, like basket weaving for the mentally ill.

The document gave historic details of three voting districts. The government had won all three seats, but by very small margins. They formed a cluster on the election map, a splash of ink in the middle of the Island. But she saw now that those seats were crucial. And in one of them, labelled Ellingham East, the candidate had won by only twenty-five votes. This was a revelation to her. When that election was held she was still working in Ottawa. The winning candidate's name wasn't familiar, probably a backbencher. But now she understood why Arthur would want Chaz to be ready with solid analysis of that area for the election night broadcast. And it wasn't in Arthur's nature to let anyone relax, just because the premier hadn't yet revealed the election date.

The numbers she was extracting and collating took time. The process helped keep her mind off yesterday's session in Jon Tillerman's office.

Something had gone very wrong there, and last night she had lain rigid in bed, going over and over what he'd said until she had to accept that the friendship she thought had existed between them was over. She felt diminished in his eyes, knowing that he thought even for a minute that she was naïve enough to be manipulated by a character like Danny.

Someone stopped behind her chair. Where bigger stations used a robot to distribute mail, the Charlotte-town newsroom had Ralphina, who also kept an eye out for moral turpitude in those around her. She leaned over Mercy's shoulder to carefully place a couple of envelopes on the desk, as if bestowing a prize on the deserving. Then she offered what Jinxy called her beatific smile and moved on.

Mercy's report about the new farm for the homeless had run near the bottom of last night's six o'clock news. So far there had been no reaction from the public or from any members of the opposing party with ambitions to unseat the government. Instead the Opposition leader focused on the delay in calling an election. He declared himself outraged, shocked, amazed, incensed, and astonished that the premier wasn't ready to name a date. The bluster earned him top spot on the newscast.

"Hey," Jinxy had said, "you have to admire a guy who can come up with so many adjectives and still appear comatose."

After another twenty minutes at the computer Mercy set aside the research and reached for the mail. A couple of standard letters from anonymous trouble-makers with hot tips for the crime reporter: the name of an ex-husband cheating on his tax return; someone informing on an ex-wife who was neglecting the kids to party with her new boyfriend. Ah, domestic bliss. She threw the letters in the shredder bin, then turned in her chair to find Ralphina's tall thin frame standing in her usual perfect posture, one hand holding out a package as if it were a gift.

"This has just come in," she said, then leaned over and added, in a conspiratorial whisper, "special delivery."

Mercy took the package, nodded a thank you, and set it aside, not willing to satisfy Ralphina's obvious curiosity by opening it right away.

Alone again, Mercy saw that the package was bound up with enough tape to keep a mummy in tip-top shape for a couple of millennia. Inside was a broadcast video, but not the usual public relations promo. It was a newsroom field tape. The label was blank. And stuck to a corner was a note addressed to her. *Thank you for talking to me on the phone*, it said. *I didn't think it was right to throw this away. If there are any pictures of Danny on it, please let us know. Sincerely, Mrs. Janice Brewer.*

Mercy picked up a red pen and wrote *erase* across the label. But on her way to the tape bin she hesitated. She went back to her desk, put the tape into the monitor, and pressed the rewind button.

Off the top were the standard colour bars and tone,

then a wide shot of a well-kept bungalow, painted pale yellow with white trim, gingerbread details along the roofline, an attempt to add style to a basic box. It was a nicely framed shot of a typical modern house in the country. In the distance sat two barns and a silo, its cover divided into red and white segments. She could hear voices on the tape, but the volume was low.

The static shot of the house held for about ten seconds, then abruptly zoomed in on a large window and refocused. Through the window she could see the profile of a man sitting at a table, not against the window but a little farther into the room. It looked like her new pal, Puck Overton, minister of tourism. And opposite him Chaz was just getting up from a chair and walking out of the shot. The camera wobbled for a couple of seconds, as if the shooter was getting ready to move the tripod to another location. But it steadied again. And she saw another man walk into the frame and lean over Puck's shoulder. Mercy couldn't see his face. Then the volume was cranked up and she could clearly make out what they were saying.

"...can't hang on forever. You have to nail this down. You know I can make it happen." The man on his feet looked agitated, his arms working, as though this wasn't the first time he'd tried to make his point.

"I'm on it." This was Puck, impatient. "Hell, it isn't even my seat. The premier asked me to handle it for a reason. He knows I can fix it."

"It's *me* doing the fixing." The man leaned closer but his voice was getting louder. "And don't you forget it! The money up front. Or no deal. You agreed."

"*Shit*, man, stop yapping. You think *we* want this delay? The media at us every day to name the date?

Panic isn't a strategy. The money's coming. Just a couple more days."

"*Hell*, it's the party's money, isn't it? Can't you get a lawyer or somebody to put the pressure on? A cop, even?" The man was whining now.

Puck stood up. "Stay cool," he hissed, and walked away. The man moved out of frame in the other direction.

A few seconds later the camera was shut down.

Mercy sat for a minute trying to digest what she had seen and heard. Had Danny shot it? He must have. But what did it mean? She rewound and watched it once more, then covered the label with a *Do not erase* sticker and locked the tape in her bottom drawer.

Danny had been interested enough to tape that private conversation. She found it intriguing herself. But it wasn't easy to know what they were talking about, other than the fact that the election call was stalled. And some kind of deal involving money seemed to be holding up the date.

This wasn't her business. The mature approach would be to turn the tape over to Chaz and back off. But the mention of a lawyer, police, and money set off bells. It had to be more than politics. If she gave the tape to Arthur, he would ask Julie to look into it. And Julie wouldn't know where to begin.

She got out a notebook and jotted down a few words, then thought about what she knew. Chaz had gone to what must be Puck's home in a rural district to do an interview.

The cameraman, let's assume it was Danny, had shot the interview inside the house as the two sat at a table. Politicians seemed to like that setting. Made them look folksy. When it was over, Chaz would have taken off his lapel microphone and left it on the table out of habit, expecting the cameraman to pick it up and pack it away. But meanwhile Danny had stepped outside for a wide exterior shot of the house, a scene-setter, to insert at the top of the interview. This was routine stuff. And Puck still sat there, wearing his microphone.

The battery for the mics might be sitting on the table, too, smaller than a pack of cigarettes. Outside, when Danny heard the new conversation start, he decided to eavesdrop. If the two men noticed the mic they wouldn't even realize that it was still recording sound whenever the tape rolled, even if the camera was outside. And Danny would have gone into the house later to gather up all the equipment.

That much she could figure out without leaving her desk. But she needed more. While Jinxy was out for lunch she wandered over to the assignment desk and looked at the logbook. This wouldn't attract attention. Filling out their time cards, reporters and technicians often checked back to see what days they had worked overtime.

She began searching backward starting with the day before the explosion, looking for Chaz's name, then a story slug that might fit. Most of the entries showed that Chaz was at the legislature or at another government building. But on May 1, about a week before the explosion, he had gone to a rural riding to interview the minister of tourism at home. The story was slugged "Tourism Preview." The cameraman was listed as Danny Brewer.

She didn't recall watching Puck's interview on the newscast. Not surprising, since her radar seldom picked up the talking heads of politicians. She found the lineup sheet for that date, looked down the page, and there it was: Tourism Preview, shelf number 1227.

Whatever she had expected, Chaz's report was a disappointment, a routine interview with the minister predicting a bumper crop of tourists, with his assurance that all accommodation, golf courses, and roads were ready for the arrival of the summer hordes. Not a clue about Puck's conversation with the unknown man once Chaz's interview was over.

Now what? Was it worth pursuing? It could take serious digging. Before now, she had turned up good stories with much less to go on. But here she was at a real disadvantage. Not only was she ignorant about the inner workings of local politics, but she couldn't pursue her own research while Arthur was keeping a vigilant eye on her. The aroma of wrongdoing wafting her way could turn out to be nothing but stale hot air. Whatever it was, the facts would be much harder to find. Her contacts in the political world were nonexistent or secondhand. There would be no jumping in with both feet, focusing all her energy with Arthur's blessing.

Maybe impossible, but why not try?

Chaz wasn't at his desk. She found him in an edit suite putting together a roundup of Opposition party nominating meetings. She watched from the door. Aside from the colour of the banners this could be a meeting of any political party. The shot showed a crowd of several hundred, most on their feet, stamping in time to canned battle-theme music, the stage jammed with people smiling and clapping, a couple of them hoisting the arms of the chosen candidate. All were caught up in the emotion, the suspense, the promise of a showdown, of winners and losers. They might have been getting ready for a big sports event. Or a war. And Chaz's attention was riveted on the screen. He loved it, too, she realized, all the rah-rah stuff.

These days she was hesitant about approaching Chaz, even for background information. She was afraid he might see it as a sign that she was ready to pick up where they had left off in January, after the episode that she tried to blame on the weather.

A huge dangerous blizzard, just before Christmas, had succeeded in putting the whole Island under a state of emergency that lasted almost a week. All leave was cancelled and Mercy missed spending the holiday with her parents in Ottawa and with the brother she hadn't seen for three years. The crisis kept news staff working full-out, reporting from the cabs of snowplows pushing through five-metre drifts and from helicopters flying over farmhouses barely visible in the mountains of snow. Adrenalin and excitement kept them going. At the end of long workdays all they could do was catch a few hours' sleep at a motel within reach of the station. Finally, on New Year's Eve, life began to return to normal, and Jinxy organized a big party in the motel's pub to help everyone decompress.

It took only a couple of glasses of wine and hearing someone singing her mother's favourite song, "The Times They Are A-Changin'," for Mercy to take herself to a corner where she gave in to homesickness and tears. Chaz noticed.

"You've been working too hard this week. We all have, but you never let up. Give yourself a pat on the back and relax. Come on, let's get out of all this noise."

He took her gently by the hand and led her to her room.

Almost at once they were on the bed and a frantic coupling was over in minutes. They lay panting, side by side, looking at the ceiling.

"Hey," Chaz said, his voice low and husky, "that was great for starters. How about...why don't you call your friend Pat? Maybe she'd like to join us. You know, share the fun?"

Had she heard right? She sat up and looked at him. He was serious.

"I'm not into that, Chaz."

"You sure? Ever tried it? You might be surprised." He smiled and waited, still lying there on his back.

She got off the bed and went into the bathroom. When she came out, wearing a robe, he pretended the idea of a threesome had been a joke. He paced the room, adjusting his clothes as he talked, opening a floodgate of information that included what sounded like his whole life story, including career plans that reinforced her opinion that television could give people an exaggerated sense of their own importance.

"There," he said. "Now you know everything about me," as if it was a parting gift. She didn't respond. Did she have to ask him to leave?

There was a long pause. He looked her up and down, slowly.

"Okay, I get the message. But you really should learn to relax." And he strolled out of the room, closing the door quietly behind him.

Now, standing at the entrance to the edit suite, Mercy watched Toby, the big strong bear of an editor, as his surprisingly agile fingers flew over the console, making the video sequences flow smoothly.

"Looks like the Opposition can't wait for the big day," she said.

Chaz turned in his chair. "Here to see the master at work?"

"Of course. Never miss a chance to watch Toby do his magic."

"I meant *me*," Chaz said.

Toby looked over his shoulder. "Flattery, I love it. Makes up for not seeing my own mug on the screen."

Chaz got up and stretched. "How about a five-minute break?"

"Okay." Toby headed for the door. "I'll grab a coffee."

"What's up? Hey, like my new glasses?" Chaz pushed his chair away from the console and leaned back, hands clasped behind his head. "By the way, you did a great job yesterday with the homeless story." Offering compliments seemed to be his latest strategy. And now her new assignment to politics would mean more time together and an even harder job keeping him at a distance.

"All this political stuff," she began. "Arthur assumes we're born with the knowledge. Would you mind filling in some of the vacuum?"

"Ah. Now there's a challenge. Get Mercy Pepper to stay awake for a lecture on politics." She welcomed the teasing. A sign that he was backing off? Then he turned on the smile that was part of his charm. Well, okay, it was *all* of his charm.

"I'm going to need more information just to keep my head above water," she said. "How about I just ask some questions?"

"I'm at your disposal. In any way that takes your fancy."

She ignored the implication.

"First, what's all this fuss about calling the election?"

"It's confusing. They've already put off the fixed election date once. And the government's five-year term is up at the end of June. The election act says the campaign has to last at least twenty-six days. So, do the math. They're cutting it pretty close."

"Okay, I'm with you so far."

Toby came in quietly, sat down, and began checking the edits to see that they were clean.

Chaz continued. "Governments don't often go down to the wire like this. Mostly they call an election in the third or fourth year, especially if they're looking okay in the polls. If not, they might hang on a bit, hope for something good to happen, like the Pope naming a new saint from among the cabinet. You get the idea."

"So what's the problem here?"

"Hard to figure. The premier keeps saying they need time to train people if it's going to be a new voting system. But he's been saying that for weeks. And still no decision."

"No scary issues out there?"

"Not lately. A couple months ago that big dairy, Haymarket Creamery, was threatening to close. A lot of jobs there. Workers trying to get a union. Owner wouldn't talk on camera but wanted a bailout. We covered the story at the time. But the government turned him down and no action since."

She recalled watching the story, but her attention had been stolen by stock shots of people sampling a dozen flavours of ice cream. She'd missed the details.

"But you always have your ear to the ground." Mercy avoided looking directly at Chaz, kept the compliment casual but maybe enough to get him going. "Any gossip?"

"Sure. Never ends. You want to hear about the satanic cult infiltrating the premier's family? Our own Saint Ralphina brought me that one this morning."

"Could the premier be waiting for signs of a bumper tourist season? Reservations way up? Something to boast about during the campaign?" She tried edging her way into the topic. "In that interview you did a couple of weeks ago the minister seemed really keen on talking about new programs."

"Sure. Puck loves to brag that he's on top of everything, a real hands-on guy. I asked him again about an election date. No hint. They haven't even given the go-ahead to the agency that shoots their ads. And those guys need lots of lead time."

It occurred to her that the "deal" mentioned on the tape might be the contract with that ad agency. Maybe the Party didn't want the public to know how much they were ready to pay for the ads. But why the delay in getting the money?

"Okay. Enough for my first day." She held up both hands. "The reluctant pupil can only absorb so much."

"For you, a pleasure. Hey, we could go for dinner. I'd let you have your way with my...um...infinite knowledge on the subject."

She was already headed for the door and pretended not to have heard, now annoyed with herself that she had learned very little, except that Chaz was still trying for a second chance. And avoiding him while she dug into the mystery of the tape would be tricky.

Chapter Nine

Half an hour later, Chaz's video editor was standing beside her desk.

"Got a minute?" He took a quick glance over his shoulder, then leaned closer.

"Sure, Toby." She was happy to be distracted from trying to sort out the churning shreds of information that filled her head.

"Chaz doesn't listen to me. Can't blame him. Ralphina's driving him nuts. A new election rumour every morning. You know what she's like. 'God isn't ready to let the premier pick a date yet.'" Toby was talking fast, his voice low, as if Mercy might stop him mid-sentence.

"Okay, Toby. I'm all ears." She pulled a chair over, but he waved it away.

"This comes from my cousin. He's a farmer, west of here, in the country. Yeah, guess that's obvious, no farmers in the city. Anyway, he's not a political type and can't understand why his neighbours can't seem to talk about anything else. But lately, he says, nobody wants to talk about politics at all. None of the usual gossip. No rumours. No stories. Nothing. Silence on the subject. Weird, he says. Makes him suspicious."

"What does he think it means?"

"Has no idea. Maybe you can figure it out."

"Would he talk to me?"

"Give him a try."

"Thanks, Toby. It's worth checking out."

Mercy picked up her notebook and wrote down the cousin's name and number as Toby gave them to her.

"Chaz should listen to you more," she said.

"If anything comes of this, don't mention that I gave it to you. He'll yell at me for going behind his back."

"Your secret's safe with me, Toby."

"Sure." He chuckled. "Always wanted to be a spy. No excitement sitting in the edit suite all day."

She watched him walk away, the now athletic man who had once weighed almost three hundred pounds and could eat and drink everybody under the table. But one day a couple of years ago he had decided to become healthy and fit. And it appeared his resolve had not wavered. Toby was now the person to go to for advice on nutrition and exercise, a walking, running, soccer-playing bundle of wholesome energy. His soccer coach had arranged for him to talk to high school kids about the dangers of energy drinks and sugar. All he needed, he had told Mercy, was a woman who could appreciate him after seeing the photo he kept in his wallet, of the whale he had once been.

Mercy was tempted to follow up Toby's lead right away. It sounded like a "people" story, and she was already feeling stymied in her search for an explanation of the scene on Danny's tape. But it felt important. So she resolved to give it more thought before she went off on the tempting tangent of Toby's cousin's suspicions. Danny may have listened in and recorded that conversation out of simple curiosity, but he had found it interesting enough to keep, wrapped carefully in his kit bag. What was he planning to do with it?

Something Danny's mother had said on the phone was teasing Mercy's memory, but her brain wasn't responding. It was as if her thoughts were attached to strings and each time she tried to follow one to see where it would lead, something yanked her back, refusing to let her go further. She knew why. Since the accident she had kept a stranglehold on her mind because it always ended up at the same place, reviewing over and over the way she had talked to Danny, the way she had pushed him into going behind the building alone to get the shots. And now that she needed her brain to run free, it wasn't budging.

Reminders of Danny seemed to be everywhere—the calls from his mother and father, Jon's insinuations, and now the tape.

Then, suddenly, there it was. The little things, the random bits of information that had clogged up her head for days, were moving into slots, organizing themselves into a pattern.

She glanced around the newsroom. Had she said something out loud when it hit her? Nobody was looking her way. She forced herself through it one step at a time, told herself it was just a theory.

Danny could have planned to blackmail somebody with that tape. If the Party's finances were in trouble, and if that got out, it would not help their image. And it could explain why the premier hadn't yet called the election. And now she remembered the remark by Danny's mother on the phone. She had said his apartment was a mess when they went to gather his belongings. But Mercy knew, in fact, that he was very careful about his personal things, always. He would let the camera van fill with junk, but Mercy had seen him at his locker lots of times. His clothes were folded or on hooks, and his time card was clipped to a special holder inside the door. A place for everything. The only reason his apartment would be a mess was if someone had turned it over, looking for something. The tape? And the man who called Danny's mother asking for property belonging to the station? He wasn't from the station at all. Management would never go to those lengths for an old tape.

And now that her brain was in overdrive it was sending her another message, that Danny's fall down the stairs behind the building might not have been an accident. The possibility was far-fetched, almost unthinkable. Only yesterday she was outraged when Jon Tillerman suggested Danny might be into something illegal. And here she was following threads through a maze like a trained rat. Working every day on crime stories had affected her judgement, and the accident had put her over the edge. Maybe Arthur was right. She was unstable. Her suspicions were off the wall.

She could see why she had been eager to leap to this conclusion. If Danny's death was *not* an accident, then her conscience would be clear. She could bury the guilt she carried for sending him behind the building alone.

First, she would have to face the facts. Danny's death was *not* murder. Stop following that possibility. The inquest had ruled his death an accident. Her guilt would remain.

And now she had to focus on the real story—the meaning of the conversation on Danny's tape. What did secret money problems have to do with the stalled election? The answer would give her a prime news story, Arthur would stop worrying, return her to the court beat, and life and work could get back to normal.

She would have to do it on her own. She couldn't even mention the tape or the blackmail theory to Arthur. He'd have her certified. Telling Chaz made no sense either. He'd just take it to Arthur. And damned if she would share this with Det. Sgt. Jon Tillerman.

Why hadn't she paid more attention to the inner workings of politics? It was no time to go asking basic questions. She did know that all political parties needed money to run an election campaign. And where did it come from? From the Party faithful, she assumed, the card-carrying members.

Chaz wasn't at his desk. She went over and flipped though his card file. Under the Party's name was a list of the executive. The treasurer was Garfield Hoodles. *Hoodles?* What kind of name was that? She checked the phone book, but Chaz had it right. And it was the only Hoodles in the book. Not oodles of Hoodles, she thought, and smiled at her own wit.

Now what? Call him up and ask him straight out if the Party was broke? Not too smart. She picked up the phone.

"Hi, Ruth, it's Mercy. Remember how you like to say there are no easy answers? Well, these will be a snap." Ruth Henderson was active in one of the left-leaning parties, the legal aid lawyer Mercy had interviewed at the courthouse with Danny just before the explosion.

"Good to hear from you, Mercy. You must have had a rough week after that awful accident with your cameraman. "

"Yes. Best to keep working, though. Keeps the mind from dwelling."

"Sure. So what can I do for you?"

"I need a quick rundown on how a political party raises money."

"Got a hot story?"

"Backgrounder. I'm starting from zero. You know me and politics. An empty corner of my brain."

"Okay." Ruth chuckled. "Well, party members pay their dues, just like any club, even the Hell's Angels. Then the party 'bagman' beats the bushes for the rest. Simple as that. Every party out there has an agenda. Up in the clouds are the ideologues. And as you descend, the motives become more pragmatic until you reach The Great Provincial Free Beer Party. But corporations are probably at the top of the list for donations to the two main parties."

"Private companies?"

"Sure. Many companies contribute to the two main parties. Hedging their bets. And there's a nice little tax incentive, too. More than you get, Mercy, with your annual donation to the animal shelter."

"And how's the money spent?"

"The election campaign, running the office, advertising, rallies, that stuff. These days they hire specialists to design a whole string of television ads. Sophisticated production. Costs a fortune."

"How much?"

"There's a limit to how much each party is allowed to spend for the whole campaign. About ten dollars per registered voter."

"Seems fairly straightforward."

"But that's not all. Each candidate can spend another

ten dollars for each voter in the district."

"That's on top of what the provincial party spends?" Mercy tried to do the math in her notebook as Ruth talked. "Sounds like a pile of money."

"Sure is. And that's just one party I'm talking about. All parties can spend that much if they have it. But whoever's in power usually has the easiest time raising money. Unless it's very obvious that they'll be turfed out and won't be dispensing big government contracts anytime soon."

"Okay, Ruth. Thanks for this. Someday when you're premier I'll say I knew you when you had time to talk to a lowly reporter."

"You're that naïve? This province will never elect a social democratic government. I just belong with the underdogs. Gotta go."

Really, Mercy thought, *this is no different from research-ing any news story.* She dialed the Elections PEI office and identified herself to the woman who answered.

"I have a couple of questions about political con-tributions."

Silence at the other end. Then, "It's not my job to be interviewed by the media. Are you recording this?"

Mercy had never heard such a hostile tone from a civil servant. She gave herself the "count to five" pa-tience reminder.

"No, this isn't an interview. Just looking for a bit of information. And I'm pretty sure it's not classified."

She heard a click, then a man's voice. "Fawcett here. Can I help you?"

Apparently he could. And he did.

"Take a look on our website," he said, cheerily. "The list of contributors is published and updated regularly.

All amounts over two hundred and fifty dollars are there to see."

"Just one more question, Mr. Fawcett. Why couldn't the woman who answered have told me?" she said.

"Sorry about that." His voice lowered a little. "We're sitting here revving our engines at the starting line, expecting an election call any minute. And when it comes we have about a million things to do all at once." He paused. "The stress is starting to show."

Chapter Ten

So, even the election bureaucrats were feeling the pressure. As Mercy hung up, Arthur came out of his office and wandered over to her desk. Was he watching for strange behaviour? Had this increased surveillance become part of his daily routine?

"Phoning?" he said, as if he had caught her doing something illegal.

"Just trying to get more information about the new internment camp." How easily the lie came.

"No sarcasm. Objectivity. Remember?"

Ah yes, she thought. A reminder. Her lack of objectivity. Arthur had never referred directly to the episode in Ottawa. But he would have seen the report in her personnel file, the highlights of which included Mercy's admission of a certain naïvety, a lack of distance from the case. It was the issue that had sent her looking for a fresh start.

It had begun when a woman approached her in the corridor outside Family Court, insisting they'd been in grade school together. And Mercy, ashamed that she couldn't remember this shabby person with the sad story, went straight to the social workers with some hard questions about why the woman's baby had been taken into care. Mercy wasn't surprised that officials refused to discuss the case. But the woman and her husband were eager to be interviewed. And Mercy's news report suggested that the pair were victims of overzealous bureaucrats. Her mistake became known within days when the parents turned up in criminal court, charged and soon convicted of fraud, drug trafficking, and child endangerment.

It was an error that Mercy knew she must never repeat. She had jumped to a conclusion without enough evidence. And she had almost done it again. But still, the conversation on that tape was intriguing. She wasn't going to let it go.

"Okay, Arthur, objectivity it is. So it must be time to get reaction from the street people. Both sides of the story. Fundamental, as you always say." She folded her arms and smiled up at him, waiting for his answer.

"Stir them up?" he said. "Not our job."

"So we just leave it hanging?"

He thought for a few seconds. "Retailers. Get comments."

"Ask them how they'll enjoy *not* having the homeless hanging around their storefronts? A little predictable, isn't it?"

"Do it!" His voice was rising dangerously.

Arguing with Arthur over points of journalism was nothing new, but why was she doing it over the homeless story? It wasn't the one she really wanted to pursue.

"Okay, Arthur. Whatever you say. A chorus of retailers." But as soon as the words were out she knew what she had to do.

She would mount an irresistible argument for going after the most intriguing story, buried in that conversation on the tape Danny had kept. Politicians as victims of blackmail on the eve of an election? She wanted to know more, a lot more, and so would the public.

A careful approach to Arthur would be vital. She could not give away too much or he might turn it over to Chaz. She was acting like a rookie, someone who manipulated and schemed. She began to scheme. Five minutes later she was standing at Arthur's desk, the door closed behind her.

"Retailers!" he barked. "Remember?"

"Listen, Arthur. Something's come up. I need just a few minutes of your time. I'm asking you to listen carefully to the small amount of information I can give you. Then I'm appealing to you, based on all the work I've done in this newsroom, to trust my judgement." She felt like a young lawyer pleading that first case.

His eyes shot to corners of the room, as if planning an escape.

"I've come across something that I'm *certain* is a good story but needs research time. It could be *really* big and implicate some very…um…prominent people."

He held up a hand. "Illegal? Julie's beat."

"This story deserves someone who can devote *all* their energy to investigating. I'm the only one you can spare."

"Free rein? No. Spill it. The story. You said big."

"I really can't. Not yet. Just give me a few days. You've always let me run with a good idea. I've never let you down, have I? And *you* can get back to the important work of planning for election night."

"Bad timing. Not now." He spun his chair to the window.

"Okay, Arthur. I give up this time, but you haven't heard the end of it." So much for her powers of persuasion. A fresh strategy was needed. Meanwhile she headed for Jinxy's desk to ask for a camera for the retailers' clips. Twenty feet away her phone was ringing. Jon Tillerman leapt to mind.

It wasn't him. A woman introduced herself as Alice Marshall, said she had watched Mercy's report on the new farm for street people.

"The government worries that homelessness makes us look bad. Cosmetics. Not a lot of thought went into this. I've seen street people in cities all over the world. Here at least we can afford to help the small numbers we've got. And some actually prefer street life to whatever it was they left."

Mercy was surprised at the sincerity in the voice. This wasn't a crank call.

"When I was a schoolteacher," the woman continued, "a couple of these people were in my class. They were children but I could see that they'd have a hard time in life. Too bad I couldn't have taught them some way to cope when they grew up. And now I give them money and they probably spend it on liquor. And it doesn't help in the long run." She paused, not in a hurry, and not trying to convince Mercy of anything, just thoughtful.

"You know, there are addicts in every family, mine included. It's just that street people don't have the respectable trappings to help them get by. So the rest of us have to look after them, don't we?"

"But not by hiding them away in the country?"

"It may be a nice idea for those who'd like to go. But someone should ask them first."

"We'll be following this story, Ms. Marshall. I'll

keep in mind what you've said. I'm very glad you phoned." She took down the caller's number. No simple solution, she had said.

Mercy tapped on Arthur's door. "Yes?" he said. And she wondered, not for the first time, why he never said "come in" or actually opened the door himself. Did he expect the knocker to state their business through the keyhole? She opened the door and took a couple of steps into the room. His eyebrows shot up.

"Still here?"

"I have an idea I know you'll like, Arthur." She didn't wait for a reaction. "This so-called problem with the street people is more complicated than it looks. I've given it a lot of thought. We're not doing the issue justice with a couple of short news stories. There are some—"

"Calm down. *Jesus.*"

She counted to five in her head and tried again. "I have an idea for another way to do it."

He sighed, as if life was one long session of dealing with loony reporters. "Write it down." He turned his chair to the window, its favourite position.

"I'll be back in half an hour."

"Don't hurry."

At her computer she began typing. In twenty minutes it was ready. She went over it and added a couple of things she knew he would like.

His door was closed again. She rapped once and walked in, holding out her proposal, all on one sheet of paper, concise, well-written. He picked it out of her hand by a corner, keeping it at arm's length, like something fished out of the toilet.

"What's this?"

"Just read it, will you? Please?"

He squirmed in his chair, a look of dread spreading over his face. Then he glanced down, started to read, and waved her to a seat. Halfway through he gave her his furrowed brow look. She could almost see the scales trembling as he weighed the possibility that she might again be capable of behaving strangely under stress, of embarrassing them all.

"Can't do it," he said, and spun his chair to the window again.

"But it's good stuff, Arthur. We *should* be doing an in-depth half-hour documentary on the street people. Nothing controversial, I swear. You'll see the script before I start editing, long before it goes to air. Information only. A real service to our audience. How other cities in Canada deal with it. Meanwhile, I'll do the short news items as they come up, as the government gives out more details." She put a little emphasis on *government* and his chair turned slowly to face her again.

His eyelids drooped in that way the news staff had come to recognize as his deep-thinking mode. She was counting on this. He was translating what she had just described into his own terms. It would mean not having to keep checking on her every day and not having to face her champing at the bit, wanting to cover controversial elements.

"Not bad. Doable."

Perfect. And he had already forgotten about getting reaction from retailers. Now so would she.

He stood up, patting the breast pockets of his jacket, like a general checking his medals. A smile of relief spread over his face, the relief of a man who's just learned that his girlfriend isn't pregnant after all.

She looked at the clock on the way back to her desk. Still time to get a start today. Three calls to national and regional tape libraries tracked down several news stories done by reporters at other stations on the plight of street people in their cities. She asked for them to be sent to her on the following day's satellite feed. Next she spent an hour talking to two producers, one in Toronto, one in Vancouver, to see how those cities provided for the homeless. She taped the conversations, so she'd have a record of details that might be needed later. Then she called an old friend in Ottawa, a psychologist who'd studied the culture of the homeless—people who had no choice and people who actually liked the freedom it gave them. He promised an interview by satellite in the next couple of weeks, whenever she was ready to book a studio at the press building on Wellington Street. By four o'clock she had a rough outline, a list of possible interviews, and some suggested local guests for a live panel to follow the airing of the documentary. She included the name of the retired teacher.

The wheels were in motion. Now she would have the freedom to dig into the story she did not want to leave alone—whether Danny's secretly recorded conversation was evidence of political corruption.

The lunch she had packed that morning sat on her desk. She ate it quickly, couldn't have said what was in it, her mind bouncing around like a racquetball. Then she flipped back through her notebook until she found the phone number.

"May I speak to Mr. Hoodles, please?"

"My husband is no longer here." This was the wife? Mercy had almost asked to speak to her father, the voice was so childlike. "This is Elspeth Tate Hoodles speaking. My husband died in March," the woman added.

Ouch.

"Oh, I'm so sorry, Mrs. Hoodles. I didn't know. My name's Mercy Pepper. I'm a journalist. I must have taken his name from an old list."

"What list was that?"

"The executive of the Party. Mr. Hoodles was listed as treasurer."

"Yes, that's correct. He was treasurer for many, many years. Until the day he died. If you tell me what you want, perhaps I can help you. I'm used to helping people." The woman didn't seem eager to hang up. Mercy hesitated.

"I'm looking for some information about the Party's fundraising. If it's not too insensitive to ask, Mrs. Hoodles, what happens to the money that your husband would have been holding for the Party, now that he's...gone?"

When the woman answered, it wasn't with the surprise Mercy had expected. It was as if she had been waiting for the question.

"Oh, that's being looked after." The statement sounded deliberately mysterious. Was she trying to drag out the conversation? Maybe she just wanted someone to talk to.

"Can you tell me more?" Mercy reminded herself not to sound too assertive. "What I mean is, exactly what happens in a case like this? I presume there's an account in the name of the Party and the funds are there, waiting to be used?"

"Well, yes. But it's a little more complicated than that. My husband was given a large amount of responsibility. Because of my family, you see."

"Sorry, I don't understand."

"My father was Selfridge Tate."

Was Mercy meant to be impressed? She had no idea who Selfridge Tate was.

"Perhaps we shouldn't be talking about these things on the telephone," the childlike voice said. "Would you like to come to my home? I could explain all this much more fully in person." A brief pause. "I could see you... tomorrow at one forty-five."

Mercy took down the address. Maybe it would be a waste of time, but with so little to go on, it was worth taking a chance that Elspeth Hoodles might have some useful information.

On the drive home from the station Mercy felt herself gradually relaxing, the farther she got from the city. The days were getting longer; the fields were getting greener, almost by the minute. And today the clouds were speeding across the sky faster than she had ever seen them move, on their way somewhere, full of purpose. There was energy at work everywhere she looked. Nature didn't sit around wondering what to do next. It just kept those seasons coming, kept the juices flowing. At that moment she was struck with a sense of well-being that she hadn't felt for what seemed like a very long time. The evening didn't stretch ahead like a grey void needing to be filled.

Chapter Eleven

She was back at the station at eight the next morning, knowing it would be torture to sit through the morning meeting, her mind racing, feet twitching to get started. She intercepted Arthur arriving at his office door.

"I'll have to skip the meeting today, Arthur. I might have a lead on the location of the country property for the homeless. I'll drive out and take a look, see if there's activity."

His lips pursed. A big decision, was it, to let her out of his sight?

"No camera. No confrontation." He reached for the doorknob.

"Absolutely. Just research."

It was a lie. She had no such lead. What she did have was an appointment to talk to Toby's cousin at his farm, made last night from her home phone.

"I wasn't trying to get myself on the news," the man had told her, his voice hesitant but not unfriendly. "Just sort of thinking out loud. Anyway, if you want to hear it, it won't be over the phone. You'll have to come out here."

And now, with Arthur out of the way, Mercy grabbed a map and headed for the door. Half an hour later she was deep in the countryside, west of the city, not as familiar to her as the area around her little schoolhouse. But the farms appeared prosperous, carefully maintained, the pride on display, houses and barns that showed no sign of giving in to the ravages of time and weather. Modern bungalows appeared along the road, too, as if some farms had sold off acreage for development. Another five minutes and she began to see village names that were familiar but she couldn't think why. The cousin's directions were good and she didn't need to look at the map. Soon she found the lane he had described, a handmade, bright red, miniature barn serving as a mailbox, the name Cox stenciled on its side.

A large border collie ran toward the car as she pulled up to a substantial white house. She hesitated. The absence of barking wasn't necessarily a good sign. But this pooch reminded her of Pat's dog, George. And now his tail was wagging frantically. She got out and the dog seemed eager to lead her to the side door, where Graeme Cox had just appeared.

They shook hands. He looked at the sky where clouds were loitering.

"Let's go in. Anyway, don't need neighbours dropping by to see who my visitor is. No such thing as privacy out here." He was smiling as he spoke, and Mercy saw a shy but relaxed man, probably late forties, hair starting to thin, a resemblance to Toby in the strong build.

He led her inside to a big comfortable kitchen. They took chairs at a round wooden table and Mercy dug out her notebook.

"I'll be out spreading manure this afternoon. Too bad you'll miss that." He laughed to himself.

"This shouldn't take long, Mr. Cox."

"Call me Graeme. We're not formal out here."

"Okay, Graeme. Now," she began, "what's this about a strange silence to do with politics that Toby was telling me about?"

"You might think it's nothing. Or maybe that people just don't like me. And I'm not keen to talk about politics at the best of times. But for the last few weeks, even a mention of the election delay and the subject is changed, fast. See, not everybody out here is farming. A lot are working at the plant. Not so long ago, a bunch of them tried to get a union certified. Couldn't see the problem myself. All the farmers around here ship milk and cream there. The owner turns a good profit, has for years. But he said a union would put him under unless he got a government bailout. That's the usual line from business people, right? Well, he didn't get that bailout and the workers were furious at the government, said they'd vote for the Opposition this time. Election was all they talked about at the time."

"Is that the big dairy that was in the news a couple of months ago? Haymarket Creamery?"

"That's the one." He shook his head. "Then the election date was put off, and suddenly everybody went silent. I couldn't figure it out."

"And you don't have any theories, yourself?" Mercy asked.

"No. Except... You might think this is foolish." He rested his arms on the table and leaned toward her a little. "I was outside the post office in the village. A guy I know who works at the plant was sitting in his car. Window was down so I crossed the street to say hello. Guess he didn't see me coming. He was writing on a clipboard and my voice caught him off guard, made him flinch, and he shoved the clipboard under the seat in a hurry, like he didn't want me to see it. So I kind of teased him. Moonlighting, was he? Doing surveillance for the Mounties? He didn't laugh. Kind of scrambled for words, then said something about getting names of people who wanted a flu shot. But he was really on edge."

"And you couldn't see what was written on the clipboard?"

"Just for a couple of seconds before he noticed me. There were names, for sure. But flu shots didn't sound right. That's done in the fall, isn't it? Then I thought they might be still working on getting a union, but quiet-like." Graeme ran a hand through what was left of his hair and heaved a sigh. "Ah, who knows? Only other thing on the paper was a couple of phrases along the top. More like what you'd write if you were just doodling, though. Know what I mean?"

"Do you remember what they were?" Mercy was ready to admit that this talk was going nowhere.

"A bunch of nonsense. One was 'Ice Cream Flu,' and the other was 'Election Virus.' Maybe you can figure it out. Toby thinks you're pretty smart. Or maybe I'm just completely out to lunch." He apologized for not having more to tell her, then offered to show her his new Jersey heifer, if she was interested.

"It's tempting, Graeme, but...maybe another time?"

"Sure enough."

He stood in the yard and she returned his wave as she drove off, but her mind was already churning. On the surface, what he had told her was silly, frivolous even. What could it possibly have to do with the election delay? And she had just wasted half the morning. Then one far-fetched idea popped up. Could "Election Virus" have something to do with the computerized voting system? But what the heck was "Ice Cream Flu" all about? Maybe the man in the car with the clipboard was just getting names for some kind of petition. But she had no idea what the issue might be. And why didn't he want Graeme to see it?

She hadn't been paying attention to her driving. The sun was now behind her and she was on the wrong road. Only herself to blame. She dug out the map to make sure. Besides showing that she was at least half an hour out of her way, something else struck her. Those village names she'd noticed on the way to Graeme Cox's farm were familiar because they were all within that one voting district, Ellingham East, which Arthur had given her to research. It was where the government's candidate had won by just a handful of ballots, the district that would be watched carefully on election night. And, of course, as Graeme had told her, the dairy plant that employed so many people was right there. She'd file that bit of information away and think about it later.

By eleven she was back at her desk. The newsroom was relatively quiet. Reporters were either out on a story or on the phone trying to get one. Mercy was surprised that she was already hungry. The country air? She ate her packed lunch and focused her thoughts on the upcoming interview with Mrs. Hoodles, hoping for something more revealing than what the morning had produced.

But at two o'clock Mercy found herself standing with her *back* to Mrs. Hoodles's front door, trying to figure

out what had just happened. Her one forty-five appointment with the treasurer's widow had lasted less
than fifteen minutes. The lady had given her the bum's
rush, and Mercy didn't know why.

Across the street a car was pulling up a few metres in
front of Mercy's. And as she walked down the winding
brick path a man got out and started toward the house.
It was Puck. He looked startled when he saw her and
paused as if he might speak. But instead he nodded and
continued toward the door. Interesting, thought Mercy.

In her car Mercy rewound the last few minutes.
She had arrived at precisely the time specified, at the
address on an old residential street not far from the
Lieutenant governor's mansion, an area of spreading
lawns and hired gardeners. The Hoodles's house was
an elaborate, blinding white, two-and-a-half storey,
with a heavy front porch and another above it, sup-
ported by mock-Grecian columns. A sparkling silver
Volvo sat in the driveway, its nose facing what looked
like a former stable, tastefully converted to a double
garage. Mercy could almost feel curtains twitching at
neighbours' windows.

The woman who opened the door was tall and heavily
built, her confident appearance not what Mercy had
expected from the little-girl voice on the phone. Elspeth
Hoodles was dressed in a pale grey tailored suit. A
silver pin in the shape of an ornately scrolled *T* sat on
a lapel. She appeared to be in her sixties, but the face
was at odds with the rest. Across a broad forehead hung
a thick fringe of blond hair, cut as straight as a plank.
The rest of her hair curled next to very pink cheeks.
The lips were an alarming shade of red. She offered
Mercy her hand and led her inside.

From down the hall crept a small dog and the woman hissed "Lie down" with such authority that the shock almost sent Mercy diving to the floor herself. At the entrance to a big room on the left Mrs. Hoodles stopped.

"Do you have a business card?" The sweet voice was back.

Mercy rummaged in her bag and handed it over.

The room they entered could only be described as a parlour. Queen Victoria might just have stepped out for a moment. Heavily framed paintings covered almost every wall surface. Mrs. Hoodles showed her to a chair with a deep round seat and a soft padded back, a little too low even for Mercy.

"I'll bring some coffee. And please feel free to look around the room."

It would have been hard not to.

The furniture was the kind rarely seen these days outside a museum. Every piece that wasn't upholstered in fussy brocade was built of dark mahogany, highly polished.

A corner cupboard with glass doors reached almost to the ceiling. It was filled with old books. Several small tables shared the burden of framed photographs and knickknacks. The decoration around the opening of a large marble fireplace reminded Mercy of the proscenium arch of a theatre stage. The play would be by Oscar Wilde.

But all this was dwarfed by the main attraction: a huge oil portrait of a middle-aged man with thick white hair and a stern expression, a male version of Elspeth Hoodles and the largest portrait of an individual Mercy had ever seen outside the Louvre. She couldn't help smiling at the sheer egotism on display.

The man was probably considered handsome in his youth. Now the chin was starting to sag and the hands had thickened. The look was serious but not unpleasant. Maybe the painter wasn't the best, the colours weren't natural, but he'd caught something of a strong personality: the erect pose, head up, looking straight out. A couple of fingers resting in the watch pocket of his vest spoke of a man to be reckoned with. He was posed but ready to act at a moment's notice.

Behind her Mercy heard the rattle of saucers and turned to find Mrs. Hoodles carrying a silver tray with matching coffeepot and delicate china cups. For her size she handled the job gracefully. She set the tray down carefully on a low table and smiled. Mercy went back to her assigned seat.

"You noticed the portrait of my father."

"It's impressive."

"Cream and sugar?" Mercy nodded and a full cup was placed in her hand.

Mrs. Hoodles poured a second cup and lowered herself, back straight, knees together, to sit on the edge of a hard-stuffed sofa.

"He was a great man, my father. He did more for this province than anybody before or since. But you're young. And your name is Pepper? That's not an Island name. You wouldn't know much about our history." She looked up at the portrait. "He was famous as a breeder of cattle. Yes, even before he entered politics." Her tone implied that the occasion of his *entering politics* had been a huge public ceremony, with the peasantry on its knees in homage.

Just as Mercy was figuring out how to get her own topic onto the agenda, the woman quickly drained her cup, placed it on the tray, and snatched up Mercy's card.

"You want to know all about the money," she said, still looking at the card.

The bald statement caught Mercy off guard.

"Oh, there's a lot I could tell you. But for now, I'll need to know a little more about you. What is it you people call it? Background." The girlish delivery was again sweet in tone. But behind it Mercy heard something else: a childish stubbornness, a sulker.

"Of course, I'll give you my background," Mercy offered, "but surely you can just tell me whether your husband, as treasurer, looked after the account that held money from contributors to the Party."

"Yes, we'll get to that. But first, where do you live?"

Okay, Mercy thought, *I'll just play along and see where it goes.* "I live in a little abandoned schoolhouse east of here."

"Oh dear, what a shame. Young people no longer seem to care about how things appear."

Mercy was on the point of parking her cup and bolting for the door when the voice went on, almost in a whisper. "My late husband was very careful about looking after the money. He was loyal, not just a book-keeper. And you may call me Elspeth."

"I don't want to offend you, um, Elspeth, but there are rumours out there. And one is that the Party has a problem with money. And that might be why the premier has delayed calling the election. Do you know anything about that?"

"I *do* know that they spend far, far too much money on election campaigns. That's the story you should be doing." Her fingers were now twisting Mercy's card as if she were wringing a tiny neck.

"In father's day *politics* was not a dirty word. A rally wasn't some gaudy event with vulgar music and circus balloons. It was a serious meeting. All candidates came, from all parties. They spoke directly to the voters. Wonderful speakers. Orators, like my father. Now it's nothing but money, money, money. They *advertise*. On *television*. Like common retailers."

"Yes, an interesting issue, Mrs. Hoodles, but can you tell me anything specific to do with the money your husband kept in trust?"

The woman glanced at her watch, stood up and went to the window. "I'm sorry," she said. "I have another appointment in a few minutes." She came back with surprising speed and took Mercy's cup, still half full.

At the door, Elspeth Hoodles apologized again, then added with great formality, "I may have more to say on the subject at a future time."

And now Mercy sat behind the wheel of her car, parked behind Puck's black Chrysler, wondering what to do next. Elspeth Hoodles obviously had an agenda of her own, but what was it? In fact, why had she even agreed to see Mercy?

Then the penny dropped. *Of course*. The woman wanted Puck to see Mercy leaving. Elspeth Hoodles had arranged it that way. To make Puck think she had been talking to the media about the money.

Mercy drove slowly down the street, around the block, and parked again a good twenty metres back from Puck's car, far enough away not to be obvious.

Half an hour later boredom had reduced her to watching a couple of pigeons performing a mating ritual, the male fanning out his tail feathers and strutting around the female, who looked as bored as Mercy felt. The guy pigeon didn't want to take no for an answer. He reminded her of Chaz, and she laughed out loud. She was still smiling when an old, rusty brown truck caught her eye as it moved slowly past her, then sped up and swung into the Hoodles's driveway beside the Volvo.

*

Skim knew he was right. It was the reporter, parked right there on his street. Well. Lucky him. *Take it cool.*

He locked the truck and strolled down the sidewalk toward her car. As he got closer she looked away. Did she even remember him? He crossed the street and went to the driver's side. The window was closed. He knocked a rat-a-tat. She looked up, shaded her eyes, and opened a thin slice of window.

"Hi. Remember me? Skim? Last Saturday at the auction." He put out his hand, ready to shake, but she didn't put the window down. So he jammed it through the opening. She shook it by the fingers, none too friendly.

"How's it going?" he asked. "Any hot news today?"

"Just taking a break."

"Looking for somebody lives around here? I know all the neighbours."

She took out a notebook and pen.

"Sorry," she said. "Maybe I don't look busy. But I've got a few things to write down while I'm...here. So I can't really sit and talk. Nice to see you again, though."

The brush-off. Like she'd done it a hundred times and was good at it.

"Got a question for you," he said. She was looking straight ahead now. "Me and the guys were just talking

117

about that explosion. Where your partner there...you know." He had her looking at him now but not in a good way.

"And, hey," he said. "What happened about that milk truck? That had the gas in it. They ever figure that one?"

"Yes, it's all sorted out. Charges are pending."

"Oh yeah? Against who?"

"Some guy out in the country."

"So, just the one guy?"

"So far."

"Didn't see it on the news."

"He hasn't appeared in court yet. That's what 'pending' means."

He could see she was getting kind of cranky now.

"So he's sitting somewhere waiting for the judge to get back from Florida?"

"Normal delays, paperwork." She didn't crack a smile, just turned away and started tapping a finger on the steering wheel.

Stop while you're ahead, boy.

"Okay. Just wondering. The guys and me. I'll let you go. Got work to do myself."

He moved away and crossed the street again, giving her a little two-finger salute as he walked to the truck. In the garage he did some sorting, thinking about what she'd said. Maybe Cab was off the hook, nothing to worry about. Then again, maybe not.

Chapter Twelve

Mercy watched the guy who called himself Skim go into Elspeth Hoodles's garage. What was he? Handyman? Gardener? All-round nuisance?

She had just wasted almost an hour. Then as she made a move to start the car Mrs. Hoodles's front door opened and Puck appeared. Alone. No lingering on the step for a polite farewell. Head down, he marched down the path and across the street, flicking a key chain against his leg, not looking in either direction, throwing himself into his car and starting it almost in one motion. Even the engine sounded indignant. Interesting, she thought, to see politicians when they think no one is looking.

As Puck pulled away Mercy followed at a distance that wouldn't attract his attention. After a few turns he appeared to be heading toward the set of modern government buildings that squatted on the west side of the city, smack in the midst of Victorian-era homes. When he pulled into an underground parking garage she found a space on the street, grabbed her bag, and went in the front door.

The elevator opened for her on the ground floor and there he was.

"Hello, Mr. Minister." She feigned surprise.

"You're a busy lady today."

"On my way to the, um, license bureau. But since I'm here, can I come up and talk to you for a minute?"

"Certainly," he said, sounding anything but certain.

Mercy was surprised that he agreed to meet without notice, but in the elevator it occurred to her that he probably wanted to find out just how much Elspeth Hoodles had revealed about the Party's money matters.

At the third floor they walked a long hall, bypassed his secretary, and went straight into the corner office. He sat at his desk and shuffled some papers. She took a seat that wasn't offered.

"And what can your government do for you today, Miss Pepper?"

"What's going on with the campaign money?" she asked.

A faint smile appeared. "What money's that again?"

"I've heard the Party doesn't have its funds lined up for the election campaign."

The smile became a laugh. Then he gazed out the big window to his left. It had a great view of the treelined road that ran along the harbour.

"You're obviously listening to the wrong people." He turned to her again. "Opposition rumours? How could we not have the money? Seen our list of contributors?" He leaned over the desk toward her, his voice low, confiding. "The truth is we're doing a great job. Our supporters know it. They're behind us a hundred-and-ten per cent."

"Is this hockey language, sir? If you get a hundred-and-ten per cent on voting day it would raise a couple of questions. Or am I being too cynical?"

"Oh, I've met dozens like you before."

"So if money isn't the problem, why the delay?"

"Promises to keep. Terrific stuff. We want to get them started. Why we were elected."

"If you're so sure of a win, why not get the election over with first?"

"We're filling out our term, that's all. Five years. That's the law. And we're not breaking it. So where's your story? You people have nothing better to report?"

He was grinning now. Back on top.

"You know that I talked to Mrs. Hoodles."

"There's not much I don't know." He picked up a paper clip and peered at it, fascinated.

"She told me some things that don't jibe with what you're saying."

"Really? And why would anybody listen to her?"

"Well, with all due respect, sir, I noticed you spent some time with her yourself."

"A courtesy call. To a recently bereaved woman." He was still examining the paper clip.

"But what about the money that Garfield Hoodles was responsible for? If the list of contributors adds up to a healthy amount, as you say, what's the problem? Is it possible that the money's gone?"

"Say that in a news report and you'll look like a complete fool. If Elspeth Hoodles told you that, she's making it up. Don't you people ever get the facts before you go shooting your mouth off in front of a camera?" The scar that connected his eyebrows was now as red as a stoplight.

"I didn't mean to upset you, Mr. Minister. I'm not reporting any of this. It's just research, asking questions." How far could she go with a cabinet minister before overstepping the bounds of civility? She leaned forward in the chair. "But I think you know what I'm talking about. Why is the truth so painful? Don't your constituents and your supporters deserve the truth?"

She imagined she could see the red scar throbbing now and the fleshy face becoming more pink as she watched. He hunched down in his chair and looked around, as if to make sure no one else was in the room.

Then, in a low snarl he said, "And you'd know the truth if you heard it? Not likely. But here's a truth for you anyway. And it shows your ignorance: the financial affairs of a political party are nobody's business but its members. It's not taxpayers' money, it's not government money. It's money that comes from party supporters. And the list of who those supporters are is public. Other than that nobody has to tell you people a goddamned thing."

She watched, fascinated, as the words twisted his mouth into interesting shapes, the thick moustache like a synthetic broom on the attack. The scar looked ready to burst open. She was tempted to tell him he looked cute when he was mad.

"Mr. Minister, I'm shocked at your language. Been hanging out at the rink again?" She deserved a penalty for that remark, but she really wanted to see what might happen if he let go.

He peered at her, his lips tight, then slowly unclenched his fists and looked down at the blood where the paper clip had cut into his palm. Two big breaths followed. He turned to the window and took another long breath, then faced her again.

"Look...Mercy." His voice softened. "May I call you that? I'm sorry if I've offended you. We're just so darned busy getting things done. I'm a little impatient when some ridiculous story like this blindsides me."

"No offense taken. I'm used to trying to get information out of people who don't want to give it."

He stood up and came around the desk, wiping the injured hand on his pant leg. "Mercy, believe me. In a couple of weeks we'll all be laughing about this. It's all in your head, or in Elspeth's head. She's a silly woman." He offered his left hand and smiled. "Now I've got to get back to the legislature. My job. For the taxpayers."

"Fine." She ignored the hand and stood up. "But, by the way, you're not my only source. And neither is Mrs. Hoodles." She left him to ponder that one.

Her enjoyment at seeing him upset had faded by the time she got out of the building. *Face it.* She'd been bluffing. All she had was the mysterious conversation on Danny's tape.

*

From the den came the noise of the television. It might have been a cartoon, the characters screeching and hissing at each other. But no. Skim recognized the voices. It was his aunt's favourite show. He stopped in the doorway.

"Caught you at it again." His teasing was an old game they played.

"Look at them in their cheap suits," she said. "Half of them are too fat to see their feet."

He held up his hands. "Heard it before. Know where you're coming from. But, hey, you keep watching, right?"

He looked at the screen. Politicians, sitting in rows in a great big old room. Marble pillars and chairs with soft cushions and red carpets and up at the front on a platform, a seat like a throne for a codger wearing a black robe. And most of the time these guys are shouting at each other, one side facing the other, calling out names like *fool* and *cheat*, then sitting down and looking like they're dozing off. First time he'd watched it with her it was as funny as anything he'd ever seen on TV. But not funny to her.

"I only watch to remind myself how much politics has decayed," she said, not taking her eyes off the screen. He knew more was coming. "When Father was in cabinet they looked *distinguished*. They said things worth listening to."

"No fat politicians in the old days?"

"People carried their weight with dignity. Just look at that fellow."

A guy was on his feet, jabbing a finger in the air, trying to make a point.

"Fat," she said. "Flabby and sweaty. In Father's time a big man was imposing. People ate good healthy home-cooked food. Now it's all hamburgers and beer."

This was how the game went. He'd lead her on, get her blabbing about the times when she was a girl. He couldn't care less about the politics and the names and stuff. But he listened when she got into the way people lived. It was why he liked the job he did for Calvin. Packing up some old tools from a barn, and next thing Skim would be wondering about the people who used them way back before there were even cars. Something to think about.

She switched the TV off and heaved herself out of the chair, shaking her head like she didn't understand what it was all about. But she'd be back again later, watching to the end.

"Did you like the lunch I packed?"

"Yeah, it was great. Think I'll make a coffee before I go out again."

"I'll make it for you."

Days like this he thought it wasn't too bad living with her. Never tried to control him, except for the questions about where he'd been, where he was going. He had answers, maybe not the truth, but enough. The stuff about chicks was a drag, though. Bring a "nice young woman" home some time, she'd say. All he could do to keep from laughing out loud picturing the one he'd been with Friday night. Big earrings and leather jacket with fringes hanging. Cowboy boots. Not exactly what his aunt had in mind. The reporter, though. Bring that one home and the aunt might be some impressed. But maybe not. She didn't like nosy people.

Lately, he'd been feeling like three years in this house was enough. Had plans for moving to his own place. If he was reading the signs right it was about time to make a pitch to Calvin. A partnership. The guy couldn't do much lifting anymore, didn't trust the kids he hired by the hour.

Skim knew it would come. Just needed to be patient. He didn't like Calvin a whole lot—the gossip, the long boring stories about families and who was related. But if he made himself listen sometimes he picked up good information. And Calvin didn't ask questions. When the time was right, he'd offer his stash of antiques that was sitting in the garage. It would be his share of the partnership. Then Skim could see them making a whole lot more money. He'd be an independent man. And one thing he was sure about. He had more good ideas in a minute than most people had in their whole lives. Get his foot in the door and the rest would be easy.

So those Sunday mornings, lying out on the cold, wet grass, they were kind of a test. Like being an apprentice. Now that it looked like it was coming to an end he was even glad he'd done it. *Made* himself do it. Was proud even. Always paid his aunt room and board, too. Insisted. Couldn't live with taking charity, even from family.

She was in a pretty good mood lately. Like she didn't even miss Uncle Garf. Well, he was no ball of fire. Too soft, not sharp. Skim figured the most money his uncle'd ever brought in was when his life insurance paid off. But he treated Skim okay. Kept his aunt out of his hair.

The house and their income came pretty much from her half of what her father left in his will. His mom back in Boston got the other half. But Skim's dad saw it as money to spend on a bunch of crazy schemes. Even as a kid Skim could see his dad's big ideas were foolish. And the money was gone before they had a chance to move to a better neighbourhood. So they stayed in the old one and lived on his dad's pay from the factory. Not a bad life, when Skim thought back. It was where he picked up some pretty good lessons about surviving and getting ahead.

"Been thinking," he said.

His aunt set the coffee down in front of him on the kitchen table, smiling.

"Don't want it to come as a big shock," he said, "but I could be looking for my own place soon."

But she did look shocked. Backed away like he'd shouted at her. He was sorry now he'd said it. Bad timing.

Her face was white, all the makeup sitting on the whiteness like a mask. *Jeezus*, maybe she was going to faint.

"What are you talking about, Roger? You can't mean *now*. Just when everything's getting better?"

"Better? What's that mean? You're still calling me Roger. People call me Skim now. You know that." He took a gulp of coffee to stop the words coming. Didn't want to argue. "Look, maybe you don't want to live alone now. But I can't stay here my whole life. I'm not a teenager anymore."

She moved closer, standing over him like she did when he first moved in, making him feel like a boy. She was quiet for a while, then walked around and pulled out the chair across from him, smoothed her skirt under her like always as she sat down.

"Perhaps I should have talked to you about this before," she said. "but I've been keeping it for a surprise."

"I'm not big on surprises."

"Yes, but you'll like this." She had the same look as when she watched him open a Christmas present. Then she sat up straighter. "Somebody is going to offer you a job soon. A job with prospects. Where you can go as high as your talents will take you. I know you have a lot to offer. All you need is a start."

"Whoa. I've got a job." He knew where this was heading. Some political flunky work.

"You're not telling me you want to stay on with that Calvin fellow? Standing up in front of people, holding second-hand furniture for sale? Like some scavenger?"

"Doesn't bother me, I said that before." He leaned back in his chair, folded his arms.

"It's never been right. I've always known that." She

sounded close to crying. "But Garfield wanted to let you try it. And I went along like a good wife. But here you are, still doing the same job. And now he's gone and there are people who will listen to me."

"I bet. But that's not how I want to get by. Working at a job somebody hatched just because your father was a big deal."

"It won't be like that at all. It will be a job that needs doing. Maybe even the work that Garfield was doing before he died."

"The party bagman? That's what they called him."

"Don't use that vulgar word. There are things you don't understand, Roger. If it weren't for what my family has stood for in the past, Garfield wouldn't even have been the party treasurer. It was only because my father convinced somebody long ago that Garfield was as loyal as a man could be."

"Well, he did the bagman job okay, didn't he?"

She looked down and took his empty cup, smiling a little.

"Oh, yes," she said.

Skim got up before she started on another rant.

"Roger, just promise me you won't do anything... foolish. I'll have more news soon." She reached over and touched his arm as he went by, smiling right at him, still living in dreamland.

Okay, for now, he thought. He didn't like arguments anyway. Waste of time. He walked over to the sink, drank a glass of tap water, and headed out to the garage.

*

Back at the office Mercy found a pile of tapes on her desk, the reports on street people in other cities that she'd requested the day before. They'd have to be looked at, but not now. She unlocked the bottom drawer and took out Danny's tape.

It was getting close to deadline. Everyone was busy, no one looking her way. She pulled her monitor closer and went through the tape again.

Maybe nothing concrete had come from talking to Elspeth Hoodles and Puck, but she was now certain of a few things. It was when she had pushed him about money that Puck had lost his cool. And what was it Mrs. Hoodles had said? Something about her husband being very careful about the money. She sounded proud saying it, not as if he had gambled it away.

But what was the "deal" Puck talked about on the tape, the one that just needed a few details ironed out? And what was the business about talking to a lawyer? That's what intrigued her most, the hint that something about the money or the lack of it might be illegal. And it must have been what got Danny's attention, too.

Something else was nagging at her, though. That outside shot of Puck's house. Chaz had used one in his report. Where did he get it? Danny must have reshot the exteriors. But she had to be sure.

At five thirty Mercy found all three edit suites busy, but Chaz wasn't in any of them. She went to the VTR centre where the day's reports were lined up for that night's show, ready for playback. Chaz wasn't there either, so he had probably gone home.

At his desk she rummaged through the stacks of old field tapes left from previous stories. By now the newscast was in full swing and the room was almost empty.

The tape box was labelled "Tourism interview, exteriors." She slipped it into Chaz's monitor. The only shots on the tape were of the outside of Puck's house. So Danny had kept the original with the overheard conversation for himself, put in a fresh tape, and given the new shots to Chaz for his edit.

Blackmail was a strange business. Offering that tape for money didn't guarantee that Danny hadn't made copies. But, of course, it wasn't the actual pictures the victim was paying for. It was to keep the blackmailer quiet, for the promise not to show and tell.

And now that Danny was dead so was his blackmail scheme. So why had his apartment been searched *after* he died? Someone was still nervous about where that tape was and who might find it. Wouldn't she love to know whom Danny had approached. Probably Puck. But she didn't feel ready to confront him with it yet. Had Danny hinted to anyone else about what he was doing?

That thought brought her to the fellow she had seen this morning. The auctioneer's helper. Skim somebody, Danny's pool hall buddy. But did she really want to look this guy up? A type who might be hard to get rid of?

She called Pat at home.

"Hi. Invented a better mousetrap yet?"

"No. But we're working on breeding a dumber mouse. What's up?"

"That auction last Saturday. Who was the auctioneer?"

"Is he in trouble?"

"No, I just need to talk to him."

"Name's Halpern. Clyde or Carson, one of those cowboy names. You'd find him under Hoodwink Auction Service. Just kidding. It's called AAA Auctions."

Finding this Skim guy would have to wait until

tomorrow. She hated when this happened. Once on a roll it was hard to slow down.

By the time she got home it was almost seven, but she wasn't ready to eat, felt keyed up, jumpy. She put on some sweats and went for a run.

The countryside around the schoolhouse wasn't hilly, and she could make the circuit of about five kilometres in under thirty minutes at a relaxed pace. It was a pleasant evening, with the sun still well above the horizon.

Most of her neighbours here were farmers, and very few cars used the back roads at this time of day. She passed Jack Murphy's neatly mown stretch of lawn, the source of that sweet scent of the first cut. Jack's acre was a shining emerald green. Even the surrounding hayfields looked thicker and more lush than yesterday.

After a couple of kilometres she did some cartwheels. It felt good, like she was a silly kid again. As she ran she planned what to make for supper, to avoid, for now, thinking about Danny and the tape.

By nine o'clock she had finished supper and her mind was again poking at what little information she had to work with. To depend on getting something out of that Skim character was a pathetic way to do research. And yet there didn't seem any better place to go. She took the problem to bed and for the second night that week, lay awake, watching the clock. At one o'clock she got up, looking for something to read, then remembered the "just in case" pills from the therapist. Half an hour later she was back in bed, drowsy.

It began as a dream, watching a symphony orchestra in a large concert hall, playing a familiar piece of music, something by Ravel, slow and sensuous. Then the strings were joined by a sharp percussive sound, a metallic clicking, then a faint scraping. Not rhythmic, but in brief spurts. Gradually the scraping became more urgent. She knew now that she was asleep and had to wake up, to find out what was causing the noise. But she couldn't move her body. She could only lie there and listen. And then she realized what it was: a mouse caught in the trap, struggling. Trying to drag itself free, pulling the trap along the floor. An awful feeling of dread crippled her. And when she tried again to move it was as if her struggle matched the one she was hearing. From far away she heard herself crying in frustration, felt tears on her cheeks. It seemed to go on for hours.

Then a bright light was coming through the windows. It was Thursday morning and she was exhausted.

Chapter Thirteen

The auction room was a former church hall, now jammed with more merchandise than Mercy had ever seen in one place. Dozens of beds and mattresses next to wardrobes, crates of dishes, appliances, bathroom fixtures, lamps, trunks, tables, and chairs of all sizes, old and new. A survey of a century of domestic life. The Skim guy was up on a stage at one end moving a dresser and directing members of what had to be the provincial wrestling team as they fetched and carried enormous pieces of furniture.

She went to the edge of the stage and waited, feeling like a groupie hoping to catch the performer's eye. On nearby tables dozens of big cardboard boxes were stacked four deep. On top of each pile stood a foot-high Anne of Green Gables doll, dressed in the predictable dress and pinafore, red braids hanging, freckled nose, little straw boater. The boxes must be full of them. Then she noticed that one eye of the doll nearest her looked off wildly toward the rafters. On top of the next box the doll had only one braid, another was missing an arm, and the next had no painted features at all, like some space creature. She looked closer, wondering whether she was hallucinating. But no, they were lined up like so many wounded soldiers, a field of disfigurement, casualties of the production line.

A headache was starting. As she had driven into town, her foot on the accelerator had felt weak, her arms heavy. There was more than one kind of impaired driving, and she had done it this morning, escaping from the house without looking into the corner where the mouse must be lying, dead in the trap.

Now one of the crew noticed her and nudged Skim. She turned away, thinking it might be smarter not to appear too eager. In seconds he was beside her.

"Sorry ma'am. The sale isn't till Saturday. But somebody like you might rate a personal tour." He was chewing gum, relaxed.

"The guy at the door said I could look around."

"No problem." He folded his arms and stood watching her.

"Don't let me interrupt your work," she said.

"Always glad to help: Unless your mind's on shoplifting."

By the time she realized he was joking, and forced a laugh, the timing was off.

"Hey, you feeling okay?" He stopped chewing and peered at her.

"Sure. Oh, by the way...while I'm...you mentioned Danny Brewer when I saw you at the auction last week."

"Yeah. Why?"

"We're just...we're having some trouble sorting out Danny's...affairs, and..."

"Don't have a clue about his sex life."

She dragged up a smile.

"Look... Skim. You're the only friend of his I've met."

"I wasn't a real buddy. Just saw him a couple of times. Didn't even know his last name."

"Well, anyway," she began again, "there are a couple of things..." She took a deep breath. "Somehow Danny... um...got hold of something and we need to find out whether he had...whether he mentioned it to his friends." *Holy Unicorn.* Had she ever done a worse job of pumping someone for answers?

"You talking about stolen property?" he asked.

"No, more like...information."

"Well, that's the business you guys are in, right?" He pushed his hands into the back pockets of his jeans. "So, what're you asking? I don't get it."

Was he dragging this out, making her work for it? Or did he really have no idea what she was talking about?

She tried again. "Did Danny ever mention anything about...well, any projects he had going? Anything like that?"

"Might have. I'd have to think about it."

"Could you maybe ask around? Quietly? Let me know? I mean, can I trust you to find out but, you know, keep it between you and me?"

"Sure. Can't promise to get anything, but then maybe you'll fill me in more when I call you back." Without waiting for her number he gave his little two-finger salute and walked off. Halfway across the room he stopped, took the gum out of his mouth, and parked it on the nose of the nearest Anne doll.

*

Well, well. Skim took the stairs two at a time and was back up on the stage. He didn't turn around. Didn't have to. The TV reporter needed a favour from him.

That was something. Might even get into an arrangement, another partnership. But he pulled back from taking that line too far. First, he'd think about what he already knew about Danny and who might know more. Then decide how much to tell her. Show he was right up there when it came to understanding the information business.

He gave the muscle boys a few more directions, then left them to it and made for the office phone near the front door. The reporter was gone. No surprise there. He was right. She wasn't there to look at the goods. She was there to talk to him.

Three of the guys he called were still in bed. Not happy to be awake, but they listened anyway. The last one was out. Skim knew where to find him later. He went back to work, whistling.

*

Mercy's car was heading for the station as if on automatic pilot, but she didn't want to go back yet, knowing the tapes for the homeless documentary were waiting to be reviewed. Instead she stopped at the nearest convenience store and picked up a tired-looking sandwich and some orange juice and headed for Victoria Park. She stopped the car, facing the harbour, dug out a couple of aspirins, and washed them down with juice.

A faint breeze barely disturbed the water. The sky was clear. Against the magnificent blue backdrop herring gulls performed impressive aerobatics. The faint saltwater smell carried a vague fishiness, but it always struck Mercy as something fresh and clean. The sun blazed directly overhead, still on "God's time," as the locals called it, while daylight saving time said it was one o'clock. The small blockhouse, a vestige of colonial days, was freshly whitewashed, and next to it sat two old cannons, looking a little ridiculous in their retirement. Hard to imagine, in a world of drones and missiles, that it used to take only a few iron balls to defend the harbour.

A couple of sailboats were out, and a group of young Japanese women strolled along the boardwalk, pointing and exclaiming, taking pictures, marvelling at sights they must have dreamt about for months.

Mercy took her lunch to a nearby bench. A couple of bites of the sandwich told her it could have been improved by adding shredded Kleenex. She broke it into pieces and put it on the grass a few metres away. The gulls arrived immediately, ignoring her but screaming warnings at each other, snatching bits and taking off. Only the fastest and most aggressive got what they came for. Survival, of course. What life was all about. But up close, not a pretty sight. Those Japanese tourists would see only the panorama of the seashore, graceful birds, nature at its most benign, everyone's image of a stress-free life.

She got up, stretched, and headed back to the car. Inside, her cellphone was ringing.

"Hell you up to?"

"Just...some research, Arthur."

"News conference. One thirty," he barked. "You're late!"

"I thought I was still on the homeless documentary."

"The details. Remember?"

"Right. Sorry, Arthur." But he'd passed the phone to Jinxy.

"The camera's already there, Mercy."

"I'm on my way."

It was the jolt she needed. Her own fault, too. She had forgotten Puck's promise to reveal the enticements designed to get the homeless out of town. It would have to be reported tonight. But now Arthur was on the warpath. And no wonder. She resolved that for the next couple of days the documentary would get her full attention. She would behave herself. Just as well. The meeting with Skim had not gone well. She had no new information but might have picked up an unwanted colleague.

This time the government media room offered no big tourism posters, no cops, no coffee and snacks. Just Puck, already at the table, reading from a news release to a scattering of bureaucrats and reporters, with Fred Fredericks hovering nearby. Luc had set up the camera and was recording.

"...and after much consideration, I'm here to explain the details of the plan to improve the streets of this beautiful city, to explain how we will relocate our less fortunate citizens to a place where they will have a chance to improve their..."

Some activity at the back of the room caught Puck's attention. He stopped talking and people turned to look. The doors were open and a group of about ten filed in, a couple of women among them. They stood at the back, looking around. Mercy recognized some of them: the fellow known as Sailor who hung around the waterfront, cadging change from members of the yacht club and welcoming tourists as they got off cruise ships. And she saw Bruno, former pride of the amateur boxing circuit, his face now lined and bloated. He was limping. Several others were familiar but she didn't know their names. A small white-haired woman helped them find seats in the back row.

Puck looked over at Fred, then smiled down at the gathering.

"This is what we're offering," he said. "Three good nutritious meals a day. Soap, toothpaste, and shaving cream, and a small allowance to cover newspapers, magazines, and snacks, all available on the premises. In the lounge, satellite TV and the latest movies. Attendance not compulsory." He waited for an expected chuckle that didn't come. "And during the day, professional counselling, help of all sorts, and the teaching of a variety of skills from woodworking to welding." He looked up. "And for the, uh, ladies, we'll have something entirely suitable to their interests: cooking, for example, gardening, quilt-making. It's all here, you can read it for yourself." He waved a clutch of papers.

"Now, you must admit your government is prepared to make life as wholesome as possible for these people and give them a chance to get back on their feet. So to speak."

From the back came the rumble of a voice. Luc quickly swung the camera around to a man who was sitting, arms folded across a big chest.

"Anything to drink out there? Any buses into town?"

"Sir, if you're referring to alcoholic beverages, I have to say we're not running a hotel."

"So we'd be stuck there?"

"There might be..." Puck looked down at civil servants in the front row. "We may be able to arrange a bus trip to the city from time to time...a sort of field trip." A bureaucrat was nodding approval.

"And what about heavy work? Me, I can't do heavy work."

"No, no." Puck swatted away the suggestion. "Just some gardening for those who are interested. In fact, by the end of the day, the...um...participants will be so tuckered out and contented, they'll look forward to that big comfy bed waiting in the dormitory at 10 p.m. A worthwhile day behind them, a good night's sleep, and another productive day ahead. The sort of life we all strive for."

"You sayin' there's a curfew?"

Puck tried to crane his thick neck to find the person who was speaking.

"Sir, let me assure you. Everything you could possibly need will be right there. No point going anywhere and certainly not in the pitch dark out in the middle of... Just wait till you see it. A beautiful big farmhouse set in acres of land, a putting green, volleyball, badminton, picnics under the trees. Truly, a kind of paradise."

Mercy was tempted to ask about singsongs around the old campfire.

"What about cigarettes?" someone called out.

"Unhealthy. But we'll provide the latest medications to help you quit the habit."

There was mumbling in the back row as Puck started to rise from his chair. "In the next few days," he added, "officials will approach the people who...uh...qualify so they can sign up for the project and—"

"May I interrupt?" It was the white-haired woman, on her feet now.

Puck sighed and sat down again.

"I don't claim to speak for all the people you have in mind for this program," she said. "But those here today feel there is room to negotiate. This program changes their lifestyle completely. You want them to give up basic human rights. And yet you haven't even discussed it with *them*."

"Well, ma'am. We're glad to see you taking an interest. But our committee of experts—"

"We've formed a committee of our own, Mr. Minister, and we've come up with a list of requests." She leaned over and took a piece of paper from someone sitting next to her. "I'll read it. Twenty cigarettes a day for those who are smokers, transportation into town and back once a day, a meeting once a week to bring up any—"

"We'll certainly take your ideas into..." He was out of his chair again, the last few words thrown over his shoulder.

"No, Mr. Minister." The woman's voice rose a little. "These are not just ideas. They're demands. They're conditions for signing on to your program. And there may be more when others hear about it."

Puck turned to face them, shoulders working. "Demands? Conditions? Where do these people get off making demands?" He looked at Fred as if the answer might be there. "This program is like winning the lottery. Most of us right here," his arm swept the room, "would be thrilled for a chance like this."

The woman was still standing. "They are willing to negotiate, but if an agreement isn't reached by two weeks from today," she looked along the row, "then perhaps *no one* will sign up."

Mercy was beside Luc. He had caught the exchange nicely, panning slowly back and forth on the tripod between the woman and Puck as they spoke.

Now Puck headed for the side door without responding, pushing Fred out of the way. There was an energy in the room that hadn't been there before. Reporters buzzed among themselves. A couple of them moved toward the group at the back, pulling tape recorders out of their bags. Mercy saw Fred coming her way.

"So, Fred. I'm dying to hear what spin you'll put on this one."

"Mercy." His hand went out. "Glad you came. Not a problem here. We're on top of it. A little blip. We might have jumped the gun a fraction. Remember we promised the details within a week. We're ahead of schedule."

"But behind the eight ball."

"So you'll be doing a report for tonight's newscast?" he said.

"Of course. How about this for a lead: 'Government thwarted in its effort to put one over on the little guy.' Sound good?"

"Now, wait. It was a simple misunderstanding."

"Right, Fred. Does the minister want to come back and say that for the camera?"

"Well, he…"

"No, I didn't think so."

Mercy's headache was gone and she was beginning to enjoy herself. Not because she knew the government would look bad on this one, but because she finally had some real people in her story. She looked around and spotted the white-haired woman among the group at the back, some of them now leaning against the wall, others still sitting. Luc was ready, the camera off the tripod and on his shoulder.

"Hello," Mercy said. "I think you must be Alice Marshall."

"Yes. I should have given my name. But I was afraid he'd cut me off before I said a word. Our talk on the phone got me all worked up. Maybe I've gone too far."

"You've certainly got the minister's attention. Would you be willing to explain your approach for my report?"

"I didn't really plan to get myself on the news, but if it helps..."

Luc rolled the tape.

"This little group has asked me to speak for them. And I thought a lot about it and decided that focusing on the human rights issue was just too vague. These people here are really more worried about the details." She glanced around and smiled. "The bread-and-butter issues, if I can call them that. You know, some of them might really want to go."

"And what happens next?"

"The people who came today will talk to the others out there. There could be more demands to put on the list."

Mercy did more interviews then, with Sailor and a couple of others. They all said the same thing, as if they had agreed ahead of time. The message was clear. Their independence was about all they had left and they wouldn't give it up without a struggle, or at least some very real compensation. As Mercy headed for the elevator with Luc he gestured back toward the room, where two street people stood, one on each side of the door, hands out, ready to accept loose change.

Chapter Fourteen

"Missed it? Well?" Arthur was waiting at her desk, glaring.

"No, we got it all. I'll have a good report for tonight." He didn't ask for details and she didn't give him any.

"Do it," he said, and walked away.

Luc offered to go downtown on his own to get shots of the areas where street people were usually found but shoot only those who had been at the news conference, since others might not want to be identified.

Julie came in, fresh from the courthouse.

"Hey, Mercy, remember that new resort chef with the reputation for chasing married women? Some husband is up on a charge of stabbing him with his own meat thermometer." Everybody within earshot laughed. Mercy was missing the daily docket. Covering provincial court was like being handed the characters for a novel.

She got through the rest of the afternoon with the help of coffee. Aside from the exhaustion, it was the kind of day she was used to, back into the old routine. Around four she called the vet college.

"I'm a mess, Pat."

"Oh? Well, here's my mess. In a minute I'll be elbow deep in cow intestines."

Mercy swallowed, aware of the rising contents of her stomach. "I've got at least one mouse carcass in residence, and I can't even look at it."

Pat laughed. "Want me to come out there after work? Bring a hearse?"

"You do have a way of putting things into perspective. Could you meet me here and follow me home? I can't face the house alone." She didn't describe her night of semi-stupor, listening to the fatal struggle.

When Pat arrived it was with the aroma of Greek takeaway filling the car and dog George drooling on the upholstery. Mercy transferred the dog to her own car out of kindness. At the end of the drive to the country, though, he would have to face the cruel fact that the two-legged creatures would eat stuffed grape leaves and moussaka and drink wine. George would get dry kibble and water.

"Can we get it over with before we eat?" Mercy pointed to the corner behind the woodstove and covered her eyes with one hand.

The ringing phone made her jump.

A loud male voice said, "So it's intimidation now? Is that your game?"

"Who is this?"

"Oh, you know, all right. Sending the cops over? Just because I got annoyed at how you people treated us?"

"Mr. Brewer."

"Who else would it be? Then again, probably all kinds out here would like to give you a piece of their minds."

"I think you've already said enough, Mr. Brewer. Apparently you've threatened our senior producer.

That's why the police talked to you."

"Just letting off steam. Don't you get it? But here's what burns me now. It was our *own* cops who came, the Moncton cops. One of 'em lives down the street, for Chrissakes. Now the whole neighbourhood thinks we're criminals."

"I'm sorry to hear that. But what exactly do you—"

"And now that guy, the company property guy or whatever the hell he is. He's calling again. I told the wife to hang up. But no, not her. She had to tell him we found that old tape. Said she already sent it to you. Special delivery! Paid by me, for God's sake. So I'm telling you. Call off your fuckin' flunkies and leave me alone." He slammed the phone down on his own shouting.

Mercy stood where she was and put the receiver back gently, as if it might give Danny's dad some solace. She watched Pat washing her hands at the kitchen sink.

"Done, Mercy. And I've set the trap again. Peanut butter this time. We don't want to bore them with the menu." George gave the corner a brief sniff and went on to investigate almost everything in the room. The only thing he didn't seem interested in was the food.

Mercy set the table and they sat down. The dog continued to prowl.

"Settle down, George. This is not the new frontier." Pat always assumed he understood sarcasm.

Mercy watched him. "Think he's bored? Maybe he wants out."

"No, he's just nosy."

Mercy glanced around, trying to imagine what the dog was after. She had been looking at the desk for several seconds before her slow brain took it in. One of the drawers wasn't quite closed and something was sticking out. She walked over and opened it. Everything was neat, but not quite right. Not the way she had left it.

Pat continued to eat. Mercy's gaze moved from one piece of furniture to the next. Within a minute the survey picked up several more hints that objects had been moved.

"Someone's been in here," she whispered, hardly believing she was saying this calmly. It was as if eyes were still watching, peering in through every pane of glass. She quickly went to the long row of windows along one wall, grabbed the drapes roughly and flung them along the wooden rod to close out the light. Then she ran to the other side of the room and did the same.

"What are you doing?" Pat said. "It's not even dark yet."

By now Mercy was shaking, standing near the wall as if it would protect her. As if walking into the middle of the room would make her vulnerable.

"Listen. Someone's been here today. Somebody's gone through my desk, opened the trunk there, turned over the cushions on the couch. Look at that painting, Pat. It's crooked!"

It took a few minutes to convince her. And pointing out each bit of evidence gave Mercy something to focus on besides the fright. By the time Pat was taking her seriously she felt calmer. Mercy had read about it, how someone comes home to discover a break-in, and how it affects them. But the feeling of having been violated in some personal, physical way was more profound than she had ever imagined it could be.

"Okay. We'll call the police," Pat announced, heading for the phone. "RCMP? They cover this area, right? Don't touch anything else. Fingerprints."

"No. Stop. I want to think about this for a minute."

"What's to think about? Get them out here now."

Mercy's first overwhelming fear was now being pushed aside by indignation.

"I might know what this is about," she said. It felt good to hear her own voice, reasonable, detached. Not quite what she was feeling, but it helped. "I'm working on a story that's...a little out of the ordinary. This could be part of it."

"Are you serious? This is ridiculous. You don't get paid enough to put up with this crap."

"You're right. But in a way this is just what I needed. It confirms that I'm on to something. Look around. Nothing's missing. If it was the usual break and enter my computer would be gone." She marched to a dresser and yanked open the drawer that held the box with her grandmother's rings. "See? It's all still here."

"Where's your camera?"

It was still there, too, on a shelf in the wardrobe.

"Then who was it? What did they want?"

"Probably the tape. To do with the story. You'll be the first to hear about it, when I've figured it out."

"So they didn't find it?"

"No, it's locked up at the office."

"But you still have to call the cops."

"Who says?"

"Mercy, this is nuts. People can't go around breaking into homes without some consequences."

Mercy was only half listening, her mind racing elsewhere. She didn't want the police in here. With nothing missing they would be polite, file a report, and that would be it. Except that the rumour might get out. Even the Mounties would gossip about a break-in at the home of a TV reporter. But if she kept it quiet, whoever did this might think it went unnoticed. And that might give her a tiny advantage.

Mercy was now feeling much better, just a little shaky from her first "fight or flight" shot of adrenalin. They looked closely and could see where the back door had been fiddled with, scratched around the jamb.

"Get a locksmith out here tomorrow," Pat said. "A better lock. And a deadbolt. Want me to stay here tonight? Of course, George isn't into confronting criminals."

"No. There's no reason for them to come back."

They actually finished their meal, although Mercy couldn't remember later what it had tasted like. Pat's car had just left when the phone rang again. If it was Mr. Brewer she would hang up. But it was Arthur.

"Nine tomorrow. My office. Be there."

"Okay. What's it about?" But he had already hung up.

By the time she went to bed there was nothing that could have kept her awake. Her first fright at the break-in had filled her head with the image of a stranger, some violent thug, his features distorted by a stocking mask. But now that she was pretty sure what this was about, that image was gone, replaced by the picture of bumbling crooks in suits. *The Gang That Couldn't Shoot Straight*. It was laughable, really.

Mercy paused outside Arthur's office, trying to guess what was bothering him. He had skipped his Friday morning squash game for this, something unheard of. She felt like an actor preparing to walk onstage for an improv scene.

For the first time ever he opened the door to her

knock, as if he'd been standing on the other side holding the knob. And he closed it behind her so fast it almost caught her heel. They took their usual seats. He didn't look at her but picked up a sheet of paper and swiveled his chair to face the window. Then he started to read.

"It has come to my attention that you have pursued research in a way that is embarrassing to this station and to the people who are the subjects of your inquiries."

"What?" she said.

Without turning he held up a hand to stop the interruption and kept on reading.

"As you well know, it is one thing to have problems within this news organization. We can deal with those episodes among ourselves. But your latest behaviour has gone beyond what is tolerable. You have lied to your superior about your work, gone behind your superior's back, and harassed people who deserve our respect. All this over some story you've invented that is so far removed from reality that you must be..." The composition must have ended there. He tossed the page onto his desk.

"Words fail me," he said to the window.

The shoddy worker always blames his tools, she thought. But this speech of Arthur's was extraordinary. She realized that what he had to say to her was so urgent that his normal three-word barking style was not capable of delivering the content without composing it ahead of time.

And she got the message. There had been a complaint. From Puck. Her session at his office wanting to know about money and the election delay, and her coverage of the homeless project. Nothing was going his way this week. Like a cornered rink rat, he was now on the attack.

"Arthur, please look at me. Can't we have a conversation like two adults? I tried to tell you about this story, but you wouldn't listen."

"Did listen. Decided no. You bypassed. Out of control."

"I came to you with a good story and you wouldn't trust my judgement. I had to start digging on my own." She heard herself pleading, even as she knew it never worked with him.

At last he turned to her, shaking his head like a doctor now ready to pronounce the patient dead.

"Okay," she said. "Now that I finally have your attention, listen to this. Danny Brewer. Yes, our own cameraman. He was blackmailing somebody. And not just anybody. The Party in power. The government. I'm sure of it. Does that get through? Are you even the least bit interested in that? In what political secrets could be cause for blackmail?" She was on her feet now, pacing, waving her arms. "*That's* the story I'm chasing. It's what I should have been doing with your support."

She had never understood the real sense of the word *dumbfounded* until she saw his face. His mouth gaped. His eyes bulged. At last it was sinking in. But long overdue. If only she had found a way to make him listen the first time, they would be well on their way to getting the facts by now. It sounded so right she was actually grateful that Arthur had caught her out. She felt dizzy with excitement and stopped pacing. They looked at each other.

She knew that in the real world lying to the boss was serious. But these days her fellow workers in the newsroom hardly thought of Arthur as "the boss" in the usual way. He had gradually become little more than an object dressed in a detour sign, an obstruction that could interfere with getting the job done. Ways were found to ignore him or trick him. The strategy had evolved, without any talk. They had become good at it, learning to use flattery to neutralize his control. It was as if someone had parked an oversized child in their midst, someone they felt a need to care for, but a child with authority. Still, they had proceeded, in ways wily or elementary, to shunt him aside, carefully. But had anyone ever actually lied to him? Maybe she hadn't been careful enough.

"You see, Arthur? It's a great story. And—"

Arthur reached for the paging button and spoke into the receiver. "Bradley. Arthur's office. Urgent."

Her union rep? "What's this, Arthur?"

His voice was shaking when he said it.

"*You*. Suspended."

Chapter Fifteen

The sun was in her eyes as she drove east, the wrong time of day to be heading home. *Suspension.* A word that sounded vaguely criminal. Why had it never occurred to her that Arthur would go this far? She felt numb. The countryside appeared alien, passing like one long fast pan shot. The car delivered her to the schoolhouse.

Inside, nothing had changed. But she was overcome by an attack of such aching loneliness that she started to cry as soon as the door was closed and for a long time was unable to stop. She would have given anything now just to hear the familiar sound from her parents' basement of her father arguing with his tools.

She couldn't remember ever feeling so alone, even in those first few weeks on the job with new colleagues still painfully polite and old friends far away in Ottawa. Missing having someone special, someone who actually cared when she was happy or exhausted or proud or discouraged.

There had been such a person once, and the mutual infatuation certainly felt like love. But they were too young. She could understand it now, that it could have lasted only if they were able to stay frozen in time, if they had somehow stopped themselves growing into the people they were to become. And just out of college, looking for work, Mercy found herself having to take a series of jobs all over the country, a situation that her hometown lover couldn't accept. When it was over the loss left her with a hollowed-out place that sat waiting.

In the early months in Charlottetown her only social life had been Friday evenings at the pub unwinding with other reporters, the talk inevitably made up of anecdotes collected during the week. Stories of lighting stands collapsing at a crucial point in an interview, told to get a laugh, relieve days of deadline tension.

Her last romantic involvement had developed over a few weeks spent with Pat's brother, visiting from Toronto. But the commitment to his practice as an architect was unshakeable, and the calls and letters that seemed so urgent at the time became less frequent and more casual. She hadn't heard from him in six months.

And thinking about the motel episode with Chaz last New Year's Eve brought no comfort. A huge mistake, her judgement off-kilter in a weak moment.

Now she went out the back door to the stone patio where she sometimes sat in the evening, looking over farm fields and at the sky, watching the cows doing what humans had decided cows were meant to do, all the features contributing to a picture of harmony, the world at peace, the seasons turning as they should. She knew now why she had wanted to live out here. It gave her solace for moments like this.

Her eyes moved off to the east, beyond acres of pasture and ploughed red soil, to a small abandoned house, partly hidden now by trees in half leaf. It might have been the detail in an artist's landscape, placed there to relieve an otherwise monotonous beauty. Her first sight of it, shortly after moving into the school-house, stirred images of a pioneer family, the pattern of their lives and daily work ruled by the elements, by how the grain and hay grew, how the animals fattened or gave milk, how much wood could be cut for the winter's heat. A life that demanded hard physical work but was straightforward and predictable. She had planned to take a closer look, one day. But she hadn't. And she wouldn't today, either.

She went back inside and splashed water on her face, feeling a little better, her mind beginning to accept what had happened in Arthur's office but not yet ready to figure out what she could do about it.

The sound of a vehicle stopping outside jolted her. *Jumpy*, she thought, putting down the coffee she had just poured. It hadn't bothered her until now, having a front door with no window. She peered out one of the big schoolroom windows to see Skim getting out of his truck. By the time she opened the door he was sitting on her steps, leaning back, enjoying the sun.

"Reporting for duty, chief." He didn't move, just looked up at her.

"What are you doing here?"

"Called your office. Told me you were likely at home."

"How did you know where I lived?" she asked.

He ignored the question. "Felt like taking a drive." He was dressed neatly, in light-coloured chinos, a brilliant blue shirt, and a navy windbreaker, his wispy hair carefully combed, looking not much like the unsavoury image she had of him in her head. In fact, looking rather familiar, like a second-string actor in an old movie. Always in the background but sometimes a comforting presence.

She wasn't pleased to see him now, though, a reminder of the research that was already spelling serious trouble, but so far, only for her.

"This isn't a good time, Skim. I'm not feeling great today."

"Yeah. You don't look so good, don't mind me saying."

"You could have phoned. Saved the trip out here."

"Rather be talking face to face." He sat up straighter and took a pack of cigarettes from his jacket and held them toward her. She shook her head and sat down at the other end of the step.

"Came across a little information for you." He paused to light up, in no hurry.

Information? And here she was temporarily out of that business. Maybe even permanently. But not quite ready to wave the white flag.

"Want some coffee?" she said.

"Sure. Black's what I drink." He nipped the end of the cigarette and followed her inside, looking around the big room, interested. Then he surprised her by admiring her collection of hooked rugs and settled in on the couch.

"Talked to a couple of guys last night who know their way around, if you follow my drift." He leaned forward and took the mug from her. "One of them heard something about a week ago to do with your pal Danny. You know where he lived?"

"Fitzroy Street, down near the end."

"Yeah, that's the place. My guy heard somebody got paid to get in there and look around." He took a couple gulps of coffee.

She felt a little buzz up her spine.

"Did your...contact know what the search was about?"

"No. One of those stories that makes the rounds. Like, some loser's flashing money, then he gets a few beers in him and can't wait to tell his buddies, an easy job. Go in there, get this thing, get out. Don't know what the thing was, though, or if he found it. But he got paid." He was looking at her as if he expected an explanation.

"Who paid him? Did your contact say?"

"Didn't know. I asked, though."

"Can you find this break-in guy and ask *him*?"

"Now wait a minute. Don't get excited. It doesn't work like that. I get too curious everything'd shut down. Might even get thumped for sticking my nose in."

"Well, interesting contacts you've got," she said. "Thanks, anyway."

"So?" He took another big drink from the mug but kept his eyes on her.

"You're not...expecting payment for this, are you? Sorry, but reporters don't pay for information. I was asking as a favour."

"Jeezus. Don't want your money. Just wondering what it's all about."

She avoided his eyes.

"I can't tell you, Skim. It's not all that clear yet. Maybe it never will be."

This was a guy she would normally avoid like the plague. His need to know made her uneasy. But nothing compared to the misery of being alone today, the hours stretching ahead like a desert. And her impression was changing. He wasn't the cocky smartass who had approached her at the country auction. And today he wasn't the "guy in charge" she had seen at the auction hall yesterday.

He looked into the coffee cup, then put it down on the low trunk in front of the couch.

"Look. I'm not trying to get in on this. Just... I don't want to fall into something that could be trouble, without knowing what I'm doing."

He had a point. And what more did she have to lose?

He sat still, listened attentively, and didn't interrupt.

"...so then I found out the treasurer of the Party died in March. A heart attack. And maybe there's money that hasn't been turned over. His widow made it sound like it wasn't a big deal, but she was trying to be mysterious about it, too, as if she was stringing me along. But..." Then Mercy remembered. "Hey, you were going into her place the other day. You do some kind of work for her?"

"I know her pretty well."

"Anyway," Mercy went on, "the cabinet minister I talked to got his shorts in a knot when I asked about it, so there's got to be more to it. Danny apparently found out the Party doesn't want whatever this is to get out, and I think he was blackmailing them, or trying to. That's about all I have so far." She didn't tell him about the tape.

No reaction. He had picked up a little stoneware jug from the trunk and was examining it, turning it over in his hands, and seemed not to be listening.

"This probably sounds like a lot of nothing to you," she said. "But it's important to me, to my...job. So I hope you'll keep it to yourself, Skim."

He put the jug down. "What do *you* think happened to the money?" He leaned back a little, as if expecting a long answer.

"I don't know. There must be safeguards to stop the treasurer from spending it, or investing it. Mrs. Hoodles is stalling for some reason. And the Party's trying to keep it all quiet. It would look pretty bad if one of their loyal followers had fiddled the books."

Skim got up quickly. "I better get going." And he walked out the door.

She went out, too, and stood on the steps wondering what his hurry was. He pulled out of the circular drive without looking at her, the tires kicking up stones as he went.

*

Fuck. What the hell was going on? Was his aunt off her rocker? Sometimes hard to believe she was a grown woman. And the stuff the reporter'd said about the cameraman? Blackmail? With what? And did this Mercy Pepper know more than she let on? He couldn't decide what to do with the stuff she'd told him. Had to think about it some more.

When he got home there was Cab, in the backyard, doing his donkey work. Shifting dirt between a wheelbarrow and a flowerbed, clumping in his big rubber boots half across the yard for every shovelful. Not enough smarts to move the barrow closer.

Skim stopped to watch. The guy was as slow as a September fly. He heard his aunt call through an open window from the kitchen.

"You can stop for lunch now, dear."

Cab looked up, then peered around the yard.

"Over there, Cab." Skim pointed. "Under the tree." Where he'd left the lunch box. But long forgotten.

Cab dropped the spade, happy to see him. Skim went

over and put an arm on Cab's shoulder and steered him around so they were facing away from the house.

"We better cancel our little job on Sunday, Cab." He kept his voice low.

"For this comin' Sunday, y' mean?" Cab whispered.

"Yeah. But we might go out again sometime. I'll let you know."

Cab drooped, then perked up.

"Got something good to tell you," he said, watching Skim's face. "A man talked to me 'bout the milk truck. My deliveries. Remember I told you? He said not to worry, I'm not in trouble. Nobody's gonna arrest me."

"That right? Who was the guy, Cab?"

"Uh, didn't say his name. Had a nice suit on, though. Came right up to me on the street. Knew all about it. Said my uncle was in trouble, but not me. He was real nice. I think my uncle's still mad at me, but I don't care." He looked as pleased as Skim had ever seen him.

"Was the guy a cop?"

"Naw, I told you. Wearin' a suit."

"Must have said who he was."

"Nope."

"He say anything else, Cab?"

"Nuh. I forget."

*

When Skim had gone Mercy sat for a while on the front steps, not ready to think what she should do next, if anything, just allowing her latest defeat to sink in. The suspension would be on her record forever, assuming she still had a job after the hearing. Her union rep had done his best in Arthur's office, but couldn't change Arthur's mind.

Inside, the phone rang. It was Jinxy.

"Hi, I just heard. You okay?"

"Not wonderful. I imagine it's the talk of the news-room."

"Well, sure. But everybody feels bad for you. You don't deserve this, Mercy. We're all ready to speak up. Could've been any of us. You never know with Arthur."

"No, I asked for it. Lying to the boss? Going behind his back? What could be worse?"

"It'll get sorted out. Don't sit around out there with a long face. Doesn't suit you. Come for a drink with us tonight."

"I don't think so, Jinx."

"I'll pick you up and drive you home. How's that?"

"Thanks. I'm just not up for it. Another time."

She felt better after the call, more like sitting down and thinking it through, the way a mature person would. Anger didn't help. Better to face her own bad behaviour, stop thinking like a spoiled child who had never heard the word *no*. Accept that if everything was going wrong it was her own doing. When she thought of her working life before the explosion she saw how easy it had been. People trusted her, cooperated when she went in search of answers. She felt capable. Now the trough of good luck had run dry. And if she got the sack the stigma would be there forever. About as much chance at another reporting job as a seamstress getting work in a nudist colony. It would be public rela-tions next, the last refuge of the washed-up journalist.

*

By five o'clock Skim was back from the auction hall to pick up Cab and drive him home. He watched the kid walk over to the truck, lunch box in one hand, his envelope of money in the other. He'd be out drinking in a couple of hours, for sure.

"So, Cab. Big night tonight?"

"Naw. Prob'ly just to the Legion."

Cab was like a third child in his sister's family, all living in the granddad's house on Water Street, near the old train station. The grandfather was getting on now but told Skim great stories about working on the railroad and what they got up to on those trains. Nowadays when Cab's old gramps looked out his front window, all the trains were gone, and the tracks, too, the old stone CNR building in the middle of a parking lot, all fixed up to give out information to tourists.

Cab's mom was dead, his old man gone off somewhere. The sister kept an eye on him, had to. Not something the family ever talked about, just knew he was a 25-watter and needed looking after. Gramps called him Cab because he used to follow behind the other kids like a fat little caboose. But Skim's aunt never called Cab anything but "the hired boy," like her famous father would have.

Skim pulled up in front of Cab's house.

"You think any more about that guy who talked to you?"

"Huh?"

Skim ran his hand around the steering wheel and let a couple of seconds pass. "The man. Said you weren't in trouble over delivering the gas."

"Oh, yeah."

"Well? You remember anything else about him?"

"Nope." Cab was looking out the window now, ready to open the truck door, get away.

"Cab. Stop right there. Look at me. Tell me more. Besides the suit. Was he tall? Was he short? Bald? Skinny? Young? Old? What?"

"Not that old." Cab's mouth closed.

"That it? Jeezus, Cab. It's sweet fuck all, you know that? You talk to a guy, he tells you something. Good news, you said it yourself. He's nice to you. You said that, too. And you're too stupid to look at him? Times I wonder how you know enough to get up in the morning."

"He had red socks, Skim. I 'member now 'cause they put me in mind of, y' know, in Boston? You told me about the baseball team."

"Red socks. For fuck's sake, Cab!"

He tried to get out of the truck then, looking scared. Skim reached over and grabbed his arm.

"No, you're not going anywhere. Sit right there. I'm gonna watch you try to think for once. You're not getting out if it takes all night."

"You're hurting my arm. Lemme go!"

"Understand what I'm saying?"

"Yeah. I'm tryin'."

It was mean, Skim knew it. But maybe the guy just needed a jolt once in a while to get his brain moving. The "man" could easily be a cop. Anyone real friendly could get Cab talking, might even start him bragging about what Skim was finding on their Sunday morning trips to those attics in the country.

"I know *somethin'*, though," Cab said. "Somethin' *you* don't know." Then he said it again, real quiet, almost under his breath. "I—know—somethin'—you—don't—know." Each word separate, determined-sounding. "It's a big thing…and it's about *you*," Cab said.

Now Skim was ready for a laugh. It was going to be something stupid for sure.

"Well?"

"Yer a-dopted."

The word took a couple of seconds to sink in. And then, in less time than it would take a computer, Skim's brain sorted it all out, whipped through his life so far, thought of his mom in Boston, looking at him as if he was from another planet, not like a real mother would, and his father, kind, but his mind somewhere else. For a few more seconds Skim argued against it in his head, like an animal trying to get free of a trap. But he knew, like he'd never really known anything in his life before. It was true.

Chapter Sixteen

Nobody home when he got there. A plate of food covered in tinfoil on the kitchen counter with a note. He didn't bother to read it. Everything in the place looked phony now, part of some huge con game, everybody in on it but him, even a kid like Cab who couldn't think straight.

And Skim the sucker, trusting. All that stuff they'd done to make it easier when he first came up from Boston. Him going along on just about everything. Stopped cursing in front of them, behaved himself. Grateful for the chance to get away from the old life so he wouldn't end up like his old man. All the paperwork Uncle Garf had sorted out, getting him a work permit, everything to make him feel like one of the family, like a *Tate*, his aunt said. Plus arranging so he could vote, one more for the Party. But Skim held the line on that. Sorry, not interested.

Pile of garbage. Knew that now. He was a charity case, furious at his own stupidity. And part of his anger was that something in him had fallen for that whole line about the Tate family and how important it used to be. Even down in Boston, his so-called dad, the factory worker, was impressed by being married to one of the Tate girls. Told Skim he should be proud of his important ancestor. The grandfather wasn't American, of course. But still. And these past three years in Canada, while Skim liked to feel he was making it on his own, way back in his mind he liked the idea he was a Tate, that he did have some kind of history. Felt sorry for Cab. How stupid was that? At least Cab knew where he came from.

Skim paced the kitchen, back and forth between the doorway and the sink, trying to think what to do, keyed up for a face-to-face with his aunt. His aunt? Now he could call her *the old bitch* if he wanted to.

He went into the dining room and looked around. Her desk was there. He yanked open the wide top drawer. Bills, all in neat piles. He looked through all the drawers, not knowing what he wanted, maybe something on paper that actually said it, that he was somebody else. Another name, another set of parents? Or taken out of an orphanage? Horrible scenes from refugee camps and old Hollywood movies crowded into his head.

He took the stairs two at a time to his aunt's bedroom. Another desk there. He was into the third drawer when it hit him. Searching here was useless. If there was an adoption paper it'd be in Boston in a drawer in *their* house, the people who took him in. What could he do about that? Call 'em up? Say thanks for feeding me, like some alley cat they found by the garbage cans? Last time he talked to them was Christmas, the call his aunt always made. He hardly ever thought about them since he came here. Was that normal? He sat on the floor for a while in front of the desk, for the first time in his life feeling like a nobody. And no plan for what to do about it.

When he tried to push the drawer back it didn't want to close. He reached in and flattened down some papers. Still jammed. He yanked this time, hard, wanting to hear the wood splinter and break. It shot out and crashed to the floor, something white stuck to the back. A big envelope. He pulled it away from the tape that held it there. Nothing written on the outside and not sealed. His hand took a long sheet of paper partway out. Just a list of names. He pushed the paper back into the envelope. None of this crap mattered now. But it was hard to slow his body down while his head was someplace else, trying to picture a man and a woman, his real parents. He couldn't. What he needed was to put his fist through a wall.

But he got the drawer back in carefully, like he always did on those Sunday mornings in a strange house. Downstairs he found the white envelope still in his hand and stuffed it in the front of his jacket, not thinking about anything except that he wanted the aunt to be there right now, standing in front of him, wanted a target for this rage. Where the fuck was she? Why'd he have to wait around like some beggar till she was ready to come home?

He backed the truck out without looking, burned rubber in first gear, and headed down the street, not sure where to go, just out of there, not liking the anger taking over, making him feel not himself. *Himself?* Well, he wasn't, was he?

He drove around, talked his breathing down, forced

his brain to start thinking, to stop *feeling* so much. He parked along the harbourfront, across from the kids' wading pool, still closed for the season, hardly anybody on the boardwalk either. Those types were all at home now, eating their family supper. He pictured them sitting round the dining table. In another hour they'd be here, out of their neat little houses, walking up and down, all knowing who they were and what they'd be doing for the rest of their lives. What would he be doing tomorrow? He couldn't see it.

It was warm. He pushed the seat back, unzipped his jacket, and found the envelope. It took him a couple of seconds to remember what it was. When he did there was another thought attached to it. What was so important somebody would hide it at the back of a drawer? It didn't just fall back there. It was taped. Well, so what? Did he give a shit about any of this stuff?

He wasn't feeling so out of control now. Didn't even want to see his aunt. Didn't care if he never saw her again. Funny now, that he used to worry about the old bitch and hurting her feelings. Some joke that was. He'd get by. *More* than get by. Think about it. He was already well on his way. Just move out, get to work on Calvin for that partnership. It was in the cards.

He looked at the envelope, then took the page out again. It was typewritten, in three columns. On the left he saw company names. There was the one Calvin rented heaters from. In the next row there was an amount of money. Then on the right his uncle's signature, Garfield Hoodles, beside each one. Money for the Party? Had to be.

He put the envelope on the seat, started the car, then headed east, out of town.

*

Mercy watched the newscast at six, trying to draw back and think of herself as just another viewer. None of the stories interested her. By now Arthur would have assigned the street people documentary to someone else, or more likely dumped it.

She walked around the big room, feeling the quiet that was usually so welcoming, now just emptiness. She got out a Bud Shank album, one of her parents' old ones: flute and oboe, recorded live when West Coast jazz was the new hot thing. Playing this music on the vintage turntable usually cheered her up. By the third cut her head was right back to Danny and the tape.

A smoldering anger had crept up on her, and with it the energy to focus her thoughts. There was a good reason to keep working on that story now. Getting it was her only hope of wiping out the suspension. And it had to be a big enough story to justify her behaviour, to prove that she was right to defy Arthur. Now she had the time to chase it.

The late sun caught the chrome of a vehicle pulling into the circular drive. She turned down the music and went to the door. Skim was standing there, looking scruffy and sweaty, not much like the guy who had shown up this morning.

"Brought you something I, um, found. Could fit in with your ideas about the money." He handed her an envelope.

"You found?"

"Just take a look. If you don't want it I'll, uh, maybe take it back."

This was getting out of hand. Did he think they were partners? Or worse, co-conspirators?

"Skim, I don't want you to get involved in this...research of mine. I only asked you to keep your ears open about Danny. Not this. You can't go digging around like it's your business. It's my *job*." Not quite, she thought.

"Didn't break anybody's arm or anything. It just kind of turned up."

"I'll look at it, but that's all. You're getting in way over your head."

She opened the envelope, saw the sheet of paper, and took it over to the table. He sat down on the couch. She could feel his eyes watching from the same spot he had sat in just a few hours ago.

"Do you know whose signature this is? I can't make it out."

"It's...it looks like *Garfield Hoodles*," he said.

"Right." She thought a minute. "This must be a contributors' list, with the amount donated to the Party beside each name." But it wasn't nearly as long as the one on the government website, the official one. Maybe it was only a partial list, before Hoodles had finished beating the bushes, as her friend Ruth had described his job.

"Where did this come from, Skim? It's not a public document."

"It was...in an old desk. Thought you'd be interested."

"Quite a coincidence, this turning up now. When I just told you about the Party's money problems this morning." *Oh, please*, she thought, *not breaking and entering*.

"Some things I didn't say before," he began. "Didn't think it mattered. But maybe now it does. Remember you said you were trusting me?"

She held up both hands. "Stop right there. This looks like trouble. I don't want to hear it. So listen, Skim. I appreciate what you've done so far. But you've got to understand. If the police start to investigate a burglary and I know something, I'll have to tell them. I'm not one of your...pool hall buddies."

"Jeezus. I'd never drop you in anything. That's not me. Just listen, and then if you want, I'll leave. Make like I've never talked to you."

She hesitated. "All right."

"Elspeth Hoodles is my aunt. Well, she *was* my aunt. Never mind. You saw me going into her house because I live there. Or I did. She had that list, and now you're saying I'm right, it has to do with the Party money. So there you are. Might help you figure out what our boy Danny was up to."

She was trying to imagine a family relationship between Mrs. Hoodles and the rough young guy sitting in front of her.

"Did she actually give it to you?"

"No, but...it was there for me to see."

She picked up the page and looked at it again. She would have to go online and compare this list with the one published on the official website. But not right now, with Skim looking over her shoulder.

"Okay, Skim. How about this? Now that the deed is done there's probably no going back. We'll think of it as a *leak*. You know what I mean?"

"Sure."

"Can you get the page photocopied and then put the

original back where you found it?"

"Yeah, I can do that."

"I'll come to the auction hall tomorrow to get it. You'll be there? I need time to study it, to figure out if it means anything."

"Okay." He got up, looking somehow not quite as tall and confident as usual.

"Skim, why are you doing this? It could look bad for your uncle, you know."

"He's dead. Can't hurt him anymore."

"What about your aunt?"

"Yeah, don't worry about her. She's a *Tate*. Cream of the crop, right?"

As he went out, a car turned into the drive. She had never had this many uninvited guests. Skim took the steps in one and was in his truck and heading out before the other vehicle stopped. Chaz was behind the wheel. Jinxy got out of the passenger side first, waving two bottles of wine. Chaz held up a bag of groceries like it was the Stanley Cup.

"Steak, Mercy. Three nice big juicy steaks," he said.

The men came in, full of good cheer, Jinxy heading straight for the kitchen to find a corkscrew.

"Wonderful," she said. "And steak. Just what a vegetarian craves on a Friday night."

"You're a vegetarian? Since when?" Chaz looked hurt.

"Trying," she said. "But I keep falling off the wagon." She kept it light, wanted to avoid any serious personal topics with Chaz.

"That'd be the hay wagon?" He chortled. "What I always say is this: if God hadn't meant us to eat animals, he wouldn't have made them of meat."

"Ah," said Jinxy, "cannibal logic." He passed them

each a glass of wine and took the groceries from Chaz.

"So who was young Superman who just flew away?" Jinxy asked.

"Big romance you haven't told us about?" Chaz sat beside Mercy on the couch.

"No, just a neighbour." She got up and went to the stereo.

"Well, as long as we didn't interrupt anything," Chaz said. "You know, nudge wink."

Jinxy was already busy at the stove. She put on a Jimmy Hendrix CD, then excused herself and picked up the phone.

"Would you go to an auction with me tomorrow? The hall on Monroe Street? Ten thirty."

"Sure," Pat said. "But how come you're the one dragging me this time?"

"Be grateful. I'll explain when I see you."

She hung up and sat at the table, a comfortable distance from Chaz. "This is terrific. Just when I was feeling Arthur had ruined my life, you two arrive to save me from throwing myself off a cliff."

"You're smiling," Jinxy called from across the room. "A good sign. Or else you're in denial." He was already setting the big round table, organizing. Didn't matter that it wasn't his house. His role was to organize. He topped up their glasses and called for a toast.

"To the quality of Mercy," Chaz offered. "May she never be strained."

The meal was good, the wine was a step above the usual plonk, and the vegetarian life was going into a fast fade.

"Thought I'd be showing up alone," Jinxy said. "Surprised Chaz didn't already have a big date."

Chaz held a hand over his eyes, faking shame. "I do," he said. "Just postponed it for a few hours." Then he grinned at Mercy. "But I'll get there for the best part." The reference made her cringe.

"So, what'll you do with all this time on your hands?" Jinxy asked.

"Oh, who knows?" she said. "Take up knitting?"

"Start going to funerals," Chaz said. "Ralphina got me thinking about it. Seen her funeral diary? She keeps track of 'em all. Figures out some connection to her own family. All those relatives."

"And what's in it for you?" Jinxy asked.

"Great way to get close to the politicians. They're always there, glad-handing," Chaz said, then shook a finger gently in Mercy's direction. "You should try it, after you get back."

"I don't think so. Sounds..."

"Deadly?" Jinxy offered.

"Joke all you like," Chaz said, "but I always pick up some info for a story."

"Well, who says I'll have a job at all, this time next week?" Mercy hadn't meant to raise the subject, but there it was.

"It'll blow over." Jinxy said. "I mean it. Arthur knows we can't do without you for long."

"Meanwhile," Chaz said, "he's dumped all the routine government junk back in my lap. Plus he's still nagging about the election date. Maybe *I* should try making wild accusations about blackmail and get suspended. Take a rest."

There was silence. Then Jinxy slammed his fist on the table. "Chaz, remind me to kick you next time."

"He told you?" Mercy was startled. "Arthur actually

told you the details?"

"Yeah, Mercy, he did," Jinxy said. "Called us both in. Ranted for half an hour. Said he couldn't have you undermining him. No surprise, his attitude. Said you were making up crazy stories about politicians. On the beat a couple of days and you were seeing criminal activity everywhere you looked."

"Sorry. None of our business." Chaz reached across the table and touched her arm. "But if you feel like talking, we're willing to listen. Well, maybe curious, too. So we can be ready for Arthur when it's our turn."

"No, I don't need to talk about it."

"Arthur's not a great manager of people," Jinxy said. "But he's been worried about what he calls your 'nervous fuming' ever since, you know...the explosion. Afraid your imagination could run wild and we'd lose credibility with our viewers."

"Our viewers?" Chaz cut in. "They'd watch news that's ten years old as long as they could see people they know. If it was local talent they'd watch monkeys tap-dancing."

"Gee, I'd watch that myself," Jinxy said.

Maybe it was the wine or just having some company, but she was feeling better now, actually looking forward to the time off, however long it lasted.

As the talk began to lose its life and they sat around dragging up old stories, Mercy kept hoping Chaz would drop some bit of information that might help her. No such luck. The political ignorance she had stubbornly protected like a kind of virginity was now a handicap.

"Let's do this again," Chaz said, as they went out the door. She didn't respond.

Alone again she turned on another lamp. From not far away came the familiar drone of Jack Murphy's tractor, probably fertilizing his young potato plants, Mercy thought. He had been at it all week, well into the evenings. The noise was welcome. Now she looked out, followed the progress of the tractor's light to the end of a field, saw it turn and make its way back, like a guard on patrol. She watched until the sound faded and the beam moved off toward the farmyard.

Chapter Seventeen

"Where's George?" Mercy asked. Normally the dog never left Pat's side.

"At home, taking a nap. He stayed up late watching *Lassie*."

They were early for the auction, but inside the hall Skim and his crew had somehow jammed in even more furniture and small goods than were there on Thursday. And it was now well organized. He was in a corner shifting boxes of dishes while a potential bidder waited to get a look at the oak table underneath.

Mercy moved in his direction, leaving Pat to examine the hinges on a pine cupboard. When he saw her coming Skim took an envelope out of his jacket and handed it over.

"I wrote on the outside where you can get me," he said.

"This isn't your aunt's place."

"No. I'm crashing at a buddy's for now. He works the night shift."

"Thanks, Skim. And...keep it to yourself, right?"

"Think you have to tell me that?"

"Sorry." She smiled and he walked away to the stage.

Cheerful chatter rippled along the rows. Mercy tried to get interested in the bidding, but it felt like an endurance test.

The auctioneer, so good at offering rural humour to the country crowd a week ago, had a different patter for the city folks. He pointed out sophisticated details on mahogany pieces, hinted that they had come from a prominent family, claimed fragile china had survived ice storms and a North Atlantic crossing. He guzzled from a bottle of water between items.

Last night Mercy had gone online at home and printed out the official pages of contributors published on the government website. Now she couldn't wait to get another look at the list in Skim's envelope. She looked around for the washroom, went into a cubicle, and dug it out of her bag.

All the names from Skim's shorter list were also on the official list, which was long but included every donation over two hundred and fifty dollars. On Garfield Hoodles's private list the total was a lot more, about five million dollars more. Was this information that the party treasurer was keeping out of the public eye?

Pat looked at her when she sat down again. "What's up? You're really jumpy."

Mercy told her about the suspension, keeping her voice low. She got no reaction.

"Trying to find a bright side to this one?" Mercy said.

"I've got to say you have a way of landing yourself in deep doo-doo."

"Well, here's the bright side. It gives me time to find out what's going on with this story."

"So, what *is* the story? Really big?"

"Could be. Political. Maybe criminal, too."

"Won't Arthur hear you're still poking around? Fire you for sure?"

"That's why I have to figure it out and be ready before I confront anybody. Once it all comes out, there's no way Arthur can fire me."

"Did you get the deadbolt for your door?"

"No time." It hadn't even crossed her mind.

Pat looked at the ceiling and shook her head.

"Nobody knows what I'm working on," Mercy whispered. "I haven't even told *you* the details."

"Well, someone knew enough to break into your place."

"Sure. And what they were looking for isn't there. No reason to come back. I explained that. And I can't get the goods by being a wimp." Just talking about it was generating the old excitement, that sensation that always got to her, of being on the edge, poised to dive, but feeling outside it all, safe.

The crowd was so thick now that people had filled all the chairs and were lined two deep down each side and along the back. Mercy felt welded into a sea of sweating bodies, the air hot and stale. Skim was on the stage, holding a dining room chair over his head, balanced in one hand.

That was when she noticed a little buzz at the entrance door.

She saw a uniform, then two. One cop looking around, the other leaning over to talk to the woman who gave out the bidders' cards. The woman pointed to the front and the officer went directly to the stage and beckoned to Skim. Behind him, the auctioneer babbled on, didn't miss a beat.

Mercy watched Skim jump down and follow the cop

as he worked his way through the bystanders along the side of the hall. Only a few seemed to be interested. Even Pat hadn't noticed. Mercy tapped her on the arm, said she would be back, and squeezed her way toward the entrance.

By the time she got there, Skim and the two constables were gone. Outside she saw the police car pull away and felt a prickle of alarm. But as she stood looking around, Skim's old brown truck went by, moving fast out of the parking lot.

Once she got to her own car it was too late to follow, so she drove to the police station. The officer at the desk was a new face but not young. When she asked for Jon Tillerman he looked at her with mock disbelief.

"A sergeant working on the weekend? Never heard of such a thing."

She told him she was a reporter. "Do you know why the officers were just at the auction hall on Monroe Street?"

"Not for me to say, ma'am." Like it was none of her business anyway.

She saw the constable who had been on maternity leave sitting at a computer in the next room, back to the door.

"Could I speak to Constable Blake, please? She's right over there."

"Hey, Blakie," he called over his shoulder, eyes still on Mercy. "Somebody here to see you." He went back to what he was doing without another word.

"Karen, hi. I need some info, fast. About half an hour ago two of your guys showed up at the auction hall on Monroe Street. Talked to a fellow called Skim."

The constable thought for a moment. "Maybe checking on a complaint about overcrowding? We've had them before."

"No, it looked more personal than that."

"Wait a minute." She went back to the computer and scrolled down. "There was an incident overnight. They were looking for some woman's nephew, next of kin. That him?"

"What kind of incident?"

"Not sure. She was found lying in her backyard. Neighbour saw her early this morning. Gave us a statement." She scrolled down the screen. "Here it is. 'The dog was barking and it woke me up. Usually a quiet dog. I went to look over the fence. Saw poor Elspeth. The back door was open...'" The constable stopped reading and looked up.

"That's already more information than I should be giving out, Mercy. Anyway, guess the dog was the only witness. The neighbour took it to her house and called 911. Thought it was a heart attack. But now it looks like somebody beaned her."

"Is it serious?"

"She's in hospital. Yeah, I can see this would be news. Older lady attacked on her own property. Pretty unusual."

Fifteen minutes later Mercy was at the Queen E., directed to the third-floor waiting room. No sign of Skim but a cop sat leafing through a magazine. She knew him. It was Reynolds, overweight and cranky, the butt of doughnut jokes.

"Hi, I'm Mercy Pepper. We've met before. What happened to Mrs. Hoodles?"

Pause while he turned a couple of pages. "Yeah, I

know who you are."

"Well?"

"Under investigation."

"Have you seen her nephew? Name's Skim."

"Why?" He took a candy out of his pocket and popped it into his mouth.

"He might know more than you do."

"Have to take your turn. He's with our guys right now."

"Where?" It was like trying to budge a mule.

He favoured her with a smug grin, teeth now candy pink, and folded his arms, settling back into the chair.

"I'll just wait with you, then," she said, and sat down beside him. "Keep you company while your colleagues do the important work."

"If you understood police work," he offered, "we always question the family first."

"Ah."

"We know what we're doing. This Skim fella lives with her, some relative. Probably a domestic dispute."

Mercy thought about that euphemistic phrase used by the British cops: *Mr. Jones is helping police with their inquiries.* What it really meant was that Mr. Jones was the prime suspect.

She didn't believe for a minute that Skim was capable of it. He had been with her last night until Jinxy and Chaz arrived. Must have been at least seven. And this morning he hadn't looked like someone who had just beaten up his own aunt.

A door opened down the hall and Skim came out, head down, followed by the two constables who had shown up at the auction. He made straight for the nearest seating without looking up, dropped into a chair, and threw his head back, staring at the ceiling.

The trio of cops left without a glance at her.

"Skim. What happened?"

Her voice startled him. For a moment he didn't seem to know where he was.

"Jeezus. What're you doing here?"

"Is she badly hurt?"

"Yeah. Unconscious. Hit her head, or somebody hit it for her. They're saying she could've been lying out there since last night." He ran both hands roughly over his face.

"Why did they question you here?"

"Came to the hall first just to tell me, 'inform next of kin,' that's what they said. Then they came here to see if she was up to talking. When they found out she was still out of it, they just started asking me questions, just casual at first, then got serious."

"They didn't want to take you to the station?"

"Maybe thought I'd call a lawyer. Clam up."

"What did they ask you?"

"The usual stuff. They all get it from the same book. You know. 'Where were you between nine last night and nine this morning?'"

"Did you tell them?"

"Sure. I was at a pub on Sydney, then went to my buddy's, to bed. He works nights. So nobody to say that's where I was. Just me saying it." He was looking around now, as if he wanted to get moving, do something. "They said not to leave town."

"You haven't been to your aunt's house at all since you left my place? You haven't put the list back?"

He turned sharply to face her. "For Chrissake! That doesn't seem like a big deal right now, y' know?" He got up and started walking away, then circled back.

"Here's you still trying to cover your ass. But I've got other things to worry about."

"I know, Skim. I'm sorry. I shouldn't have brought it up. Do they really think you did it?"

He stood over her.

"Why not? They look around, can't see anything missing like the TV and that. So they figure it's a family fight. A bunch of drinking and somebody loses his temper. They see that a lot." He started pacing. "The doctor says it could be a long haul. I'm going to the house to look around."

"Do you want me to come with you?"

"Suit yourself. We can't go into the backyard, though, unless they're gone."

They went in separate cars. Everything was quiet. The police had left. Mercy and Skim stood on the stone path behind the house. The extensive garden was filled with the colour and scent of spring blossoms. A deep purple lilac bush was the star attraction, with brilliant yellow tulips in full bloom and a magnificent pink magnolia tree competing for attention. It looked like the last place for a violent act. No sign of where Elspeth Hoodles had been lying.

An open porch covered the full width of the rear of the house, built long before decks came into fashion. It was substantial, like Elspeth herself. A heavy balustrade fenced it in. Evenly spaced thick wooden columns reached up to support a balcony on the second floor.

Skim opened the back door with a key. In the kitchen everything was tidy. Nothing unusual that Mercy could see. He went to the counter, picked up a plate covered with tinfoil, and put it in the sink. Then he moved into the hall. Mercy followed. He walked around, standing for a few seconds in the doorway of each room, but not really looking.

"I'd better get back to the auction, Skim."

He didn't respond, maybe hadn't been listening. Mercy put a hand on his arm and he looked at her, but his face was blank.

"I didn't tell my friend where I was going. She'll be wondering."

He nodded, still in fogland, and she left him there.

*

Skim figured it was time to say it out loud. He turned around and the reporter was gone. He went to the kitchen and looked out the window. No sign of her. Just as well. Keep his ideas to himself for a while. See what the cops were planning first. But he knew what this was about. Only an idiot could miss the connection between the money his uncle collected for the Party and his aunt getting hurt. He'd never believe Uncle Garf spent it. Just wasn't him. Now he was gone his aunt didn't want to turn it over, that was it. Playing some kind of game with them. Make them plead. Get her some attention. And the Party just got tired of it? Wanted to give her a scare and maybe went too far?

Then, still at the window, he realized something. Saturday. Cab should be here, working in the garden. Maybe he did come, then left because she wasn't home? Had his own key, though. Could have got started without her. Except that first somebody'd have to tell him his chore for the day. Another possibility: Cab came and saw the cops and got scared. Maybe they even talked to him. And what would he tell them?

Likely everything he could think of, which might not be much. Then again, he could spill a few beans about their Sunday jobs.

Skim picked up the phone on the kitchen wall.

"Hey, Gramps. Cab there? Oh, yeah? Since when? No. Okay, I'll keep an eye out."

He hung up and stood there, still with his hand on the receiver. Cab didn't go home last night. Maybe he got drunk, forgot where he was, like the night he was driving the milk truck. Pretty weird, though. First time not sleeping in his own bed. That's what old Gramps said.

Skim added another worry to his list, as if there weren't enough already.

* * *

Mrs. Hoodles's back garden had worked its magic on Mercy again as she had walked toward the gate. She'd stopped to look around. Set between flowerbeds and on each step up to the house, large terracotta planters overflowed with pansies and marigolds and other brilliant annuals that Mercy couldn't identify. She could imagine Elspeth on a summer day, sitting in the shade of the maple tree on the weathered wooden bench, wearing a Victorian straw bonnet, sipping tea and reading a letter written on deckle-edged vellum.

Harder to imagine her lying there with blood seeping from her head onto the grass. Mercy turned to listen to the sweet notes of a bird's song and she looked up, thinking of Elspeth's little-girl voice. Along the upstairs balcony every column was topped with a big planter of ivy. Except one. She went over to look at the spot below. Nothing. She headed back to the auction.

Pat was still there but now there were many empty seats. Only a few items were left to sell. Excitement had flagged long ago. Mercy whispered that someone she knew was involved in an accident, but everything was under control. Pat looked at her hard.

A man and woman made several trips past them, carrying out the boxes of damaged Anne dolls. Another time, in different circumstances, Mercy and Pat might have had a good laugh, creating stories about what plans those people might have for five hundred deformed dolls.

It felt like forever since Mercy had had anything to laugh about.

Chapter Eighteen

The big room was chilly with late spring air that had a way of creeping in after the sun went down. Mercy turned on a couple more lamps and set a small fire in the woodstove, leaving the iron doors open to watch the flames. On the stereo Dizzie Gillespie's big band was playing "I Can't Get Started." Car headlights swept along the wall, picking out bright colours in the Klee print hanging there.

Mercy still had the poker in her hand when the knock came. It wasn't loud. She counted to five and found her heart had stopped pounding. She opened the door.

And there was Jon Tillerman. The surprise, or maybe something else, made her tongue-tied.

"Well, you haven't keeled over with shock," he said. A cold gust blew into the room. "Mind if I come in?"

"Got a warrant?" It came without a thought. He frowned.

"Sorry," she said, and stepped back, out of the way. "That passes for humour out here in the country."

He didn't move. "Is this bad timing?"

"No, I'm not doing anything special." At that moment

she couldn't actually remember what she'd been doing.

He stepped inside, eyes on the poker.

"Hope that's not your idea of a defensive weapon."

She looked at the poker and laughed but couldn't find a clever comeback, thinking instead that she had only ever seen him in daylight before. Why was he here? She had left his office on such bad terms.

Jon followed her to one of the big chairs facing the fireplace, but stood looking around the room while she looked at him. Casual clothes, jeans, and a dark pullover. *Brown. The colour of his eyes.* Her first sight of him without a sports jacket or suit.

"I haven't seen your place before." Then he smiled. "But I guess you know that." He sat down, then immediately got up to give her a small plastic bag. It didn't look like a summons.

"You mentioned once at the courthouse that you liked jazz." He pointed at the stereo. "Gillespie, right? Anyway, I came across that recording by Buddy Rich, done years ago. On CD now. The title caught my eye."

She took it out of the bag. On the cover was a picture of the drummer himself, looking a little ridiculous in a Nehru-style jacket with beads around his neck. He was posed against a background of bright East Indian fabrics. Definitely a shot from the sixties. Above his head was the title, *Mercy, Mercy, Mercy*.

"I think he was better in the fifties," Jon said. "When he was playing with Monk and some of those guys."

"This is wonderful, Jon." When she looked up he was watching her.

"It's kind of a peace offering. I've been feeling bad about our argument the other day. Didn't want to leave it like that and..." His voice trailed off and he looked down at his shoes.

She shook her head. "No, my fault. It really was. I've been too defensive lately. This is a nice gift." She was very touched that he had even remembered that she liked jazz. And something else. A feeling of being restored, as if someone she had known as a reassuring presence, held in the back of her consciousness, had gone away but was now back. The person she had thought he was all along.

"Hardly expected to find you here." He sat down. "Saturday night, thought you'd be out on the town." He was looking at her again in that direct way he had, like nobody else did.

"I lead a very quiet life, remember? Your colleagues did the research."

"Bad move. Wish we'd never done it."

"And what about you? Where's your, um, significant other? You used to mention someone."

"Brenda. Well, she's gone. Left a couple of months ago for a good job in Winnipeg. Can't blame her. It was a real chance to move on."

"Did you think about going, too?"

"No." He hesitated. "There were other problems. Happened about the same time I shaved my head." He ran his hand over the stubble and grinned. "Hair was very important to her. Anyway, isn't this where I'm supposed to say I was just in the neighbourhood?"

"I'd be flattered if you've made a special trip."

"Be flattered, then."

She turned toward the fire, picked up another log, and set it gently on top of the flames. Strange how a fire could be used as a prop to cover awkward situations. Did the cave people do this? Jon would have had time to think ahead about this visit, prepare for how she might react. But she was still trying to absorb his actually being there.

"Heard you were looking for me today at the station," he said.

She moved to sit in the other chair and pushed her mind back to the afternoon. Skim's list was still lying on the table beside her empty plate.

"I forgot you wouldn't be at work on Saturday," she said.

"But I still have to know about serious incidents. It wasn't the usual Friday night street fight where one thug hammers another one with a beer bottle. If that woman dies it could be murder, manslaughter at least."

"Is her nephew a suspect?"

"Right now he's only a possibility. Until we get a better idea what happened."

Now Mercy edged around the thought that Jon might have already connected her to Skim and was staging this whole scene to get information about him. The awful feeling of disappointment that idea carried told her how much she wanted this visit to be genuine.

Better to face it head on.

"Jon, I might know something. I'm not sure if it's important. Do you want to hear it?"

"Sure." But he sounded more like a doctor listening to symptoms at a cocktail party.

She sifted through what she knew and decided not to mention Danny's tape, or the break-ins to his place and to her own. She wanted to hang on to what she'd figured out and continue to dig for more without the cops telling her to back off. She did tell him about the rumours that the election date was delayed because

Party funds were missing, or at least unavailable, and about her interview with Elspeth Hoodles. Then she brought the list from the table and showed him the company names and large dollar amounts signed off by Garfield Hoodles. Jon was leaning forward in the armchair, more interested now.

"How did you get that document?" he said.

"The usual way." She laughed. "From an unnamed source."

"I had to ask the question."

"Your job to ask. Mine to evade. Nothing criminal was involved."

"So, what's the big deal here? Explain to me why you think it's important."

"First," she began, "you have to understand that this is *not* the contribution list that's published on the Elections PEI website. That's where all political parties have to report every contribution over two hundred and fifty dollars. And there's no limit to how much money the parties can accept.

"But this list," she handed it to him, "is special. It's all company names, no individuals, with an amount of money beside each name that's much bigger than what these same companies have given according to the official list."

"So?"

"See what they have in common? A computer firm, a building contractor, a caterer, a janitorial service, car dealership, and my favourite: SuperShredders. Almost three dozen businesses. And all of them probably eager to bid on contracts for a service or product that the government will buy with taxpayers' money. These companies have given the Party more than five million dollars extra. They probably consider it a cost of doing business."

"So why the secrecy?"

"I think it's because the Party doesn't want these names to stand out. It would be obvious when contracts are awarded that these bidders had an advantage because they gave the big bucks. This is the list of those favoured few. These companies will win the contracts to build government offices and roads and schools. Even catering in all the school cafeterias. At least, that's my theory."

Jon was frowning now but still watching her. "Hey, wait a minute. Tenders for government contracts are sealed, aren't they? That's how it works with the police committee."

She considered for a moment. "There must be a way around that. Maybe, for each contract that these guys bid on, someone in the know slips the favoured bidder information about the other bids." Then she remembered something else. "And don't all the calls for tenders have a line at the bottom that says something like 'lowest bid not necessarily accepted'?"

"So back to this five million dollars in the Party special account," said Jon. "I can't see what's illegal there. Isn't it what's called a 'slush fund'?"

"I think so. But only the party insiders know about it."

He sat back and folded his arms. "Having a slush fund isn't illegal, though. I think our union has one. For retirement parties and other special events."

"No, so far the only illegal part is not declaring these contributions. And they seem to need that money right now. Before they're willing to call the election. But why? Anybody can see on the official website that the contributions are already up to the limit allowed by the *Elections Act*."

"What limit?" Jon shook his head, as if it was all getting too involved and he didn't want to hear any more.

"Okay. I'll stop this," she said. "I've been thinking about it too much anyway. Making me crazy."

"No. It's okay. Just explain that last bit. Then maybe we can go back to listening to the music." A little twitch around his mouth was trying to become a full-on smile.

"I'll be quick. The *Elections Act* limits all parties and all candidates to spending no more than ten dollars for each registered voter during a campaign. They have to account for every nickel they spend. And the Party now in power already has enough for the campaign. That's obvious from the website. So that's not why they need this slush fund. They want that money for something else."

"I have trouble thinking this way, Mercy. It's speculation. Give me an actual crime like an armed robbery. Then I know what to do. Bank accounts, moving money around? That's work for a commercial crime unit. Maybe the RCMP. Anyway, what's the connection to what happened to Mrs. Hoodles? Just that she was married to the Party treasurer?"

"Did your guys find any evidence in her backyard?"

"No weapon. But I shouldn't be telling you this. We've only given out the basics. Your reporter, Julie what's-her-name, got them this afternoon. As far as the media is concerned it's still an accident. The woman could have tripped and hit her head. But now that doesn't look likely."

"Where exactly did they find her?"

"On the stone path behind the house, near the porch. Her injury's at the back of her head. So we figure 'blunt instrument trauma.' They found signs that somebody left in a hurry. A rug was pushed against a wall, maybe a struggle. And the front door was wide open. We're thinking now that she could have been assaulted inside the house, then tried to get away via the back door and collapsed out there. But where's the motive? No valuables seem to be missing. I've already said too much. You have a way of..."

He peered down at his shoes, frowning, and took a deep breath before looking at her again. "Your story about the Party money is interesting, but nobody keeps that kind of cash in the house."

"No, you're right. They'd have all the *declared* money in one Party account. And Mr. Hoodles must have made his own arrangements for the slush fund. Now he's dead, it might be part of his estate and they can't get at it without Elspeth Hoodles's say-so. I think she's holding out on them." Mercy waved the sheet of paper. "And now here's the list that goes with the money. Together this is really incriminating. If this gets out they might lose the election." She would have to figure out for herself what the argument on Danny's tape meant, why the unknown man wanted money up front to "fix" something.

"Does your boss think you're on to a hot news story?" Jon said.

"I didn't go into details." She was agitated now, had to stop herself getting up and pacing. "Anyway, he's not a good listener. Not like you."

Jon didn't respond, but the look was back, serious. Should she reach for another log?

"Sorry, Jon. I haven't even offered you a drink. How about some wine? Or...I think there's a beer in there somewhere." She headed for the fridge.

"Sure. A beer would be good."

Two bottles of Heineken were hiding behind a cabbage. She poured herself some red wine then opened a beer and set it with a glass on the low table between the two chairs. He poured. She wondered whether men only drank beer from a glass when they were on their best behaviour.

"We'd need hard evidence to connect the assault on Mrs. Hoodles, if that's what it was, and all this stuff to do with the Party money," he said. It sounded like the subject was now closed.

Then a detail floated to the surface of her brain. It seemed more significant now.

"I was at her house this afternoon, with Skim."

"The nephew? What—"

"I noticed something. A planter was missing from the upstairs balcony, at the back, right over that path. Nothing on the ground, though."

"Sounds like you took a better look than our guys did."

"I wasn't searching. It just caught my eye. Somebody who wasn't interested in plants might not notice. And it could have been moved weeks ago. Or knocked over by a cat."

"And then the cat came down and cleaned it up?" He grinned.

She was enjoying this. Bouncing ideas around, like their work overlapped. She got a flash of what it would be like over a breakfast table. The music ended and the awkward pause returned.

"Maybe I should be going," he offered. But he didn't get up. "I didn't plan to walk in and take over."

"No, it's fine. I'm glad...of the company. I'll put on Buddy Rich before you go."

The opening drum solo filled the room for half a minute. "Mercy, Mercy, Mercy" was the first cut, with a sound that couldn't be anything but sixties. Witty, sexy, downtown jazz, but with more guitar than the earlier big band era. How strange she would have this in common with Jon. She'd met men on this island who listened to what she called cowboy music, and even one who preferred Pablo Casals torturing his cello. But nobody who was seriously interested in jazz. She turned the volume down a little.

"It's good, the way you have everything in one big room here," he said, looking around.

"I wanted to keep it that way. The carpenter just took down the ceiling to show the beams. Then he insulated around them and built that loft at the end." One day, if she got to know him better, she might tell him about the ghosts of long departed schoolchildren who sometimes kept her company. About the whiff of soggy mittens drying on a pot-bellied stove in the middle of the room, rubber boots giving off the heavy steam of melting snow, and bits of farm mud tracked in from the fields.

"A lot of women wouldn't stay out here by themselves," he said. "But I'd say you're not like a lot of women."

"It feels pretty safe. You're the one who sees the scary stuff."

"More like depressing. Mindless vandalism, beatings. Domestic violence. Kids living like you wouldn't treat a dog. Sometimes wonder why we call ourselves a civilized society. It can keep you awake at night."

"Have you ever been really afraid?"

He didn't answer right away, let out a long breath.

"Not exactly. I've never had to draw my firearm, even in my days in uniform. Never had anybody point a gun at me, either. But sometimes I get this feeling that it's happened before. It's like...it's as if I *know* what it actually feels like to have that point of cold steel pressed against the back of my neck, right there." He put his hand up to the spot.

At that moment he seemed the most vulnerable she had ever seen a man. She could picture him as a child, his dad standing over him, a hand on his shoulder, maybe giving him a little squeeze on the neck the way fathers do to show affection, at the very place where the boy, now grown up, fears the cold steel.

His head was down, looking at his hands clasped loosely between his knees. He was quiet, maybe even embarrassed. She wanted to sit there and keep looking at him. Instead she made herself say something.

"I'm glad you told me that." She said it softly, not wanting to break the mood.

"Never told anybody before." He looked up. "Not even Brenda." A hint of a smile crept to the corners of his mouth. "She wouldn't have wanted to hear that anyway. Thought detective work should be figuring things out from train timetables. Like old *Colombo* shows. Or Miss Marple. She didn't see why I had to get dirty. That's what she called it. Last straw was one night when a fink with some information came hammering on the back door in the middle of her book club meeting." He looked up and the smile came on full. "Couldn't blame her. I had to apologize. Had to say sorry that the fink didn't come about literature, only life and death." He drained his glass.

"I should make a call," he said, and got up from the chair. "Better get them to take another look at that backyard in the morning. And go over there myself. I won't mention the stuff about politics for now." It came out like an apology, as if she had expected more of him. The early excitement about her theory began to fade.

He excused himself and took his cellphone to a corner. She poked at the fire, then went outside to bring in more logs from under the porch. When she came in with her arms stacked the chill wind followed her. She pushed the door closed with her hip, dropped the load into the woodbox, then knelt on the floor facing the fire and heard his footsteps coming nearer.

"I really should go this time. I've stayed too long." He stopped somewhere behind her.

"You've said that twice." She poked at the fire and didn't look around. "Is there somewhere you have to be?"

Silence. Then, "Maybe coming out here tonight was a really stupid move. Don't know why, but I didn't want to phone first. A couple of times I almost turned around and went back. A guy showing up uninvited on a Saturday night at the door of a woman who lives alone? Some would call it harassment. And I'm never sure how you'll react." He took a couple of steps and carefully chose a small log, crouched down beside her, and put it on the fire. "Didn't even know if we were still friends." He was looking at the fire. She was admiring his profile when he said, "Guess I was looking for some small sign."

"How's this for a sign?" she said, and leaned over slowly and kissed the back of his neck. Before she could straighten up his arms were holding her so tight she thought she would never take another breath, and didn't care, just knew that this was it, what she'd wanted for a long time. No more keeping a careful distance. No more trying to hide her attraction to him. As if anything could stop them now. And she realized she had already imagined this and how it would be, like the best jazz, more urgent and moving than anything she had ever felt. But even knowing that they had crossed the line and now had all the time in the world, there was no way to slow down what was happening.

Chapter Nineteen

Skim couldn't remember the last time he stayed home on a Saturday night. Maybe never. Pretty weird, the way things could change so fast. Here he was back in the house he never wanted to see again, still in the life that was a big fucking lie. And waiting for a phone call about a woman who was nobody to him now. He tried saying *stupid old cow, serves her right,* but that didn't sound right. Not good anyway, thinking about this stuff, feelings and all that, getting him mad. He should just call her Mrs. Hoodles like all her other charity cases did.

But it was hard to stop going over how he'd ended up in all this, living where he didn't belong. Going over how it used to be when he coasted down the block back in Boston. Not one person made eye contact, but it felt good anyway. Had street smarts, knew what he was doing. Here on this island, at the start, he didn't get it. That first day when he walked around Charlottetown, checking it out, the smallness of everything, the way people stared right at him. No sweat at all to look you in the eye. And driving by, too, giving you the once-over. After a few weeks he noticed they just checked *everybody* out, looking to wave, maybe at a neighbour or some relative. First it felt like they all knew his business, maybe were even following him. But then he saw he could check out other people the same way. And you could roam around in the middle of the night and feel like you were in a dream. Like it was Toytown, with all the little dollies and toy soldiers tucked into bed till morning. It was that quiet. In Boston the night was never quiet. More like some mean old bear, just taking a snooze, but growling and jerking in its sleep, still dangerous.

Had to decide what to do when this was over. When the cops figured out what happened and he could leave. Go back to Boston? Would the guys still be there? Maybe they'd all be in college or have good jobs. Or even joined the army. They all had real families.

Three years was a long time to be away. He'd be on the outs with everything. When he talked to his so-called parents at Christmas they never mentioned his friends. Anyway, by then his mom probably figured it was a big mistake trying to bring up an orphan or whatever the hell he was.

The phone rang. He picked up in the kitchen, braced himself for something bad. He said hello, heard nothing.

Then, "That you, Skim? I was gonna hang up if it wasn't you."

"Cab? Jeezus, where you been?"

"I need help, Skim." The voice was low and shaky. "I'm real sorry. You know, what I said about you yesterday." Skim was surprised Cab even remembered. Almost forgot *himself* that it was a dimwit told him the truth.

"So what kind of trouble you in now?"

"Don't know what I'm gonna do. Scared to go home or anywheres."

Skim could hear the voice way past panic now. The guy was actually crying, big gulps in between words.

"Take it easy, Cab. Can't be that bad. Where are you?"

"In a phone booth."

"Where, Cab? Where?"

"Um, near Victoria Park. Hid in the woods last night. Almost froze. And today a big dog came after me."

"I have to make a call. Then I'll come for you."

"Come soon. It's dark again."

"Wait by the tennis courts. Hear that? Wait."

He dialed the hospital number, had to say yes, he was a relative, then hang on, leaning on the kitchen wall, noticing the wallpaper flowers for the first time, how small they were. Finally a nurse told him there was no change. Still unconscious.

He left a couple of lights on in the house and went out to the truck. At Victoria Park, just before the baseball diamond, he turned left and pulled over in the lane between the woods and the tennis courts. The only light came from the street lamp along the boardwalk. Black as hell all around. No sign of a moon. Skim could just make out Cab's thick shape, sitting on a bench, hunched down and looking his way now, seeing the headlights. Nobody else in sight.

As he walked closer Cab turned away. Skim sat down beside him.

"Okay, Cab. What's going on?"

"Scared to tell you." He was still looking toward the water, stiff with fear, the words shaky, his fists in a tight ball against his stomach.

"Well, you better. Or I'll leave you right here. Think I got nothing else to do?"

"Don't get mad at me again." He took his time to face Skim, eyes big and wet. "I shouldn't've said yer adopted. Only, everybody knows. I didn't tell a lie. You were hurtin' my arm, that's why."

"Never mind that. Is this about the gas truck again?"

"Worse."

"Okay, I'm not going to ask another question, Cab. You better start at the beginning and tell me, or I'm walking. Got it?"

"Yuh." He took a gulp of air. "That man talked to me again." Cab was looking at Skim now, watching his face to see how he was taking it. "He was waitin' near my house. It was dark and I wanted to get to the Legion." Skim didn't interrupt. "He talked different this time, the man. Said I was in shit after all. But he'd fix it if I did somethin'."

"Like what?"

Cab's eyes slid away toward the harbour again. "He wanted me to go in the house for him, *your* house." His voice was shaking again. "He knows lots about me. Like about the key she gave me so I can use the downstairs toilet and everything."

Skim was already way ahead, impatient now for details.

"So you went into the house. How'd you know she wasn't home?"

"Told me in the afternoon she was going to the Uni... Uni..."

"UNICEF?"

"Yeah. Big dinner and everything. She'd be sittin' at the head table."

He stopped, settling down into himself like he'd finished.

"Keep going, Cab."

"The man give me a piece of paper with some writing on it. I was supposed to look in all the drawers and desks where she had letters and stuff. He said to look for words like what he wrote out for me. I was scared to tell him I couldn't. That I never learned my words in writing. But then I did tell him and he was cursing and saying now he had to come in with me."

"Why didn't you just give him your key?"

"Said he was in a hurry. Needed for me to show him all the desks. And we got in and the little dog started barking and the man got mad again because I never said nothin' about a dog. Then we got upstairs in her room and I hear the key in the back door. I got so scared I almost pissed myself, Skim." Cab was into the telling now, couldn't get it out fast enough. "I got on the balcony, out the door from the bedroom. Real quiet, like you showed me to do on Sundays. I was lookin' for how to get down into the yard. Mrs. Hoodles, she musta heard me and she came out the back door again, lookin' around and..." He took a big gulp of air. "One of them big pots fell off and right onto her." He started to cry again, big gulps and sobs.

Cab's gramps had it right. You had to look after him.

"Okay, Cab. Stop the waterworks. You didn't do it on purpose."

"I didn't wanna hurt her, Skim. I was too scared to even look at her. I went back in the bedroom and ran down the stairs and out the front door."

"Where was the man?"

"Already out. In his car across the street, watchin' for me. He started to yell when I got in and he saw me cryin'. Made me sit there and say what I did. Then he went into the yard and...don't know what he was doin'." Cab had to stop talking to catch his breath. "But then he said he'd call the amb...the amblyance after he drove me home. Told me I was in the most trouble a person could get in if I didn't keep quiet. And he let me out but I was afraid to see my granddad even. So I came to the park and stayed here." His whole body was shaking now, from the cold or from remembering.

"The car." Skim said, trying to keep his voice low. "You saw it near your house last week, then you saw it again when he picked you up last night. Remember anything about it now? The colour?"

"First I'm thinkin' it was brown, but..."

"Never mind. Where's the paper he gave you with the words you were supposed to look for?"

Cab's eyes got smaller. His lips pressed tight, concentrating, really trying. He looked down at his pockets. "He musta took it back from me after."

"Now, listen. Cab, you listening?"

"Yuh."

"You have to do what I tell you now. Got that? Even if it makes you scared."

Cab let out a loud sob. "Is she dead, Skim?"

"No. But she's in the hospital."

"She was nice to me. I'd'a never hurt her."

"Yeah, I know. Now listen up. First we're going back to the house."

Cab moved off the bench like Skim had punched him. "I can't."

"Yes, you can. Get you warmed up, something to eat. Got any better ideas?"

"Nuh."

"Didn't think so. Let's go."

It was almost eleven by the time they got there. No messages on the phone. Skim wasn't used to doing for somebody else, but he made Cab a sandwich and a coffee. The guy's jacket smelled like wet leaves and sweat. He got an old coat of Uncle Garf's from the basement. Cab did what he was told, put it on.

Then Skim did something he'd never done in his life before. He called the cops.

Cab was on his second cup of coffee when the cops got there. Two constables, not the same as the two at the hospital this morning. But they knew what it was all about, took Cab into the dining room and closed the big sliding doors.

Skim left them to it, turned on the back porch light, and went out to the yard. Wanted to see for himself. He looked up at the balcony and saw where the planter was missing. Nothing on the path. He went back in for gloves and a flashlight, poked it into corners, under bushes. He found what he was looking for at the end of the garden, stuck deep in the compost box behind the garage. Pieces of clay pot in big chunks, soil sticking to them. He'd have to show it to those two inside, probably have to spell it out for them, too. Cab's fingerprints wouldn't be on it, just bumped it, he said. But maybe they'd come up with somebody else's. *Jeezus*. Never thought he'd find himself helping the cops.

He left the broken pieces where they were and went back in the house, stopped to listen outside the dining room. Still at it but he couldn't make out what they were saying. Cab's voice didn't sound too upset. Maybe it was taking a big chance, expecting them to believe the kid. But Cab never lied. He'd try not to talk about something but always told the truth in the end. The cops'd see that, too.

They didn't. When they came out ten minutes later, Cab looked like he was in a fog.

Number One steered Skim to a corner. "You know anything about this?"

"He told me what happened. Makes sense."

"That so? Says a man put him up to it. But he can't remember what man. Says the guy drove him here. Can't tell us what kind of car. The story about the flying flowerpot sounds like a winner, too."

"Look, we called you, didn't we?" Skim said.

"You his keeper or what?"

Skim shrugged. No points for arguing. He knew that much.

"Well, we're here," Number One said. "Might as well take a look." He headed for the back door and Skim followed. Number Two stayed with Cab, sitting down at the kitchen table now.

Outside Skim pointed up to the empty spot on top of the pillar, then to the spot on the path. The cop grunted. Skim said he'd show him something else and led him down behind the garage to the compost. The guy acted like he was all on his own, figuring it out for himself. When he saw the pieces he turned to Skim.

"Did you handle this? It's evidence."

Skim held up his hands, still with the gloves on. "*Christ!* I *found* it for you."

"Go back inside and stay there while I get it wrapped up."

Skim did as he was told, tasting something nasty, four-letter words he was forcing himself to swallow. Cab sat there, playing train with the salt and pepper. Number Two was looking around, bored.

Number One came in carrying a parcel wrapped in plastic and together the cops herded Cab to the door. He turned to look back at Skim, his eyes begging, but something else there, too, like he knew there was no more help coming.

Cab was getting a good scare, but Skim figured it this way: the cops wouldn't hold him, no more than they went after him about driving the gas truck. Somebody down at the station knew Cab for what he was, one of those sad buggers that never gets into trouble on his own, just there to be used. And Skim had used him, too. Not something he was proud of, now he realized it. But he thought he knew how it would go. Some lawyer would talk to Cab's sister, make her promise to look after him better, something like that. Once they found "the man" they'd forget about Cab, might not even think he was smart enough to be a witness in court.

For sure Skim would never be taking him out on a Sunday again. Didn't matter. Skim's own life was going to be different from here on, too.

He didn't want the aunt to die, felt the same as he would for anybody in bad shape. Nothing special, nothing real personal. Anyway, he figured she'd be okay, knowing how strong she was, in her body and in her head.

It was way past midnight now. He locked up the house, turned out lights, and took the same old stairs to his bed. He'd just keep an ear out in case the hospital called.

Chapter Twenty

Waking on a Sunday with such a sense of optimism felt vaguely sinful. Outside the day was beginning well, too, sun blazing. Mercy took her coffee out to the stone patio.

Jack Murphy's big herd of Holsteins was coming out of the barn, relieved of hundreds of kilos of dead weight. No machinery assaulted the fields. A sabbatical silence hung over everything. But along the horizon a dark haze loitered, the hint of clouds with plans.

She looked off toward the abandoned farmhouse, tiny, almost hidden by trees. Happiness was spilling out of her, too much for one person's body to contain. She checked for the trembling in her chest, present for more than two weeks. Not there.

Last night, long after the logs had burned down to ash and mugs of cocoa grown cold in front of them, Jon still sat close to her on the couch. They weren't able to keep from touching each other, small light gestures there was no time for earlier. He picked up her hand and wrapped it in his. She trailed her fingers gently over the top of his head. He buried his face in her hair and told her how good it smelled.

But it had to stop. This time he really should go. Officers were discouraged from spending the night outside the city limits without letting the desk know.

He had already tried to convince her to keep out of the Hoodles incident.

"Is that an order?" She could tease Jon now but knew that keeping herself from confronting Puck Overton and his political secrets was like telling a boa constrictor to relax.

"If your theory is right," Jon had warned, "these people could be violent. I'll worry about you." Then he grinned. "Anything happens I'll be the prime suspect. My lip prints are all over you."

When he was gone it felt as if some vital part of her body had been removed.

She made sure the door was locked, then opened the curtains and watched as he drove away, watched until she couldn't see the red tail lights anymore. And all she could hear was the echo of that last jazz melody.

Today the hours ahead loomed like a huge obstacle. She reverted to the trick invented during her stress leave, of assigning herself a series of domestic tasks to fill the time. Tomorrow she would face Puck, but at a disadvantage. No means now to go in with a camera rolling to record him trying to squirm his way out of trouble as she waved the list of slush fund contributors under his nose.

Around six the rain started. Violent gusts blew it against the windows, assaults that paused only to regroup for another try. Water distorted the scene outside.

She had just finished eating when Skim called.

"She's awake," he said, sounding weary. "I'm at the hospital."

"You've seen her?"

"Still doesn't know why she's here. But they don't think she broke her brainpan or anything. Just needs time."

"That's great news, Skim."

"There's been other things happen. We know how she got hurt."

"Oh?"

"Don't want to go into it on the phone. There's people waiting around here." He lowered his voice. "Bunch of her friends. Like buzzards. Love it when somebody's sick. Meet me at the house?"

"Did the police come back this morning to take another look?"

"I'll fill you in when I see you."

The rain drummed hard on the car roof all the way in, and she had to hold on tight to keep the Toyota from being blown into the ditch. The Hoodles's house didn't look welcoming on the gloomy street, a light over the front door the only sign of life. The rain had stopped but a strong wind kept on, and near the driveway a couple of huge green recycling bins on wheels spun in circles like newly arrived aliens in a slow ballet. A third slid along on its back. A woman struggled along the sidewalk, trying to keep her footing against the wind, cowering inside her raincoat, collar up, head down. Mercy pushed through the gusts and up the path.

She followed Skim through to the kitchen, the only room that wasn't dark. She had expected to find him relieved and happy. He wasn't.

"Cab's involved in this," he said, looking at his hands.

"Cab? Who's Cab?"

"Does odd jobs around here. Thought I told you."

"Involved how?"

"Well, he's dim. Spaces between his brain cells, big ones. He can be real maddening at times."

Then he told her Cab's story.

"Never thought the cops'd give him a hard time." He rubbed at his meagre beard. "I should've seen it coming. When he can't remember a goddamn thing about this 'man' they don't go for it."

By now, she thought, Jon would know all about this latest development. It must have been happening about the time he was driving home from her place last night.

Skim reached the part about finding the broken pot in the compost and delivered it like a punch line. He watched her digest it.

"Have they charged this guy Cab?" she said.

"No. Cops kept him till this morning. He's home now with his gramps. But no way he's off the hook yet."

"Listen," she said. "You say he can't describe this man. But if we showed Cab a picture of the fellow I think it is, do you think Cab could recognize him?"

"Maybe. Can't say for sure. But then what? They didn't like it when I found the broken planter for them. Think they'll want us showing up with a picture of some guy?"

"No. We'll show it to Cab, then depending what he says, I'd like to use the information myself, not tell the police right away. Where's your computer?"

"Don't have one. The aunt thinks they're dangerous."

"Never mind." She patted a pocket for her phone, forgetting that since her suspension it was in a drawer in the newsroom.

"Where's the landline?" she asked, then followed Skim into the kitchen and saw the phone on the wall and a phone book on the counter. She looked up the number and dialed before she had second thoughts.

"Hi, Luc. Sorry to bother you on a Sunday. I need a favour. But I'll understand if you say no. You'd be in hot water if Arthur finds out."

"What is it?" He sounded wary.

"That interview with Puck at the first news conference. Tuesday, I think. No, Monday. It was Monday. The tape's still on my desk. Can you cue it up to a head and shoulders near the beginning? Before his mouth starts diving for the microphone. I need you to dub that shot to a home videotape."

"*C'est tout?* Thought you wanted me to murder Arthur."

"We'll save that."

He laughed. "Hope your phone's not, how do you say, buggered?"

"No worries. I'm not at home." She gave him Skim's address and he promised to deliver the tape there after work the next day.

"Luc, are you sure you're comfortable with this?"

"No problem. Easy. And... I'll be glad when you're back. I'm stuck with Chaz. Friday we had to go all the way to Summerside to shoot his stand-up again. He didn't like how his hairs were looking in the first one."

"Vanity. Goes with the territory." It made her squirm when colleagues criticized each other. Somewhere, she suspected, someone was listing her own shortcomings.

When she hung up, Skim said, "Not sure we can count on Cab. And if the cops don't find somebody else's prints on that planter, Cab'll be their boy."

"So why did you call them?" His dark mood was beginning to annoy her.

"Figured they'd see he couldn't hurt anybody. But those two couldn't find an elephant with a nosebleed in a foot of snow."

She wanted to leave then, before he managed to crush her enthusiasm. But she stayed a while, tried to talk him round. His aunt was going to recover, the police might find fingerprints, and by Tuesday she could have her story and they'd be able to present the police with Puck's big head on a platter.

When she opened the door to go, the wind had dropped to a warm breeze and Luc was coming up the walk, the light from the doorway sparkling in his round granny glasses.

"Better I got it tonight," he said. "Nobody around." He handed her the tape and she almost hugged him, grateful that tomorrow wouldn't be another day of waiting. He went away without asking for details.

Skim was standing behind her when she turned around. "Why not get Cab over here right now? Can we?" she asked.

"Maybe."

Twenty minutes later Skim was back and Mercy got her first look at Cab. A short bulky kid in his late teens but with the body language of a much younger boy, moving nervously from one foot to the other, something between a shuffle and a hop. It was distracting. And he seemed too eager to please. In other words, not a reliable witness. But he knew why he was there. Skim put the tape into Elspeth's machine.

"Remember, we just want you to say whether this is the man you brought into the house," he said. "Okay?"

"Yep." Cab was wringing his hands. They were shaking.

Luc had picked a good clip. There was Puck, well into his long-winded answer, his head just starting to lower. She almost laughed out loud, remembering. Cab leaned toward the screen, intent, his face damp with perspiration. After about thirty seconds the screen went blank. Skim and Mercy looked at him.

"Naw. I couldn't get it, what he was sayin' there." Panic in his voice, as if tears were just a moment away. It was cruel to put him through this, she thought.

Skim got between the kid and the TV screen. "Doesn't matter what he was saying, Cab. Was that the man or not?"

"Yeah, that was him." He turned to look at Mercy, a smile blooming like a giant sunflower on his big face. Skim gave him a couple of gentle slaps on the shoulder.

"Way to go, Cab."

"In the back there," said Cab. "The man." He pointed to the blank screen.

Mercy rewound the tape. And there he was, just a glimpse over Puck's shoulder, in the back, as Cab said, watching. Fred Fredericks.

Chapter Twenty-One

"Where we living, New York City?" Calvin had picked up the phone when Skim called in the morning to say he'd be late. "Hoodlums roaming the town, trying to kill women home alone? It's all the talk," said Calvin.

At the hospital a nurse told Skim "the patient" was getting better by the hour. Knew where she was now, called the staff by name. Calling them a lot, the nurse said, showing him a little grin, like she understood the lady must be a bitch to live with. He waited while the nurse made sure his aunt was "presentable."

It was only after he dropped Cab off last night that it hit Skim how lousy he felt. Wished a part of him could be like the kid, happy now, thinking he was out of trouble because he was home with his gramps, the memory of his night in jail gone like yesterday's TV show. At the door he asked Skim if they'd go out to the country again next Sunday.

"Probably won't be doing that anymore, Cab."

Just a small thing, maybe the smallest way Skim's life would be different from here on. Those mornings in the spring and fall, lying in wet grass, getting dirty and cold, complaining. He'd forget *that* part easy enough. Trouble was, other things were stuck in his head now.

Those times in summer, the friggin' sun only up for an hour but already warm, pushing its heat right through his body, beaming like it was there just for him. And the air like wet earth, flowers every colour, every-place you looked. Cows hanging around watching and moaning. And birds, too many to count, cackling and whistling like they were drunk and couldn't keep it quiet. Jeezus. He'd have those maniac chirpers in his head forever. And the hay smell up his nose like some babe's perfume. He knew now what happened to him. There was a word, what was it? Seduced, that was it. He was seduced by fucking *nature!*

Might even miss Cab's company. That made him smile. Maybe get himself a dog, to go with him wher-ever he ended up going. Become a hobo like in some old movie, all his stuff on his shoulder, tied up in a rag at the end of a stick.

Not feeling too great about Mercy, either. She was working up a head of steam over all this stuff, but who says she needed him anymore? Here he was calling her every time he had something new to tell. But it only gave her ideas she kept to herself. Not even talking to him about that list, like he was too stupid to understand. Wouldn't have it at all if not for him. So he didn't put the original back yet like she ordered. So what?

For now he was jammed, spinning his wheels. Couldn't leave the aunt yet, not the state she was in and the cops keeping tabs. He'd hold his anger for a while. Lots of time to take it out and look at it later. When all this was over. But soon as he could he wanted to get clear of this place, get himself untangled. No handouts. Nobody smoothing the way for him. *Keep your eyes open and your brain moving.* He said it under his breath.

Now, he stood by the bed and watched as the aunt gradually focused on him and smiled. She seemed smaller lying there, not such a big deal.

"They haven't told me what kind of accident I had. I remember Elsie Patterson dropped me off at the house, and I remember going to the back door, but that's all."

"You fell."

"Fell? I've never fallen in my life."

"First time for everything. Banged the old skull. Won't be playing hockey for a while." He could see it hurt her head even to smile.

"Just make sure you look after the house. Give the hired boy jobs to keep him busy. I'm not paying him to sit around."

"Right."

"Get him to sift the compost. And he can get the dahlia bulbs ready. They're hanging in a bag in the basement. You'll have to get it for him. And Mitzi. Half a cup of kibble, twice a day. And take her for her little walk to do her business. First thing in the morning and again at night. And don't forget to take her little plastic bags to pick it up."

No way. "Right."

All the "do this" and "do that" was coming out her usual way. He could see how she'd be driving the nurses nuts. A cranky lady with a voice like a bossy ten-year-old.

When he first moved in it got to him. Till he figured what set her off and cut back on certain four-letter words in the house. Saw it wasn't like Boston where he needed those words, where guys had to come up with new ones if possible. Also, he never liked to stun Uncle Garf. He was so limp the wrong word might give him a heart attack. Then he had one anyway and it was only from putting in a light bulb.

And now the friggin' dog? Taking the little yapper out in public on the end of a leash? Then he remembered the dog was over at Mrs. Belliveau's house. He'd leave it where it was.

"We have to discuss certain things, Roger."

Roger. Here we go again. "Like what?"

"Your future."

He didn't need this shit now. When she got home, maybe they'd have it out. Or maybe he'd just disappear. He looked away to show he wasn't interested.

"I told you something good was going to come up for you soon. But it depends on...did Garfield ever mention a certain document?"

"No."

"I'm told it's quite important. It's all part of...well, arranging your job. That's one thing. But there's something else that's nothing to do with you. I have to find that document."

"And you don't know where it is?"

"Garfield never mentioned it. So, I...well, I told a certain person he would just have to wait. But I need to find it soon."

"And the money? Having trouble finding that, too?" Skim couldn't stop the question.

"Money?"

"You know what I'm talking about. Uncle Garf's job. The Party's money. Where is it?"

She was trying to get her head off the pillow, stirred up now.

"Roger, the money's there." She was gasping, trying to get the words out. "How can you think we'd spend it? That would be stealing. Those accounts were sacred to Garfield. The main one is in the Party's name. It's just the other one, that he had to put in another name to protect them from...well, bad publicity, he said."

Skim could have walked out then, left her to stew.

"Yeah? And why'd there be bad publicity?"

"Garfield was prepared. Loyalty. You wouldn't understand. You're too young." She was lying back again, her head turned away from him. He saw she was starting to cry, quietly. It was the first time he'd seen it. When she turned back her face was wet and her voice sounded small and broken-down.

"The Party's going to give you a good job. I told you, remember? That's one reason I kept the money back. And I'll transfer it to them as soon as I'm home again. But there's something else I've asked for. It's important to me and to the memory of our family. It's the other part of the agreement. And they won't do it without that paper."

"So. Blackmail. Spending their money's stealing. But blackmail's okay, that right?" He felt like a bully but couldn't stop. "What makes you so important you can run the way other people have to live? Because your father was some big politician? You're pathetic, you know that?"

He'd never been so fired up before. She was crying again, with her hand on her head, maybe in real pain. He went to the door and shouted for a nurse.

"Give her a pill or something," he said, and got out of there fast.

He felt like throwing something. Maybe go down to that Fred guy's office and tell him she was a nut case. He could see himself chucking the goddamn list on the jerk's big shiny desk. *Never wanted your fuckin' job.* But showing up at somebody's fancy office? Not smart. The guy might call the cops.

Instead he went to work, spent the whole day slogging hard in the warehouse, moving, carrying, hauling, pushing, still going even when the muscle boys stopped for their breaks.

Then he went out and got drunk.

*

Mercy hadn't called ahead, got to Fred's office a little after nine on Monday morning and was ready to march straight in. His secretary, a neat young woman dressed head to foot in beige, popped out of her chair and blocked the door.

"He's in a meeting," she revealed in a hushed voice.

"Aren't they always?" Mercy said, hoping for a little smile. She got a hostile stare.

"Could you get a message to him? I think he'll want to see me. Otherwise I'll be sitting here all day." Mercy grinned. "Spoiling your view."

In response the woman stood where she was and waited with her hand out while Mercy jotted, *Fred, you're in big trouble. We have to talk. Mercy Pepper.* She folded it carefully and put it into the outstretched paw.

"Don't peek, now," she said.

The secretary was back in under a minute, Fred right behind her. He walked Mercy briskly into his private office and closed the door.

"Now, what the hell is this? Weren't you called off by your handler?"

"Hello, Fred. I notice your charm level is set on low this morning."

"I've just left an important meeting. You've got three minutes to say your piece. That's it." He folded his arms and sat down behind his desk.

Mercy stood where she was. "Okay. Here it is. I know you were at Elspeth Hoodles's house Friday night. That you got someone to take you in and search the place. I know what you were looking for. And I know why. Your, shall-we-say, *accomplice* has told the police what happened." She dug into her bag for a pen and note-book. "And I have a great story." She smiled pleasantly, pen poised. "Any comment?"

He stared. Incapable of answering a direct question? Not a good trait in an information officer.

"You're nuts. You know that?" He was on his feet again, voice just below a shout now. "Think you can come in here and say whatever you like? Let me tell you..." He paused, realizing he was loud enough to be heard down the hall, and dropped his tone to a snarl. "Your boss has already decided that you're history."

She was taken aback at the rage in his words.

"Is that so? What happens when the police come calling, Fred?"

"You think they'd believe a story from some moron kid? Don't make me laugh."

"Who said anything about a kid?" She kept her voice steady, civil.

Then she leaned forward and spoke just above a whisper, as if they were co-conspirators.

"You left the woman lying there, Fred. She could have died."

He didn't flinch. But did she see a new wariness in his eyes? Was the bravado gone?

"Your three minutes are up." He was half out of his

chair, ready to leave her there.

"Hold on, Fred. One more wrinkle. What about this? The object of your search?" She pulled out the photo-copy of the list and waved it in his direction.

He seemed nailed to the spot, like the statue of some pint-sized dictator, ripe to be felled by a coup. She could taste victory, and it was sweet.

"Don't I have a duty to tell the public about this little fundraising project?" It was to be her finest moment.

Then Fred surprised her. He walked out.

She sat now, stunned, and clutched the sides of the chair to keep from running after him. Well, what did she expect? That he would just cave? That they would have a cozy chat and he would turn himself in, ashamed and penitent? He needed a moment, that was it, to absorb the shock, get a drink of water. Minutes passed. How long could she stay there, stupid now, as well as arrogant?

Face it. Fred wasn't scared. Probably at this moment on the phone to Arthur. She stood up, feeling like a punch-drunk boxer tottering toward a neutral corner. On the way out she avoided looking at his secretary but felt the eyes, imagined the smug expression.

Nothing left now but to go to Jon with what she had. But what she had was no more than her own absolute conviction that Fred was the man who had used Cab to get into the house.

She parked across from the police station and remem-bered a day two years ago. She had been here on the sidewalk doing a stand-up to camera when a screech of tires made everybody turn to look. A half-ton truck was stopped in the pedestrian crossing. The driver, hair framing his face like dirty curtains, was shouting at a woman with a toddler who stood transfixed, inches from his fender. A man in a jacket and tie appeared from nowhere, wrenched the truck's door open, hauled the guy out, and left him staring in disbelief while he led the mom and kid across the street. It had been her first sight of Detective Sergeant Jon Tillerman.

Now she put some quarters in the meter and went into the building.

Jon got up fast, smiling, as she entered his office. Then he closed the door and put his arms around her.

"Better not make this a habit," he said. "Neither of us will get any work done. Some kind of contact is important, though." He dropped his arms and put out a hand. She shook it and laughed.

He sat on the edge of his desk and listened to what she told him. She was glad to have a chair. Just being with him again made her a little lightheaded. When she stopped talking he looked at her for what seemed like a long time, something in his eyes that she took for disappointment.

"Maybe I should have been more forceful with the warning the other night. *If* this guy Fredericks was actually there when Mrs. Hoodles was hurt, then you've put yourself in the middle of this case and questioned a witness." His look seemed to beg her for some explanation that he could accept.

"My job is to get good stories, Jon. To ask questions. So I can tell the public what's going on. Not to wait till someone gives me permission."

"Just calm down for a minute, will you? I know your reputation for getting good stories. But you seem to think you can go wherever your nose takes you."

"So I don't have the right to ask questions?"

"Sure you do. But not to harass people, maybe spoil an arrest. I know you have instincts and you want to act on them. So do I. But you dig up something, write up your report, and put it on the air. And as long as you don't libel anybody and if you use the word 'alleged' then you've done your job. And the public will tune in the next night to hear more. Think I don't know what ratings are all about?"

She felt her defenses rising, was tempted to leave him in mid-sentence.

"So I'm no different from the *National Enquirer* and those trash TV talk shows? How would you like it if I thought you were as brutal as the cops who beat up Rodney King?"

"I'm just saying, you and I don't work the same way. Sure, we both do research. But *my* story isn't ready until somebody's arrested and convicted. *Convicted.* You've spent enough time in court to know what that takes. We can be sitting on a file full of lab results, photos, witness statements, solid circumstantial evidence, and we still can't get him." He stood up and walked to the window, looked out. She remembered the last time he had done that.

"Jon, I'm not just after a news story. I'm trying to help." *And trying to save my job.*

"Let me lay this out for you." He turned to face her, leaning back on the sill. "You've taken this kid Cab, somebody who has admitted involvement in an assault that could turn out to be as serious as attempted murder. You've shown him the picture of another suspect. You haven't given him a choice of six or seven in a lineup so he can point and say, 'number four.' You've shown him *one* guy."

"Two guys, actually. He picked Fred."

"You pointed him in a direction. You did this with a kid so eager to please he'd jump into a vat of wet concrete if you smiled at him."

"How do you know so much about him?"

"He's been in trouble before. We talked to him about the gas truck after the fire. He was driving it for his uncle. I told you about that."

"That was *him*? You didn't tell me that part. Now it makes sense. That's how Fred Fredericks got onto him. The gas fraud file you said was making the rounds of government departments. He saw Cab's name there. And he's probably seen him working at Mrs. Hoodles's house. So he scares the kid by talking about the gas truck. Then he uses him to get into the house. It explains a lot." She tried to contain her excitement.

"Could be. But thanks to your episode in Mr. Fredericks's office this morning, he now has time to prepare for a visit from us."

"What about fingerprints? On the flowerpot."

"There weren't any we could use."

"But you've still got Cab. He'll identify Fred in court."

"And within two minutes any defense lawyer would have him so confused he'd be pointing at the judge."

"At least I'm doing something. Are you?"

"You know I can't give you details. But it's not all running around shouting, 'Hey, I've got a great idea. Let's storm the government buildings and see what happens.'"

Okay, she thought, *I'm getting nowhere.* Before Jon got a second wind Mercy made what she hoped was a dignified exit. Their parting had none of the warmth of last Saturday night.

Chapter Twenty-Two

Driving through town toward the Hillsborough Bridge she was so distracted she almost clipped the end of an extension ladder sticking out behind a truck that was angle-parked. When she started to pay attention there seemed to be ladders everywhere, six along a couple of blocks on Queen Street alone, all propped against storefronts, holding painters who were touching up the artwork, getting ready for the tourists. Three were adding 'Olde' to their signs. And there was the mayor, planted on the steps outside the library, chatting with Bruno, the homeless ex-boxer.

By the time she got to the bridge her mind was back to Fred Fredericks. Did he know that she couldn't get a story on the air until her suspension was sorted out? If he didn't know, was he sure Arthur would keep her under control? Mercy was certain that for all his weird ways, Arthur wouldn't deliberately suppress a good story once she had nailed it.

As she came into the house the phone was ringing. The voice was cool.

"They tell me you've taken a few days off."

Her brain leapt to attention. "Things to do. Spring

cleaning."

"You free for a meeting? I might have something that would interest you."

"Always ready to talk, Fred." She was on the point of saying something clever but couldn't risk another shutdown.

"Three o'clock?" he offered.

"Your office?"

"No. Someplace more private. The parking garage on Kent. Drive to the top. I'll come to your car. Old Toyota, right?" He said *Toyota* as if it were a synonym for *cockroach*.

She looked at her watch. "Can you make it four o'clock instead?"

"Yes." He hung up.

She stood beside the phone, waiting. For what? A note to come shooting through the mail slot of her brain with a plan spelled out for her? It didn't happen like that. But it did happen. Twenty minutes later that plan appeared like a beautiful flower opening in time-lapse photography, and she could see the details in every petal. Another two hours of research on the phone confirmed that it was doable, but she would need every element to fall into place, and in a very short time.

Luc answered his cellphone.

"Are you busy?"

"Not yet. Chaz has something to shoot, but he's waiting for calls."

"Thanks again for getting that clip last night. It was perfect. I have another favour to ask. Bigger this time. Something that could get both of us into...well, anyway, it involves a shoot this afternoon, for me. In other words, on company time, unauthorized."

"*Tabernouche!*"

It wasn't fair to ask. But his role was crucial. So she took a deep breath and told him everything, all the background on Elspeth, the money, Skim, Cab, Fred, everything except Danny. It took up another fifteen minutes. He promised to keep it to himself. And when she described what she wanted him to do he caught on right away, even had a couple of good suggestions. But first, the next hurdle.

"Hi, Chaz. Thought you might be at lunch."

"Ha. What lunch? How soon you forget. I'm still trying to book an interview."

"I need a big favour. Are you using Luc this afternoon?"

"Yeah, later. Why?" He sounded suspicious.

"I'd like to borrow him for, oh, an hour-and-a-half, at the most. I'm begging. And you said if I needed anything, just to call."

"Yeah, well. People say those things, Mercy. This is... *Jesus.* Using company property and staff while you're on suspension? That's serious stuff."

"Not a chance I'll get caught. And I swear your name will never come up. You know nothing about it. This is really important. Otherwise, I'd never ask."

"God, don't you ever relax? This must be some story. What's it about?"

"Can't tell you yet. Later, I promise. It's got a few interesting elements. But no sex, sorry." She hated herself for making the joke but hoped it might soften him up.

"I'd have to get my stuff shot first. I'll think about it, get back to you."

"Call me at home. I'll need to get into town fast, so please make it soon."

It was now almost one o'clock and anxiety was setting in. She ate an apple and started on another round of calls, nailing down more details of her plan. The most important call was to Pat's brother, the architect in Toronto. She had talked to him a couple of hours ago and this time he was ready to confirm that what she wanted could actually be done. And he was sending all the files she would need to make it happen. Then she loaded everything into her big leather bag and waited for Chaz to come through. Ten minutes later he phoned back and agreed to release Luc at three thirty.

"You owe me one here, Mercy. I mean *really* owe me."

She called Luc, arranged to meet him, and headed out the door.

By three forty-five she was ready and waiting, parked on the roof level of the parking garage, at the back, away from the street and happy to see there were only a few cars around. She knew it was important to be calm, to appear in control. But she couldn't sit still, got out, and walked to the low concrete wall that ran around the edge. Her mind was on the meeting ahead, hardly taking in the scene below. Then, when she did, it seemed like an omen. From here she was looking down on the core of the block where the explosion had happened, at the back of the building where the milk truck containing gas was left. She could see the concrete steps down to the basement. The door at the bottom looked new, still unpainted. No sign now that someone died there. It was from this spot that Chaz's cameraman took the shots to use in the newscast that night. Her legs felt weak.

Still ten minutes. Pacing back and forth behind the car, breathing deeply, brought her heart rate down.

She heard a car engine growing louder, coming from the level below. She got back into the car and waited.

Fred parked several spaces away, as if to avoid contamination. She leaned a little on her leather bag between the seats.

"This won't take long," he said, as soon as he got into the Toyota.

"Good." She was ready. "I've got a proposal, Fred."

He stopped her. "No, you're the one looking for the offer. I've got it. No negotiating."

She wasn't sure what he meant. It was yanking her off course.

"A job as chief information officer," he began, "with your own department to be set up right after we win the election." He didn't look at her, but stared through the windshield at a large concrete post. "With a staff of maybe a dozen people. A deputy minister's salary."

What in...? He thought she was here for a job?

"You've got it very wrong, Fred."

"I said no negotiating." Then, under his breath, "*Christ*, you people are something else."

"Well, let me surprise you. It's not a job I'm after. What I want is this: tell me exactly what happened on the night Elspeth Hoodles was hurt. If it happened the way this kid Cab said it did, you're not in big trouble. Maybe you don't realize it, but at the moment the cops think it was attempted murder. But if it really was an accident, then all you can be charged with is trespassing or leaving the scene. Not a big deal, Fred. Just come forward. The police will understand. But if I give them your name and they have to come and get you? Let me put it this way. I've seen a corpse with a better chance at a long and happy life."

She felt more confident now. "You can tell the police whatever you like about why you asked Cab to go into that house. He can hardly remember that part."

"And this is in exchange for what?"

"I'll put Garfield Hoodles's donations list in your hands and promise never to mention it again. Think, Fred. The premier will be so grateful he might even offer *you* that new department you had in mind for me."

"Why should I trust you?"

"Do you have a choice?"

He appeared to be thinking hard, eyes darting to corners, one hand tight on the door handle. She waited a few minutes for it to sink in.

"But there is one more thing I want from you, Fred."

His head cranked slowly to look at her.

"Listen carefully," she said calmly.

This "one more thing" was the most important, what she was most proud of, the idea that had burst from what she thought was the barren soil of her brain. She talked to him for another fifteen minutes, explained how it would work. She did it carefully, patiently, mentioning details that she had gleaned from her research and the excellent contacts provided by Pat's brother in Toronto. It wasn't a commitment that Fred could make himself. She went over it again and again so that Fred could explain it to his bosses. Then she passed him a thumb drive that held all the information he would need to answer their questions. He sat stone-faced, his eyes narrowed. Maybe a good sign. Then he turned to her.

"You must be nuts. What, for Jesus's sake, makes you think a party in power would go for a hare-brained idea hatched by someone like you? A nobody. The whole cabinet would have to agree to it, maybe the whole caucus. It'll never happen."

"Fred, I know you can sell it. You're probably smarter than all of them put together. And they know that. I've laid the whole plan out for you. All you have to do is work out the logistics. In the end, everybody's happy."

"Happy? We could lose the election. And I don't know what you think your big threat is. So we have a slush fund. Nothing wrong with that."

"Ah, but I know what that five million will be spent on, Fred." She would have to be careful now. From here on she would be using sheer bluff.

"This is some kind of scare tactic? I have no clue what you're talking about. And neither do you. You think the premier would cave to an empty threat? Hah. You've got nothing."

"We need to get this thing moving, Fred. So let me give you just a small hint about what I know. A taste. A couple of key words: *Election* and *Virus*. Get it now?"

She heard a chortle start in his chest and become a full loud laugh as it escaped from his mouth.

"That's evidence? Boy, you must be desperate. Are we characters in a comic strip? You're making stuff up. Ridiculous." He chuckled again.

She wasn't surprised the hint didn't register with him. It was a long shot to use the words Graeme Cox had seen on the plant worker's clipboard. She had no idea what it meant herself. Apparently nothing. And now she was truly desperate.

"Okay, Fred. Maybe I've been too vague. I'll have to be more explicit." She hesitated. It was now or never. Her final bluff.

"I have a witness, a good, reliable, upstanding member

234

of the community. He wants to do an interview on the subject of...you listening? This witness will explain, on videotape, all about the Ice Cream Flu."

Fred's lingering chuckle caught in his throat. He coughed once, then again. His face reddened and his eyes bulged behind the designer glasses. Mercy waited for the coughing fit to end while he fiddled with his tie and cleared his throat of the final obstruction.

And now her heart seemed to be trying to escape from her chest. She had hit the target, felt like Ali Baba opening the treasure cave of the forty thieves. Somehow Ice Cream Flu was the magic phrase. She didn't know why or how. But she could almost see inside his head, Fred's brain trying to figure out which side his bread was buttered on, or if there was any bread left at all.

It was time to get Luc involved. She lifted her arm to look at her watch and turned on the overhead light, as if she needed it to see the time. It was the signal for Luc to start recording their conversation. She took a big breath and leaned a little toward Fred.

"We'll come back to this again, I'm sure. But on the other matter, I have to say, Fred, I thought you were too smart to get involved with that kid. You knew what you were looking for at the Hoodles's place. You could have done a thorough search yourself. Why didn't you just get the key from Cab and go in alone?"

He began talking in an offhand way, as if her questions were interfering with more important thoughts.

"No way. I never wanted to be involved myself. But the moron couldn't even read what I'd written for him to look for. So I had to go with him. And the dog was going nuts barking. Had to give it a chunk of raw meat from the fridge to shut it up. But listen. I didn't break in. It wasn't theft. That document belongs to us. And if Mrs. Hoodles came back I'd be able to say the kid let me in to wait for her. But when we heard the key we were upstairs and how could I explain that? So I bolted. Got out the front while she was on the back porch. Then I worried about what the kid would say to her. But he was out by the time I got to the car. Terrified. Crying. She wasn't supposed to get hurt. I'm not a violent person."

"And then you went back."

"I just went into the yard and hid the smashed pot. Spread the soil under the bush. Got dirt all over my jacket, too. Wasn't thinking straight."

Mercy kept to herself what she thought of someone who would bend over an unconscious woman's body to gather up pieces of evidence.

As if he could read her thoughts he said, "But I did call the ambulance as soon as I could."

"So why didn't they show up?"

"I told them the street. But they wanted my name. I panicked and hung up. I really thought they'd find her."

*

Alone again, heading out of the city, Mercy sang out loud. Every so often she reached over to her bag and gave it a little pat. Fred hadn't noticed Luc's car parked twenty metres away, a good spot to shoot Fred walking over to Mercy's car and getting in. Then he rolled tape again on her signal and picked up the audio of the last part of the conversation, just like Danny had done the day of Chaz's interview at Puck's house. Fred didn't notice the tiny wireless mic, black like the zipper on the bag it was clipped to, sitting between them in the front seat. Luc's tape had Fred's confession about what happened at the Hoodles's house. And it was Mercy's insurance.

Her joy that the scheme could work got her to the edge of town. Then something began to nag at her enthusiasm. Was her own audacity really much different from Danny's? Or Elspeth's? Blackmail was blackmail, even if it turned out to be in the interest of the taxpayers. And then, as she pulled into the yard of her little house, she had another revelation that brought her down with a thud. The promise to give Fred the list and never reveal what the money was for put an end to her big story. And it was only because Fred now *believed* she knew the truth about what the slush fund was for that they might agree to her plan. Her big story was now forever out of reach. She had no way to get the suspension lifted and get back into Arthur's good books. Somehow, her enthusiasm for the grand scheme had made her forget about her own shaky situation.

Chapter Twenty-Three

The phone sat on the table like some sacred object on an altar. As the hours passed it seemed to get bigger, until its presence filled the whole room. If she hadn't been told to turn in her cellphone at work she could have roamed with it, not be kept a prisoner here, tied to the landline. By morning she was lecturing herself on the virtues of patience. This scheme was bound to take time. One or two of the slower cabinet ministers might need a half-speed explanation and extra convincing. She almost wished for a religion. Earnest praying would give her something to do, the time passing in semi-conscious rapture.

The phone rang around noon. But it was Skim.

"Found out something you were wrong about," he said. "Uncle Garf never spent that money. The aunt just wasn't ready to hand it over yet. Says she'll do that when she gets home."

"Did she mention the list? Did you ask her about it?"

"What would I ask her? You never told me why it's so *fuckin'* important."

"I can't talk now, Skim. And I need the original of that list."

"I made you the copy. *Jeezus*, aren't you ever satisfied?" There was nastiness in his voice.

"What's wrong, Skim? I thought you'd be pleased that your aunt is better. But you sound angry."

"Look, I turned Cab in, a dumb kid. Wouldn't hurt a fly. And I did it figuring to help *you*. That was real stupid. I'm running around like a jerk, maybe getting myself in shit, and you're still not telling me what's going on."

"You're right." Silence at the other end. "I'd come to your place," she said, "but I can't leave my home phone. Waiting for a call. And it's really important. If you could bring the list here, Skim, I'll tell you everything that's going on. Everything."

"I got my own work to do."

"But you'll come?"

"Can't say when, though."

Waiting was torture. She cleaned all the inside windows. That ate up the afternoon. Skim didn't show. Her doubts about the scheme kept her awake for hours that night. In the morning she left the main door open to listen for the call, then washed all the schoolhouse windows on the outside, dragging the ladder around the building so she could reach the top panes. At noon, exhausted, she began to doze on the couch, only to be launched to her feet by a dull bang on the window above her. Seconds later she was cowering in a corner, heart kicking at her ribs. She waited. Heard nothing more. Crept along the edge of the room, peering out like a prisoner. No vehicles. Quiet.

Finally, feeling like an idiot, she understood what had happened and went outside to pick up the lifeless body of a small bird. It had crashed against the newly cleaned pane. She knew it by the little yellow cap: a bobolink. She fetched a trowel and dug a deep hole where it had fallen, deep enough to keep it safe from any roaming foxes. But as soon as she was finished, depressing thoughts began to take over.

So much depended on every step of this scheme falling into place. Fred would have to keep his side of the bargain: to go to the police and explain. Then Jon might understand that her probing had brought results. But even if it did work out, she was still on suspension. And what she was doing now would in no way restore her job and Arthur's respect.

By the evening she was shaking her watch to see whether it had stopped. Two more interminable days went by. Skim didn't show. Her house was as spotless as it had ever been. And she was still trapped. Now she was taking the whole scheme apart to see where she had gone wrong. By the time the phone rang she had already given up.

"Everything's in place. Press conference tomorrow afternoon."

"What? Really?" Was she dreaming? "Where, Fred? What time?"

"Check your own newscast at six. And bring the document to my office tomorrow morning."

"No. You'll get it right after the news conference."

"And you'll be in serious trouble if I don't." He had found some gangster voice somewhere and Mercy wanted to giggle.

"Believe me, Fred. After you've told the police what happened to Mrs. Hoodles and when the news conference is over, there's not another thing I want from you."

The excitement that followed made her want to call Jon, call Skim, call everybody she knew. But how could she? If the plan worked no one must ever know that she had engineered it.

At five to six she waited in front of the TV, jumpy as a kid. The opening theme began as usual, with the wide studio shot, followed by a slow zoom in to Bill Wordsworth promising an important announcement by the premier the next afternoon at two. Then a throw to Chaz standing in front of the legislature. He looked a little sweaty. Maybe there was no time to feed Bill the questions before they went on air. Chaz tried to boost the suspense by mentioning several possibilities for the news conference, before finally settling on his choice—an election call—pointing out that the premier had just decided against using a computerized voting system. Then she watched Chaz working up to one of his favourite closing phrases. It would be "Only time will tell" or "One thing is certain, we'll know tomorrow." He chose the latter. Mercy laughed and turned it off.

Now she was starving, but the inside of the fridge looked like a stronghold on the last day of a siege, just before the embattled soldiers decide they can't hold out another hour. Peanut butter on stale bread and a glass of white wine and she felt like a new person. Formidable. Indestructible. But she still had to fill another eighteen hours before that news conference. And the excitement was almost unbearable. Was it what a horse felt on the night before a big race? No. She had already won this contest but could hardly believe it, couldn't imagine where she had found the audacity to propose the scheme.

She poured another glass of wine, stood, and toasted herself, her nerve, her ingenuity. The second glass went down more slowly. She savoured it and looked around the room for something to pass the time, spotted the Buddy Rich CD sitting on the stereo. She had avoided listening to it since the latest episode in Jon's office. When the music filled the room, she turned up the volume, then considered calling Skim to say she could pick up the list herself in the morning.

She thought she heard a light tap in the silence between two tracks of music but wasn't sure. Then a second knock, a little louder. She moved automatically to answer, executing a little two-step on the way to open the door. There hadn't been car lights. It could only be Jack Murphy's wife walking over from the farm.

*

Skim figured he'd made Mercy wait long enough. She'd know now that he was nobody's flunky. And he hardly gave her a thought all week. Just went out and ran into some of the guys, had a few beers, shot some pool. Relaxed. He owed it to himself. For all the stuff he'd been doing lately for everybody else: the aunt, Cab, Mercy, Calvin, too.

His body was still aching from all the work since Monday, no let-up. Calvin asked a couple of times what the hell was the rush but looked pleased, dropped another hint about maybe needing a partner. But Skim had to ask himself the big question: did he want to stick around this island at all? Funny how you could plan so long for something, then it fell in your lap when you weren't ready.

For sure he'd get his own place now, like he'd said. Get out from all that political stuff, the Hoodles and the Tates. Elspeth sure knew the ropes. He could see that now. The old girl would get along just fine.

The list was still in the truck. Not sure he believed the aunt, lying in that hospital bed, saying she didn't know a thing about it. But so what? She was still a liar and a blackmailer. Still trying to organize his life. What a family.

He drove slow, proving to himself he wasn't in a hurry. Close now, he could see the house all lit up. Then he made out that another car was there, parked right at the door, red tail lights on. Maybe he should've called.

He pulled over, ready to do a U-ey, go back home, not walk in on something looking like a dope. Could be the car just got there. Or maybe ready to leave. He cut his lights, shut off the engine, and got out, started to walk on the shoulder, wanting to know more than he wanted to go home. A big car, maybe black but not for sure, two people in it. Just outlines against the light from the front beams shining off into a field. A guy at the wheel. The other one was smaller, a woman leaning her head on his shoulder. He was thinking it was Mercy, but it could be anybody. Anyway, what the hell was he doing, sneaking along a road in the dark to spy on some chick? Was he one of those stalkers? The kind of loser the neighbours say was real nice and quiet until they find out he's wacko?

Skim trotted back to the truck, staying to the pavement for speed. Just got the door closed when the tail lights started moving along the curved drive, slow, and out onto the road. He followed without lights, keeping well back, no plan. As he passed Mercy's house on the right he saw the front door was wide open, heard music. When he rolled down his window it was real loud. Maybe a party, people inside. But only one car there, hers. He kept following.

It was hard to see. No moon. Still cloudy after some rain, the road wet. At the next corner brake lights came on. It was a T-intersection. Left was paved. Right was gravel, but not too muddy. The car turned right. Maybe the people in the car lived down there, neighbours, just going home now.

He could go left on the pavement, take it back to the main road to town. Instead he turned around, snapped on his lights and headed back to her house, feeling like a jerk. She had to be home. When he got there it was the same scene. Door open, loud music, lights on.

He pulled into the yard and could see right inside through the big school windows where zero was happening. The music was getting on his nerves.

At the door he banged on the frame even though nothing could get through the noise of that goddamned trumpet. He stepped inside, looked around, called her name, shouted it. Nothing. He went over and turned off the music, saw one glass with some wine in it. Not what *he'd* call a party. Checked the bathroom, took a couple of steps up to the loft. He shouted again, this time into silence, took five minutes to find a flashlight then got out fast, slamming the door so it locked, to hell with the lights.

At the T-intersection, headlights on now, he turned right onto the gravel, not caring about who saw him. Mostly fields on one side, no farmhouses. Woods on the left then more fields. He drove until the road ended suddenly at the water, at a sign that said you'd be fined for taking any sand. Frig. Who'd want it? He took a look with the flashlight. Nothing but shale and creepy-looking seaweed.

Driving back, about halfway, just at the edge of the woods on his right now, was a track he hadn't noticed before, all grown over, lumpy. He pulled over. Fresh tracks went into the lane, trailing mud. He could see where it had backed out again. Had to be the same car. Hadn't seen another one anywhere near here. So. Mercy came down here with a guy to park and make out? Like some teenager? He couldn't buy it.

He walked in as far as the tracks went, saw where the other car must have stopped and backed out. It was too rough to drive any further. He could just make out the dark shape of an old wreck of a house beyond the woods. Ahead, nothing but black trees, lots of them. Why did he feel he had to go in there? And in the dark? The moon came out from behind a cloud like some kind of signal to him, as sharp as a laser and scarier than a cop's searchlight.

He started in, swinging the flashlight from side to side. Watching it made him dizzy, so he kept the beam along one side, every so often shouted her name. Didn't think about how far he'd go.

*

Mercy was staring into blackness. It was hard to keep looking because of the pain behind her eyes. Her ankle hurt. Her back ached, too. And it was cold. She tried to think but couldn't. Her ankles were bound and her hands were tied behind her. It seemed important not to move.

Her head was the worst. Even closing her eyes was torture. She was lying on her side on something soft and damp, her cheek resting on wet sponginess that smelled of spruce gum and fetid vegetation.

Not enough air. Her mouth was taped. Fear of suffocating led to the edge of panic. She concentrated on long slow breaths through her nose until her heart stopped slamming at her ribs. Her eyes searched again for something, anything. But the pain was excruciating. Better staring straight ahead. Her brain became frantic, racing backward and forward as if stuck in a track with no sense even of the season, or the day, or what had brought her to this. The terror just below the surface was oddly familiar.

She tried to put her thoughts into a kind of order. Dark. Night. What was her last memory? At first nothing. Then the phone. Talking to Fred. After that, watching the news, eating something, listening to music. A knock on the door. Expecting to see her neighbour's smiling face when she opened it. That was all.

But what about right now? *Lie still. You're all right. Figure this out one step at a time.* She almost lost it when out of nowhere appeared an image of the mouse struggling in the trap.

Her shoulders were stretched and aching. When she swallowed she could taste blood. *Don't think about it.* The biggest hurt was her head. Each time her eyes moved, even closed, the pain kicked in. Her hands were numb. She was shivering.

And she was naked.

The awareness came as a shock. Had she been raped? Didn't feel like it.

She turned her head carefully, looked up, and made out black shapes of tall trees, the tops waving slowly against a dark grey sky, the only sound an eerie creaking. Then the sky wheeled and her stomach heaved.

She heard a new sound, a feeble drone, and saw through the trees faraway lights of a plane, blinking red, white, red, white, inching across the night. All those people, sitting in rows. Watching a movie? It seemed like a miracle. She saw herself now as if from up there, and sobs threatened to choke her.

Would she die here, somebody find her body? Or just her bones? She longed for the hours to speed by so she could know how it was to end. Only two choices, really. Survive somehow, or die here. Struggling. Choking on her own vomit or tears. Not a gentle death. More like the ragged unravelling of a dirty string, until the last strand frays and the stitch to life is gone.

She could give up now. Just go to sleep. Not so bad when you thought about it like that. How long could it take? Days? No water, cold nights. *Just get through this, whatever the ending, let it be over.*

But anger followed. At whoever had done this, but mostly at herself. She would suffer, deserved to suffer, for the selfish pursuit of what brought her to this. But others would suffer, too. She pictured the police breaking the news to her parents, saw the shock on their faces, felt their grief, the grief Danny's parents must have felt, the same for any parent, no matter how the child had lived its life.

Concentrate. Hold nothing in your head but the possibility of getting free. For a moment the job seemed so great she didn't feel capable of any of it, of even beginning. Start again. *Focus.* Begin with the gag.

If she could uncover her mouth someone might be able to hear her scream. She listened. Among the tree sounds she heard something else, faint whirring. Birds? Could it be almost dawn? Not birds. Bats. She tried rubbing the side of her face against the ground to move the gag. It made her skin raw and the tape didn't budge. *Try the hands.* How long would it take before there was serious damage with the blood flow cut off? Could she wait for daylight?

She moved her fingers a little. The binding felt like light plastic rope. A chill was spreading through her body. She squirmed and twisted her way onto her stomach and over to the other side. A cool breeze drifted across her damp skin. The shivering was constant.

One hand felt something hard and her fingers scrambled to grasp it. Felt like a door knob. The next thing her fingers touched was a slim piece of metal, wider at one end. She thought it could be part of a butterfly hinge. Maybe she could use it. But she'd have to sit up. It took all her strength, knees bent and abs cramping, to do it. But now she could push the narrow end of the metal piece into the mossy ground. When the piece was stable she stopped to rest her aching arms. Then she manoeuvred the wider end up inside the plastic cord that bound her hands. Now it was very tight but it gave her some leverage. She twisted her shoulders a few times and the cord seemed to be stretching. She tried again and the metal collapsed, stabbing into her back like a thick blade. Another source of pain now.

But the cord was much looser. By pressing her wrists together tightly and dragging the binding along the ground, she was able to pull her hands free. It felt like the greatest accomplishment of her life. But with it came another bout of vertigo. She stopped, didn't dare move a muscle, counted to thirty before the nausea subsided.

The now familiar pain blasted her head again, then settled into the worst headache she could have imagined. She struggled with the tape on her mouth, fingers clumsy. But it didn't take long, and she sat for a while, taking in great gulps of air. Her whole body now shook uncontrollably.

A small sound somewhere behind her stopped her hands, still on the binding at her ankles, heart knocking. She waited. Nothing more. A small animal? She worked her feet free and was tempted to jump up and begin running but knew better. Sitting on cold sticky leaves she rubbed her ankles and feet. Her hands found wet blood at her Achilles tendon. She ignored it and kept rubbing, then pulled herself into a crouch and very slowly stood up. A new wave of nausea made her double up. It was while she stood there, bent over, that she noticed details on the ground becoming clearer.

When she straightened up a light was moving in the distance, illuminating parts of the woods away from her, but some of it reaching her. *Oh, please. Let them not be coming back.* She got down on her hands and knees and crawled to the nearest big tree, crouched on the side away from the light and waited.

Someone was calling her name.

Chapter Twenty-Four

Jeezus. She was one helluva lucky lady. But not looking too foxy right now, with her face all scraped and the hair a mess. Happy to be sitting here, though, jacked up in a hospital bed on clean sheets, dopey from the painkillers, but alive and kicking.

Skim was still hyped, couldn't come down yet from what happened. Kind of proud of himself, too, like he'd just been in a big scene from some movie where the main guy is cool all the way through and does the smart thing every time.

Out there when he saw she had no clothes he didn't want to shine the light right on her but needed to check to see how bad she was hurt. Looked real small, hunched down like she was trying to disappear. Took off his sweatshirt and passed it over and tried not to watch while she got it on. Then thought of something and moved the light around looking for her clothes. No luck. He took off his belt and looped it on a tree branch hanging down, to mark the spot where he found her, for the cops. Thinking ahead. Another smart move. When she was ready and standing up, the shirt came almost to her knees.

And boy was she stubborn, walking to the car in her

bare feet, only letting him hold her under one arm. It was tough going, too slow. And these little moans were coming out even though she was trying not to let on it hurt. Finally he just picked her up and carried her over his shoulder. She didn't weigh more than a five-by-eight rolled-up carpet.

She even laughed once, when he said, "We're not out of the woods yet." But mostly she kept thanking him once they were in the truck. Then she'd try to take a big breath and couldn't stop another groan. He couldn't tell how bad she was hurt.

When they got to the T-intersection he wanted to go straight ahead, the fastest way to the hospital. But she made him go by her house, and he had to do his magic on the lock. Women, eh? Go figure. Could be ready to croak for all she knew but had to get into some clean jeans. Couldn't go without her reporter bag either, full of god-knows-what.

At Emergency it was a wait before they put her in a wheelchair and took her for an X-ray. He walked up and down near the nurses' desk, trying to stay away from the coughers and wheezers in the chairs.

It was then he remembered he'd have to call the cops. Weird. He was spending more time with cops these days than with his buddies. Maybe he was living somebody else's life and didn't know it.

The guy who answered the phone acted real cool. Just said somebody would be over. So far not a word from Mercy on who did it. Now here she was all fixed up in the bed. An old lady in the next one snoring like a buzz saw.

It was crazy. Couple of weeks ago she was only a face on TV. Now here he was sitting beside her like they were buddies.

"Who was it took you down there?" He watched her face to make sure she was listening. Her mouth looked sore from the tape.

"I don't know, Skim."

"*Frig* that. You were sitting in the car with him. I saw you." Was she back to the old game, keeping stuff from him?

"I don't remember a thing after I opened the door."

He thought that was possible. He probably had more to tell the cops than she did. Hoped it wasn't the same pair that came to the house about Cab. They already figured him for a smartass about finding the broken flowerpot. Then it struck him funny that the two females taking up most of his time lately were in the same hospital with head damage. Wouldn't be surprised if the cops jumped on that little fluke.

Better get some thinking done before they get here. For starters he couldn't finger the guy *or* his car. Couldn't say the real colour, only dark. Never was close enough to see the plates. Now, remembering, he wondered if he had seen it before somewhere. Not likely. Only thought he did because of all the following and looking on those roads.

The cops would go back to the woods and search, find the tape and the rope and maybe her clothes. Would they give him points for hanging his belt in the tree?

It went like he figured. Except only one cop showed up, asked for their stories, separate. Then said somebody'd get on it first thing tomorrow. But looking more like he was glad it wouldn't be him.

As soon as the cop left, Mercy dozed off and he felt

like crawling in beside her. No threat there. He was so bushed now he could've slept on an escalator.

The clock at the nurses' desk showed two a.m. as he went out the door. In the truck he found the envelope with the list in it, lying on the seat, wrinkled and dirty where she'd sat on it without knowing. Seemed like a year since he'd left it there.

*

A light was making coloured patterns on the inside of her eyelids. Almost every part of her body hurt. She remembered where she was, then who had brought her here. What if he hadn't come? She opened her eyes to the smell of food.

The nurse called it breakfast but who could tell? She was hungry and ate it all, something mushy in a bowl, something dry and stiff on a plate. No coffee allowed. But what were the chances it would be drinkable anyway? The woman in the next bed didn't recognize Mercy, probably took for granted that her husband had beaten her up and didn't ask questions.

Around nine her own doctor showed up, closed the curtains and checked off damage to parts of her body as if it was a shopping list: shoulder dislocated but now back in place, would hurt for a while; mild concussion and thirteen stitches on her scalp where she had been hit; deep cut to her ankle, no permanent tendon damage but another thirteen stitches, her lucky number, apparently. Oh, yes, and a huge bruise on her back, as if she had been kicked.

"You'll feel a lot better by next week," he said, looking at her over the top of his glasses.

"But will it affect my wrestling career?"

"No injury to your funny bone, I guess." He seemed to want to hang around. Maybe his other patients had life-threatening illnesses and he couldn't face them right now.

"What happened, Mercy? Since when is reporting a high-risk job?"

"It's turning out to be more dangerous at home. I'll tell you all about it when I figure it out myself. Right now, I just need to get out of here for a really important event at two o'clock."

"I'd say as a result of last night's event, you won't be at today's. We need to run a couple more tests. That bruise could have damaged the kidneys."

He left the curtain drawn. On the way out he must have passed Jon coming in.

Even without a mirror she knew she was a mess. He looked more concerned than the doc, standing over her, asking about each injury and if there was a lot of pain. She brushed it off and tried to keep up a light banter, but when he asked who had done it and why, she suddenly couldn't talk, felt a lump in her throat.

"Sorry," he said, and sat down close to the bed. "Didn't mean to take you through it again. I'm not the investigating officer. I'm too close to the victim to be objective." He reached over and put his hand on her good shoulder, giving it a little rub.

"Jon, is there a way to keep this quiet for now?"

"Never thought I'd hear a reporter say that, but you read my mind. Whoever did this thinks you're still out there. Days before anybody notices you're gone. None of my business, maybe, but your boss was worried about you even before this."

"You called Arthur?"

"I was at your office yesterday. Guess you were out. Your boss thought you needed more stress leave. Well, now you've got it."

"Why were you there?"

"Just looking at some tapes. The reports of the explosion. Wrapping things up, paperwork." He hesitated. "Are you working on any story besides that slush fund thing? Something more, you know, personal?"

"Not unless you consider my session in Fred Fredericks's office to be personal."

"You think Fredericks could have done this over a bunch of names? Kidnapping and forcible confinement's about as serious as you can get, short of... Anyway, we talked to him the same day you told me about him. Like interviewing a wall. We checked 911. There was a call about an incident on the Hoodles's street but not enough details."

"So *somebody* called. Doesn't that confirm that Cab wasn't alone?"

"Or the kid made the call himself, then forgot. We still have to check the voice. If it's not the boy, we'd need a voice sample from Fredericks. He could refuse. We'd need that evidence."

Jon was going to be surprised when that evidence showed up in the form of Fred himself, with an explanation for Elspeth's injuries. And she could even provide the voice sample. But it would be a last resort. She really didn't want Jon to know about her taped conversation with Fred in the parking garage. Meanwhile, the two o'clock news conference looked like proof that Fred was sticking to their bargain. But did he have another trick up his sleeve? Why accept her conditions, then leave her in the woods? It was beyond comprehension, and her head hurt even to think about it.

Jon told her they weren't finished with Skim either. "Your rescuer," he called him, a little edge to his voice. Then he planted a gentle kiss on her forehead, said she was looking better by the minute, and was gone.

She struggled to get out of bed, wanting to find a phone. Before her feet hit the floor a nurse was there. She brought the phone and opened the curtains.

Pat listened, only interrupting with a couple of expressions of outrage at her attacker. "I'll be right over."

"No, wait. Can you bring me some clothes? I need a big sweater to cover the sling. And some sunglasses and a hat? Something casual."

"A disguise? Wow!"

"Don't go overboard. Just enough to cover the head bandage and some of the scratches on my face."

"My God. How bad is it?"

"Not so bad."

After that the room got busier. Nurses whizzing in and out, her neighbour sitting up, perky, gabbing nonstop about her granddaughter at cosmetology school in Halifax.

"Great," Mercy said. "So she's going to be an astronaut."

The woman looked at her as if she was from an alien planet, reached for a magazine, and limped off down the hall.

Mercy must have dozed. She opened her eyes to see Skim holding out the envelope. He now appeared as familiar as her own brother. It was then they had the long talk that should have happened last night. She filled him in on everything. He looked serious and thoughtful and watched her with a new kind of confidence. They arranged to meet in front of Province House before two. A minute later, in walked a female officer. She listened to Mercy's story again, then went off with Skim to find the lane and what Mercy now thought of as her personal dumpsite.

Tests were done but no results expected today. She looked at the lunch tray and set it aside.

Pat showed up and was suitably shocked. Hidden by the curtains Mercy got up slowly, dizzy at first. As long as she didn't move too fast her head was bearable. The clothes were fine for blending into a crowd, and the hat was old and tweedy like the one her father called his "ratter's cap." All she needed was a Jack Russell terrier.

While the hall was buzzing with visitors, Pat and Mercy escaped, giggling like a couple of teenagers.

At Province House they sat on a bench twenty metres from a large riser and podium, installed in front of the main entrance. Technicians were setting up a sound system in front of a sparse crowd. Skim joined them, and Mercy introduced him to Pat. She should have felt safe here, hemmed in by her old friend and her new one. The warm sun should have been comforting. But she couldn't stop the trembling in her chest, and even the usual sound checks made her jerk to attention.

The small crowd grew slowly. Most were in suits, civil servants and local business owners, standing, arms folded, waiting. The usual gaggle of reporters paced and chatted. Luc arrived, laden down with gear. He didn't recognize Mercy until he was almost in front of her.

"*Merde.* You look like a bag lady."

"Household accident."

"You must have been tanked." He lowered his voice. "Hey, anything new on our shoot in the parkade?

Did it work out?"

"I think we'll know in a few minutes. So where's Chaz?"

"Supposed to meet me here."

It was almost two. Luc went off to add his microphone to the others on the podium.

Through the main door of Province House came a stream of politicians—what must have been the entire government caucus, mostly men, three women. As soon as they were in chairs, strung along the back of the riser, Fred appeared, leading another group that was a little smaller. They gathered in a cluster to one side, like a Greek chorus. Fred scurried to adjust the podium. The premier stepped forward. The sun broke through a cloud as if cued by a stage manager, the light shining on his thick grey hair as he smiled and nodded at the crowd. He was a good-looking man, Mercy thought, with a personal charm that could attract attention and exude calm without apparent effort.

At the other end of the charm scale was the muscular presence of Puck, who stood nearby like a bouncer poised for action. Seeing him again, it struck Mercy that he, more than Fred, was the type to solve a problem by using violence and could easily overpower someone and tie them up.

The premier interrupted that thought.

"Ladies and gentlemen, citizens of our wonderful province," the premier began, getting immediate quiet. "We have two very important announcements today. The first has to do with a commitment we made a couple of weeks ago. We've listened to the people, we've taken it to heart, and we're here to tell you about an impressive new project that will please everyone."

A racket that included whistles, bells, rattles, bagpipes, and rhythmic clapping began to compete with the loudspeaker carrying the premier's voice. People turned to look down Great George Street toward the waterfront. The premier mouthed a few more sentences, then stopped as a crowd of about two hundred people moved closer. Mercy got a mental flash of a similar stroll by John A. Macdonald and the gang on their way up the same street to that first historic meeting about Confederation.

Some marchers carried signs. She could read crude hand-lettering in heavy strokes: *Homeless Not Hopeless, You Never Lissen,* and *Stuff Your Country Living.* Other placards bore logos of well-known protest groups. Many faces were familiar, expert activists who had an opinion to express on every issue. "Citizens Against Everything," Jinxy called them. Three marchers sang an old Johnny Cash song in clever harmony.

Mercy searched the protesters for the teacher, Alice Marshall, but couldn't see her. A prominent church leader headed the procession, setting a tone of calm and order. Subtract the noise and he might have been guiding his obedient flock to the annual picnic. Well before they reached the platform he held up his hand and the followers stopped, and, except for a couple of stray toots, so did the racket. Mercy caught sight of Alice Marshall and two of the homeless men, standing near the back. The premier beamed down.

"I can't tell you how glad I am to see that our citizens of…the great outdoors…have taken the time from their… um…busy lives to join us. Because…" He paused, then went confidently back to his text. "Because today I'm here to announce a wonderful new housing project designed especially for those among you with the greatest need. Yes, you heard right. Only for the homeless of this city. We have listened, we have understood, and we are taking action. The farm for the unhoused will not go ahead. There will be no move to the countryside, as lovely as that idea was. Instead, you will have a place to sleep right here in the heart of the city. A shelter like none you have ever seen, a showpiece, a shining example to other cities.

"This new facility will be located in the former brick-making factory. You all know it. Empty for years but begging to be preserved. And just a few hundred metres from where we are now." He turned, his head now in Grecian profile, and pointed along Richmond Street. And every political head looked in that direction, as if they could actually see the derelict building, miraculously transformed.

"And this is what makes it so special." He returned his gaze to the crowd.

"The huge space inside will become a community, a grid of streets. And the rooms where the homeless can sleep will have windows that look onto those streets. The doors open into those streets. And herein lies the beauty of this concept. The people who use this facility will have a choice. If a room feels too confining, then they can choose to sleep on one of the indoor streets.

"In the centre of the building, a large open square, like a town park, will be open to the sky. People will have a place to gather, to talk, to enjoy musical entertainment, to engage in any number of social activities, as I'm sure they do now, but protected from rain, snow, and cold by a retractable dome, when needed." Here the premier left his speech and looked around. The audience buzzed.

"But I want to tell you this. My government does not claim all the credit for this wonderful project. Taxpayers' money has been spent in the planning. But the real credit must go to a small group of our province's finest business interests." Here he gestured toward the group standing to his right. He looked at a paper and named each of the companies. The man from SuperShredders waved. So did the owner of Great Big C Computers. The air was thick with benevolence.

"And to remind our future citizens what a fine example has been set by the generosity of these people," he nodded toward the Greek chorus again, "a plaque bearing their company names will be mounted on the outside of the building."

Mercy looked over at Luc. He was shooting it all. But still no sign of Chaz. He'd be kicking himself for missing this.

Skim leaned over. "Is that them? The guys on the list?"

"Every single one," she said, and couldn't stop grinning. And neither could the company men on the platform. And why not? she thought. They were no longer secret contributors to a mysterious slush fund. They could now bask in a glorious public relations image as supporters of the unfortunate homeless. And very likely receive a fat tax write-off for their charitable donation. But would she be back in her job by then? Would the government start a new slush fund? And would she ever find out what the original plan was for this one?

"The new shelter is not the only big piece of news today," the premier went on. "I've asked the Lieutenant governor to dissolve this legislature so that we can now go to the polls in a general election on June

28." He waited for reaction. His caucus applauded enthusiastically, as if it was a wonderful surprise to them, too. Below, the suits gabbed to each other. The protesters drooped, then began to wander away, disappointed perhaps at being denied a confrontation with the premier.

Reporters moved closer, shouting questions, like shoppers rushing through the doors to a once-in-a-lifetime sale. The premier held up a hand for quiet and smoothed back his perfect hair.

"First, I want to say that I am aware of the questions about why we have delayed setting the election date. I can tell you now that we've had a very good reason. We have been working day and night over the past few months on a plan for an election campaign like no other you have seen in your lifetime." *Boy, he's good*, Mercy thought. *Soon he'll be parting the Red Sea.*

"Gone is the extravagant spending on television, radio, and newspaper advertising. Only our opponents will continue to waste money on that. Gone are the rallies in rented halls with costly entertainment. Our opponents can stick with that if they like. Gone are the days when we were known to spend as much on a campaign as it takes to..." He looked around. Did she see him wink at Puck? "...well, to make a home for the homeless." He was flying now, confident, smooth, high on anticipated glory.

Mercy was astonished. This campaign-on-a-diet wasn't her idea. But she remembered Elspeth's anger at how campaign money was spent.

The premier's voice softened. He might have been declaring he had just "found the Lord."

"We have taken a remarkable step here with a

responsible campaign on a very modest budget. Our rallies will be held outdoors, in parks and playgrounds, in farmyards and on wharves. We will speak from hay wagons and tractors and flatbed trucks. We invite our opponents to join us, to take part in large public meetings in fields and tents, where the voters can listen to *all* candidates and decide who best represents their interests. Our own candidates will travel together. Yes, all twenty-seven of them. They will cover the length and breadth of this province on one large bus, our only expense. And joining us, their time and talent given free of charge, will be the Island's most popular band, Frost Heaves!"

As if on cue, applause burst from the caucus and they leapt to their feet, beaming, nodding, shaking hands, ready to get on that bus right now—bring it on.

Reporters got their questions answered. Most were about the new election campaign, little interest now in the homeless shelter.

Meanwhile, the protesters seemed to have dissolved before Mercy's eyes, a few placards on the pavement were now the only evidence that they had been there. Alice Marshall and a couple of the street people stood abandoned on the pavement. But they were now deep in excited conversation. Mercy thought she heard the word *ghetto*.

In the fun of watching the premier perform Mercy had almost forgotten her pain and what she still had to do. She turned to Skim, hoping to take courage from his presence. But he was gone. Bored? And Pat was off talking to a teenager holding a pet ferret on a leash.

Mercy walked slowly, legs trembling, to the edge of the stage.

Chapter Twenty-Five

Fred was talking to a couple of politicians, his arms waving like semaphore flags, but keeping an eye on what was left of the crowd. He appeared guileless, just another young keener sniffing around the seat of power. What did she expect? That he would now have fangs like the hound of the Baskervilles? He looked no more dangerous than an energetic puppy, though perhaps one that might grow up to be a full-throttle pit bull. This twerp couldn't have tried to kill her less than twenty-four hours ago. But both Fred and Puck were capable of hiring some thug to do the job. She couldn't think about it. *Focus.*

Fred's scan of the crowd passed over her without recognition, then whipped back. She took off the hat and sunglasses. He didn't miss a beat, came trotting to the edge of the platform to peer down at her, showing no shock that she was there, only surprise at how she looked.

"Well, well. Somebody slam a door in your face?" His voice was teasing, a man without a care in the world.

She tried to control her wobbly legs as he hopped off the riser and stood in front of her.

"So, we've delivered our side of the deal," he said. "With bells on." He looked around, rubbed his palms together. "This could work out even better than expected." His smugness was beyond belief. She wanted to smack him.

"Another minute and you'll claim it was all your idea," she hissed. The envelope holding the list shook in her hands. She held it out.

He put a hand to his mouth and faked a yawn. "Maybe you're not as clever as you thought. You can do what you want with that piece of paper. Now it's just a list of businesses that planned all along to give to a big civic-minded project. Great publicity for them, too."

It really did hit home to her then. The big news story that had become her all-consuming motivation was truly gone. And he was right. She was *not* clever. She was still under suspension and didn't have the remnants of a story, even if Arthur suddenly decided to change his mind and listen. There was nothing to listen to. If the slush fund and the "fix" that Puck talked about on Danny's tape were originally meant to be spent on some illegal scheme to do with the election, all that was cancelled now. The slush fund was going to a worthwhile cause.

"And the other part, Fred? Where you tell the police how you went into Elspeth's house and she got clobbered?"

He looked away. "The premier says there's no need for me to get involved in all that."

"What? *Get* involved? You *were* involved." He was gazing off at some faraway tree.

"Ah," she said. "Now I get it. The premier didn't say that at all. He doesn't know about your little caper at the Hoodles's place, does he? And Puck doesn't know either. All they've heard is the gossip: that she was injured in a fall. Or maybe they suspect something but don't want to say it out loud. She was ready to give back the money, but they still wanted the document. And you wanted the brownie points for delivering it. So you used that kid, Cab, and it all went wrong. And you think Puck and the premier don't have to know."

No reaction. He was still studying the treetops.

And her aching head was speeding off in new directions, finding more bits of the puzzle that were starting to fit.

"Well, Fred, apparently there's no end to your problem solving skills. I'm beginning to understand. You're now pretending this new homeless project was also to satisfy Elspeth Hoodles." Mercy took a long breath. Not a good idea to do her thinking aloud, but her brain wouldn't stop and neither would her mouth.

"And you must have told the premier that this was the price Elspeth was demanding to keep quiet about the Ice Cream Flu." He brought his gaze back to her now and offered a stiff smile, as if bored. But Mercy had to be careful about throwing that phrase around. So far that's all she had, but it had been enough to convince Fred that she knew what it meant.

And she doubted that Elspeth Hoodles had any idea what the slush fund was for. Not the kind of political detail Puck would share. She shook her head. But maybe Elspeth was good at bluffing, too. Maybe she had hinted at other political secrets passed on by her late husband that would be revealed if she wasn't satisfied.

"You're amazing, Fred. You leap from one shaky raft to the next and never expect to get your toes wet."

She could see how determined he was to protect himself. And he was clever. But he didn't frighten her now, though she couldn't explain why.

"So," she said, "you're getting the list today, but the premier thinks it's coming from Elspeth."

"It doesn't matter what the premier believes," he hissed. "You've got your goddamn building."

"And they think you're a genius."

He glared at her. "And why not? You imagine it was easy getting all this arranged in a few days?" He lowered his voice and threw a furtive glance at the group on the stage. "And to get the premier to agree to pay some guy in Toronto for the rights to use the plans?" His hands went into his pockets and he rocked back on his heels, the picture of triumph. "And the election campaign? All that organizing? I did all of it. Nobody else could have done it."

"Well, congratulations, Fred. The no-frills campaign was a real surprise."

"Shows how little you know about the cost of a building project. There wasn't nearly enough money in that fund to cover the renovations. We had to take the rest from the regular campaign budget. Now we don't even have enough for advertising."

"No big loss, I'd say. The old-style campaign gets my vote." But as her thoughts drifted into an image of the premier charming the crowds from the bed of a hay wagon, she remembered Elspeth's rant about campaign spending. Was this her plan all along? Had she refused to give up that slush fund money unless she was promised an election straight out of the good old days? When her daddy was an orator and everybody gathered round? Mercy almost laughed out loud. She felt a new respect for Elspeth Hoodles, yet another blackmailer in a world apparently awash with them. But, in fact, it was her own meeting with Fred in the car, and her dropping of the words *Ice Cream Flu*, that had convinced him that Mercy knew the truth about how the slush fund was to be used.

Fred was turning away now.

"Wait a minute, little man. You haven't completed the bargain. You're going to the police. Remember?"

The sneer was already plastered on his face when he looked over his shoulder. "No need for that now. You're no longer the big threat you thought you were. Who'd be interested in some story you call 'Ice Cream Flu,' a fantasy with no evidence, invented by a shaky reporter just back from stress leave?"

"But I have more." She got the words out before he was three steps away. He turned just as she took the videotape out of her bag. "Oh my, what's this, Fred? If you want to talk, I'll be right over there." She limped to the nearest bench, the stitches in her ankle throbbing loud enough to be heard. The tape went back into her bag. He followed and stood over her.

"That tape isn't worth a thing anymore." His mouth formed a nasty smile. "You and your buddy missed the boat. You should have taken the first offer. Irrelevant now. Blackmail's cancelled. Gone."

It took a few seconds. Then it dawned on her that he meant Danny.

"Fred, this isn't the tape from Puck's house. This is something else. And it's about you. Interested?"

He looked around, then quickly sat down on the bench, leaving a good space between them.

It was over in ten minutes. She watched his sharp

little face as he realized what was on the tape, as he went over in his head just what he had admitted, sitting there with Mercy at the top of the parking garage, with Luc not far away, recording everything.

"Be a good boy now, Fred. As you agreed. Tell the police you were at Elspeth's house. Say you asked Cab to let you in to wait. A nice evening so you sat out on the upstairs balcony. Explain the accident as it really happened. Give that poor kid the first break he's ever had. If you don't? Well, use that wonderful mind of yours, Fred. Imagine your life once the police have this tape."

When he was gone all she wanted was to lie down right there and sleep for a week, tired of thinking, tired of wondering how she had ended up in the woods, almost too tired to move. Pat appeared and asked if she was ready to go back to the hospital. She nodded dumbly, sounds coming from a great distance away.

"Stay here," Pat ordered. "I'll bring the car over."

"Where's Skim?" She didn't want to be left alone.

"Don't know. He took off half an hour ago like he was being chased by bees. Missed the whole speech."

Mercy put her head back against the rough wood and closed her eyes. Would she ever find out what that money was meant to pay for? And did it matter now? She was not proud of herself. A first-rate manipulator, not a journalist. She thought of the abandoned factory that would soon be a shelter for street people. Maybe she should try a career with the Salvation Army.

The next thing she was aware of was Jon's voice.

"You okay?"

"Sure." She struggled to sit up straight. "Pat's getting her car."

"I'm surprised they let you out so soon. But look, something's come up. Can you come to the station? I need to talk to you. But not here."

"Can't it wait?"

"It's pretty important. Actually, it's *very* important. Sorry. I'll fill you in there."

She didn't have the energy to argue. "Oh, all right. Half an hour."

He waited with her. When Pat came they walked her carefully to the car. She felt like a drunk being led away after a brawl, headed for a stay in the overnight tank.

After Pat dropped them at the station, Jon put Mercy gently into a chair in his office, the place where, lately, it always seemed to end badly. He brought another chair to sit in front of her, leaning in, their knees almost touching.

"Have you remembered anything else about last night? How you got to the woods? Anything at all about a car?" He was so close she wanted to put her arms around his neck and lean her bruised head against his shoulder.

"I didn't see a car. Or any other person until Skim showed up. Why are we going over this again? I thought this wasn't your case."

"It's getting complicated. I've just brought someone in on another charge. Now I think there's a connection. I was hoping you'd remember some little thing I could use to go for a confession." Jon looked more tense than she had ever seen him. "We need the surprise element. Some detail he doesn't know we have."

"Who is it, Jon? You have to tell me."

"No, I don't want you to know yet. You might start connecting things that aren't relevant."

She thought it was just possible they had arrested Skim. But could they be that wrong?

"Listen to me, Jon. You wanted the surprise element. I'm it. Let me face whoever it is. See what the reaction is." Had she just said that? At this moment her pain and exhaustion were gone.

"No." He shook his head, impatient now. "Don't even think that. You're a victim. We don't do that." He took her hands as if trying to keep her calm.

"Please, Jon. There's not a person I'd be afraid to face right now. I'll sign a release form. Anything. I trust you."

"It's not a question of trust. You're my responsibility. I'd be using you, taking advantage of you, to get my job done. Not to mention the personal side. Even the chief has that figured out. That time we were talking at the news conference? 'Can't take your eyes off her.' That's what he said. And he was right. I won't put you at risk." He gently tightened his hands around hers.

"But just think," she said, her voice now pleading. "I'm *here*, right in front of him. How did I survive? That's the surprise. It's what you need. This monster will think I *wasn't* unconscious the whole time. That I can identify him."

"Not that simple, Mercy. This suspect is not your average violent thug. We know how to handle that type, the mindless low-life who's not thinking, just lashing out. What happened to you was planned, and carefully. This guy is way beyond needing anger management. He's a psychopath. And he's probably convinced that he did a good job. Right now he thinks he's only here on another charge. And even the evidence we've got on that is circumstantial at best."

"I have to go in." She felt her eyes filling with tears,

and Jon looked away. Was she being childish? There was a long silence. He dropped her hands, stood up and paced to the window. *That damned window*. She dug a tissue out of her bag and wiped her cheeks.

When he came back he stood over her. "Try again. Remember just one detail that I can confront him with."

"No. Nothing. Just me, Jon. And I'll feel perfectly safe with you outside the door."

She tried to sound as if she meant it.

Chapter Twenty-Six

Jon kept her in the chair until she understood exactly how she would have to act. He warned her to expect the unexpected but stressed that he would be just an arm's length away, on the other side of the closed door. Then he went out to make arrangements, and she felt herself starting on a new tank of adrenalin.

When he came back they went downstairs, to an area of the station she'd never seen before. As they walked down a long hall he reached for her hand, then they stopped outside an unmarked door. He pointed to the one-way glass next to it, covered by a curtain. But she didn't want to see who was in there yet, in case she lost her nerve. Jon showed her the audio connection, then gave her hand a squeeze and opened the door quietly. She stepped in alone and it closed behind her.

Sitting behind a small table in the opposite corner, a safe five metres away, was someone she didn't recognize at first. He was sweaty and dishevelled, hair falling over his eyes. He was ripping a Styrofoam cup into little pieces. It was Chaz.

He looked up. His mouth gaped but nothing came out. He dropped the shreds of cup and tried to bring a hand to his mouth. It was shaking and he stopped with it midair and clenched his fists instead. Then he looked wildly around the room, as if not knowing where he was.

"Bloody hell, Mercy. Somebody has to get me out of here."

She stayed where she was and focused on what the next step was to be, her back pressed against the strong wood of the door. She felt for the chair beside her, exactly where Jon had said it would be. She eased herself into it and folded her arms, tried to look relaxed but felt her arms tight against her chest.

"Surprised to see me, Chaz?" The words caught in her throat and she had to cough.

"I thought maybe Arthur would come, or…"

How would she manage to control herself long enough to have a conversation with this animal? A guy who could flirt and flatter, who tried to charm her, then suddenly decide to kill her. It was beyond her understanding. And now he was pretending not to notice her bruised face?

"Mercy, this is a nightmare. What am I doing here? Like some bum off the street." But he wasn't looking at her. One hand was on his forehead, shading his eyes.

Complete calm was important. She understood this. But with every fibre of her body she wanted to scream obscenities at him. If a weapon had been available she would have attacked. She wanted to pick up the chair and smash it over his head, watch his pain. For the first time she felt her own capacity for real violence.

"You might as well tell them," she said.

"Tell them what? I don't know what you're talking about." The voice was stronger now, almost the rich baritone television viewers heard every night on the news.

"I think you do." This felt like stalling. She wanted to mow him down with words, go straight to it. But Jon had said it was vital not to lose control, to follow the steps one after another.

"I know you and Danny were blackmailing the government. I have the tape."

He didn't even pretend surprise, actually looked relieved. Did he think this was only about the blackmail?

"For God's sake, Mercy. Danny's idea of a practical joke. Never came to anything. He wouldn't even show me what was on the tape."

"So Danny had to describe it to you? That must have been frustrating. A lowly cameraman standing between you and a sensational story. You could have wowed us all. Exposing government corruption? A reporter's dream."

"Friggin' Danny. You'd never believe it, Mercy. Tried to tease me with words from the tape. But I could tell he had no idea what that conversation was about." Chaz was sitting up straighter now. As if he might be able to convince her to help him. "A bottom-feeder, Mercy. That's all he was. Thought as long as he had the tape, Puck would give him anything he wanted. Clueless." Chaz looked up toward the small window near the ceiling in the wall beside him. The hint of a smile played at one side of his mouth.

"The jerk just wanted money. Cash for turning over the tape. He was a slimy upstart, had no idea that the tape itself wasn't the weapon. He could have made copies. And Puck would realize that. 'Course he would. He's not stupid. It would need a subtle approach, not say a word about the tape. Just that someone had spilled the beans, told us everything about why the election was stalled. It was the *knowledge* that was worth something, and it was ours. No limit to what the Party would do to keep it quiet."

He was more confident now, but winding down. She had to keep him talking.

"So you didn't actually know what was said on that tape?"

"Danny didn't understand the details, but he could tell it was important. He should have given me the tape. Just the hint of a scandal so close to an election, and—"

"And you knew the Party would be desperate to keep it quiet."

He picked up the plastic water bottle sitting at the edge of the table, examined the label, and took a small sip, watching Mercy as he set it carefully back in place. "I never got involved."

"No? Danny was too quick for you. Wanted the fast buck, as you said." She kept emotion out of her voice, just a conversation. "But you were after the big job, the status job, designed just for you. Head of public relations. Big staff, including Fred Fredericks, who would do all the work while you took all the credit."

"In your dreams," Chaz said, now examining his fingernails. He had pushed his chair back from the table, crossed his legs.

"Danny couldn't wait, could he?" She continued to recite, thinking as she did that Jon was hearing all this for the first time. "And after he died you had to find the tape so you hired somebody to search his apartment. Even called his parents, pretending to be from the station. You were desperate to hear the actual conversation on that tape."

Chaz was now gazing at the ceiling as if it were a work of art, but listening, she knew, to every word.

"When you called Mrs. Brewer a second time, you found out she'd sent the tape to me. So you searched my place, too." She paused to get her voice under control. "Gee, Chaz, that kind of scared me at the time. But it shouldn't have. It was only you...a complete zero."

He looked directly at her then, no longer pale, eyes snapping into focus. His fist pounded the table. The water bottle trembled.

"That so? If I'm such a zero why was it you couldn't wait to get into bed with me?"

She stared at him, not sure what was coming.

"Bet you think about that a lot," he continued. "New Year's Eve? Don't pretend you can't remember. Five minutes after we got to your room at the motel. A little attention from me and you thought you'd gone to heaven." His sneer held such malevolence she felt herself shrinking in the chair.

"It didn't take long to figure out my mistake, though." She kept her voice low and reasonable. "Chaz, you haven't asked me why I'm all bandaged up. Not even curious?"

"I have other things on my mind. Don't you get it? What am I doing here? It's not right. I've got a reputation. You think people tune in to our newscast every night to look at *you?* Some chick who likes to hang around the cops? You're pathetic." He smoothed his hair back with both hands, sat up straighter.

"If I'm that pathetic, Chaz, why do you keep coming on to me? Like Friday night when you showed up with Jinxy? You're still trying. You didn't get the message."

"That's a laugh." And he did laugh, and it was a nasty one. "Amusing myself. To get through a boring couple of hours."

This was moving away from her focus. She had tried to corner him about the blackmail, but he had admitted nothing. Put it all on Danny.

"Frankly, I never understood why *any* woman would be interested in you. You're not very bright, and you have the personality of white bread. You might not know this, Chaz." She leaned in his direction just a little, sharing a confidence. "A lot of people think you wear a hairpiece."

Maybe she had gone too far. It sounded ridiculous. But no, red blotches were appearing on his neck, and his hands tightened on the edge of the table.

Suddenly he was on his feet and her shock sent her head back with such force that it hit the wall. Her stomach heaved and she was afraid of what might happen next, that Jon might not be able to protect her after all. But Chaz stayed behind the table, pacing. Three steps, turn, three steps, turn.

"Got your clothes off anyway, though, didn't I?" It came out in a rush as if escaping without his consent. Jon said this is what might happen. Her little jabs would get to him and once he let go and really started talking she should not interrupt. A familiar tingle in her back reminded her of the turning point in a difficult interview.

"Yes," she said. "And I did wonder. What kind of man needs to knock a woman out before he can get her clothes off? I've never known anyone that desperate."

The pacing stopped. His fists clenched and unclenched. Four times. Counting kept her calm.

"You think you know men?" he snarled. "You've got no idea. No fucking idea what we have to put up with. Always waiting for the lady to say, 'Okay, you can have a treat tonight because you've been a good boy.' Always in control of the precious jewels you keep between your legs." His body was doing some impression of a woman, swaying and wiggling his shoulders. "Then, one day you decide there won't be any more treats. You shut everything down and put it all away, till the next poor jerk comes along who has to go through the audition."

His voice got louder with each word. Now he was shouting, leaning over from the waist in her direction, his face red, white spittle gathering at the corners of his mouth. She had never heard such venom coming from another human being.

Then the wave of temper receded and he was calm. A hand went up to smooth his hair again. "You think you're the only journalist with brains? I taught you a thing or two, remember? When you were still wet behind the ears. And that day you came asking questions about the election? I knew right away you were up to something." He was boasting like a schoolboy. "And I knew other things you'd never guess."

He was standing behind the chair now and moved it closer to the table as if wrapping up a meeting, preparing to leave. But ready to share one last confidential bit of wisdom, something important.

"It was really interesting watching you lose your cool when Danny died." Then he lowered his voice to a hiss. "You weren't smart enough to figure that one out, were you? An accident? Not a chance. I was Johnny-on-the-spot. I looked down from the roof of the parking garage after we got the overview shots.

The smoke was clearing and there he was behind the building. Like it was preordained, just for me. That kind of luck only happens once in a lifetime. And only to people who deserve it. All I had to do was send the cameraman away and go down there myself. One shove and it was over." Chaz actually smiled as he watched her absorb this.

"And when I let you take Luc on that shoot while you were suspended? Think I'd be that dumb? I watched every move. Saw you go into the parking garage. Saw Fred follow you. Knew exactly what you were after. The job that was supposed to be mine." He stopped talking, was looking off somewhere.

"Yes," she said, "I can see how you'd think that, Chaz, in your world of the ethically challenged, where the only motive is self-interest."

He went on as if he hadn't heard.

"Anyway, I didn't hit you that hard. Just wanted to make you pay attention. Tell you about how it could be for us. But you wouldn't wake up. Still in control, shutting me out." Chaz was talking to himself now. Crazy talk. "So I had to leave you. It made sense. I know it did. Nobody'd miss you. You could have gone away, taken a plane somewhere. Or even suicide. Arthur would buy that one."

Without warning his hand slapped the plastic bottle off the table. It shot into the corner, sending water over the floor. Then he collapsed into the chair and looked at her as if pleading for something. His head went down on his hands as the door opened.

Jon took her out. By now she was shaking but knew it had worked. An hour later Chaz made a formal confession.

Chapter Twenty-Seven

For sure this wasn't Skim's idea of celebrating. Sitting on Mercy's patio around a big table like at one of his aunt's special events. Only came tonight because Mercy said it wouldn't be a party without him. It was cool hearing her say that. The team, she called them, like they'd just won the playoffs. But still lots of questions he'd likely never get answers for. Anyway, he knew more than this cop did. All the stuff about how the shelter got paid for? The guy had no clue that Mercy was up to her eyeballs in *that*. Wasn't a bad dude, though, for a cop. But how did a guy with no hair get hooked up with the likes of Mercy?

And that reporter, Chaz. He was something else. On TV he looked smart and cool. Lots of hair and the sharp clothes—had it all. And then it turns out he's a friggin' maniac. Just shows you. Maybe a lot of celebrities are nuts. Well, sure, Skim could see it with rock stars, the drugs and that. But probably a shitload of others, too, like those TV preachers.

Saturday night. Skim could've been out with the guys, letting loose. But maybe that stuff was over, now he was a businessman for real. Word got out fast that he was the one found Mercy in the woods.

"Big hero, that's the news out there," Calvin said, on Skim's first day back at work. "Everybody's talking about it. 'Hey, your fella there. That the guy saved the reporter?' They'll be breaking the doors down to get into the auctions. Just to get a look at you. Good for sales, the bottom line."

So Skim didn't even have to bring it up himself. Calvin said, "I can see it, Skim. Halpern & Tate. Sounds classy."

"*Tate?*" Skim said. "Jeezus. Where'd that come from?"

"Well, sorry, Skim, but it's your real name, right? Your mom's name might be Hoodles now, but it was Tate when you were born. A big name around here. Why not make it work for you? It's your right."

Skim stayed cool, let on it was no shock, all the time his head spinning, like the night Cab gave him the "adopted" news, only this time, he didn't know why, it didn't seem like a real big surprise. Next thing Skim was feeling pretty good, telling himself he knew all along, way down somewhere. He might have a talk with the old girl, though, about why she kept him in the dark. But she wasn't so bad. Let her be for now. Maybe he'd just start calling her Mom one day and see what happened.

Probably he had to thank Mercy for some of the way it turned out. And here they were now, all her pals around this table, having what he figured was called "conversations" and eating food that somebody cooked special. It was the Oriental-or-whatever chick that must have done the cooking, from the way she was dishing it up. And the French cameraman was there, and one other guy not arrived yet, name of Toby, whom Skim didn't know, the one who did the job of putting the TV pictures together for the reporters.

Then, 'course, the cop and Mercy. What a crew. He figured the cop was after Mercy, the way he never stopped looking at her. And it turned out the Asian babe was an animal doctor. Boy, turn me into a sick dog, quick.

Food was good. And enough beer. Luc the camera guy was doing the driving so no drinking there. The cop came alone but he was on call and no booze for him either. Skim offered himself as the "designated drinker." Got a laugh for that. But this sitting looking at the sun go down was a drag. Started him thinking about stuff, like his latest stupid move. When he'd run off like a fool in the middle of the premier's big announcement to tell the cops he finally knew whose car it was that took Mercy. That it was the one pulled into her yard with the two guys in it that Friday night when he was just leaving. He should've twigged way sooner. Same kind of dumb mistake as that morning lying in the field with Cab when he didn't pick up that the farmer wasn't dressed for church. Losing his edge. Good time to turn respectable.

Be in his own place this time next month. Could hardly believe it. Seemed like only a few weeks ago he was a teenager, checking his chin every morning for zits.

For now he was getting a kick out of watching his "mother," or Elspeth as everybody called her now, watching her running around nuts, sticking her nose into plans for the street bums' shelter. Wanting window boxes and plants everywhere, all that stuff. First she bugged the hell out of everybody to name it the Tate Centre. Pretty funny when they told her it'd be named after Uncle Garf, for all the years he looked after the money, and for croaking, obviously. Jokes already flying about "Hoodles Hotel." She'd never get away from that name now. Almost got to be chairman of the board till the so-called residents had another protest and picked one of their own. Then *that* guy remembered he was living on the street in the first place to get out of the same kind of duty with his family. So he quit. Now a private company might get a contract to run it.

*

Mercy was glad to see Skim enjoying himself. She caught him in a smile a couple of times.

She was sitting with her back to the long view of those woods near the abandoned house, now well hidden by trees in full leaf, but she might put a screen up in the fall, forget the place even existed.

Chaz's crimes made Puck and his cohorts look positively wholesome by comparison. She now understood that they were going about their petty political corruption the way their types had done for centuries. An art that was never actually taught, just passed on, like the ability to play the fiddle. And in a hundred years the citizens would revere these important characters from the province's past, their artifacts collected as valuable witness to the times. Local historians would wash them of their sins.

But she wasn't surprised that Chaz's moment of fame came immediately. And it didn't hurt that he was as photogenic as ever. Media reps descended on Charlottetown from places never before heard of, to cover the story of a journalist who killed a cameraman and tried to kill a fellow reporter. It was international news, Jinxy said, because, as loathed as they were, journalists were not commonly thought of as murderers. Julie covered the brief court appearance and was amazed at what *didn't* come out. Chaz's guilty plea meant no preliminary hearing, no trial, no witnesses appearing, and no evidence introduced.

Jinxy had already warned Mercy. "It won't stop the rumours. People don't want details confirmed. They want to speculate without fear of contradiction." But one rumour did hit the mark: that after Mercy had faced Chaz in the interview room, Jon was able to get a search warrant that uncovered her missing clothing in Chaz's apartment.

The only line that could be quoted came from the judge when he remarked that twenty-five years should give Chaz plenty of time to work his charm on new colleagues in a federal prison.

Jinxy had called the day after the sentencing. "Arthur wants you back ASAP." And at the first morning meeting he had piled on the praise.

"Look at her. Mercy. Our Joan of Arc. Our beacon. Indispensible."

"Okay, Arthur," Jinxy said. "We get the idea."

Meanwhile, from the day the election was called, Arthur was chubby-knee-deep in the preps for coverage, wringing his fat little hands but coping nicely, never once uttering Chaz's name or bringing up Mercy's suspension.

And the new folksy-style election campaign soon dominated television coverage every night. Gone were the usual politicians' talking heads. Now it was fast-paced, colourful musical entertainment, sprinkled lightly with ten-second clips of candidates trying to get a few words heard over the rowdy crowds in a roadside field. Rural families jumping and jiving to the music of dozens of local bands keen to be part of the action.

Reporters from the newsroom were soon vying for a chance to cover an election event. And the Opposition candidates now realized their television ads were wasted. So they began to compete with outdoor entertainment of their own.

"We're witness to a phenomenon," Jinxy declared. "Elections will never be the same. Much as I hate to admit it, the victory goes to style over substance. Soon nobody will remember the days when politicians had to promise protection from terrorists who might blow up the Confederation Bridge."

Soon Mercy saw that the tone of the campaign probably wasn't what Elspeth Hoodles had in mind. Orators were scarce, and, in any case, impossible to be heard above the musicians and roaring spectators. By the end of the first week the politicians began to look like groupies, followers of the bands that included not only the original group, Frost Heaves, but also The Miracles and the new favourite, Judas and The Snowblowers.

Mercy was happy to be out of it, back covering the courts again.

The only cloud over the scene was an almost total absence of tourists, scared away by word that the highways were choked with cavalcades of local cars following the campaign wagons that lumbered up and down rural routes. The government tried to blame Fred Fredericks for the tourist decline, since he had taken credit for designing the folksy campaign. But after accepting the praise for getting it off to a brilliant start, he disappeared. A rumour spread that he was now selling ads for a low-watt radio station in northern Alberta. The police were happy to forget him. Their budget didn't allow for trips to western Canada. And in her excitement over the homeless shelter, Mrs. Hoodles was happy to forgive Cab for the backyard incident.

The shelter was a favourite with Arthur, too. He saw it as a healthy influence on the local culture.

"Terrific," he said. "Hoboes uplifted? Retrained? Respectable? Looking for jobs?"

"We have an opening here," Mercy said.

He had already offered that vacant political reporter's job to Mercy, but she hadn't dignified it with an answer, simply patted him on the shoulder and walked away to her desk.

There she found a couple of fresh newspaper typos for her collection. In the first front-page story about Chaz's appearance in court he was not called "the accused." He was "the accursed." And Jinxy had dropped off his latest find. Directly under a big ad for a cure for erectile dysfunction, the Junior Farmers' Union was given space to announce the topic for their next meeting: "Why Not Try Sheep?"

By the day of the election, the pollsters were proved right. The voter turnout was a phenomenal eighty per cent, and the sitting government won by a landslide. Only two Opposition candidates won seats. A majority was declared less than an hour after the polls closed.

Now, holding out her wine glass for a topping up, Pat interrupted Mercy's reverie with a question. "Whatever happened to that big story you were working on before Chaz...you know. Political, you said."

"Oh. Well, it didn't really go anywhere."

"Ah."

Mercy turned to find Toby coming around the corner of the house, smiling and waving a large bottle of Scotch. And right behind him was Jinxy, armed with a box of chocolate eclairs he claimed to have made himself.

"Welcome, guys," she said, and waved them to the table to meet the few they didn't know. Toby sat beside Pat and within minutes they were deep into a discussion about border collies.

"Hey, Mercy," Pat called. "Toby's related to that farmer who donated the cow carcass for my postmortem seminar."

A couple of minutes later Toby caught Mercy's eye and motioned toward the back door. When he got up she saw that he wanted her to follow. He stopped at the door, out of hearing range of the others.

"Got something interesting to tell you," he said.

She nodded and waited.

"Remember that money, the slush fund you told me about?"

"How could I forget? The loose end. Still don't know what the Party planned to do with that money."

"I think my cousin Graeme finally got the facts."

"Are you kidding me, Toby? I'm dying to hear this."

They went inside, sat on the couch, and he unzipped his hoodie. Mercy thought he might be giving her a document, but he was just getting comfortable.

"Nothing on paper," he said. "But here goes. Those guys who work at Haymarket Creamery, the ones who wanted a union? As soon as the government won, right then, on election night, they suddenly wanted to talk. No more secrets. They were steamed, really angry, whining to anybody who would listen. Said they'd been cheated. Promises broken. Not by the politicians." Toby chuckled. "We know the government didn't make a single promise. No, the workers' target was the plant owner."

"The one who wanted money to expand?" Mercy tried to remember. "I don't even know his name. He was only in the news once, I think. When he didn't get the grant and threatened to shut down."

"Well, that's it. He was really mad at the government at the time. And he ranted about it to the workers. Wasn't his fault, he said. It was the damned government. So they all agreed that when the election came they'd vote for the Opposition. Punishment. They knew the results could hinge on the vote in that one district because it was so close last time.

"But then, the plant owner decided to go a step further. He got some of the workers to sign a pledge. Got dozens of names. Then he went to Puck, demanded money again for his expansion and revealed his fool-proof plan to ensure the election win.

"Get this, Mercy. He wasn't buying votes, he said. Fifty workers just wouldn't show up at the polls. They'd come down with the flu on election day. Fifty votes that *wouldn't* go to the Opposition. In that crucial district it could guarantee a government win." Toby's face was now slick with the effort to keep the story on track. He stopped and took off his sweater.

"Go on, Toby. Is there more?"

"Apparently the government liked the idea. But the plant owner wanted the money *before* the election and under the table. Refused to take a chance that once re-elected the government might not pay up."

Mercy felt a rising excitement. The conversation on

the tape that Danny got at Puck's house now made sense. The other man must have been the plant owner. And the "fix" was what Toby had just described. Elspeth Hoodles was the holdout. It had been a lot of money, but the owner would take a sizeable amount off the top for himself. And would the rest go to the fifty names on the pledge? Still a lot of money to buy fifty votes. But seen from Puck's angle, worth an election win.

"Here's the part I like best," Toby said. "The workers expected cash in exchange for staying home, but the plant owner was afraid it would look like he was paying people *not* to vote. So here's what he would do: he'd declare a summer worker's bonus, as a celebration that the plant had supposedly won a big new ice cream contract. Each of the fifty workers who had signed the pledge would get a trip to an NHL final game of their choice in June. It would appear on his books as a perk. No cash involved."

Mercy remembered what Graeme Cox had seen on the union man's clipboard. Ice Cream Flu. Code words for the pledge. And she'd found a use for those words herself by throwing them out at Fred Fredericks to convince him she knew what the slush fund was for.

"Clever, don't you think?" Toby said.

It *was* clever, Mercy had to admit. And it might have worked. But as soon as the slush fund money went toward the homeless shelter, the deal with Haymarket Creamery fell apart. It would have been a terrific story. But even a good journalist couldn't make a news story out of something that didn't happen. And the irony was that the government was re-elected anyway.

Mercy thanked Toby, gave him an affectionate hug, and they went out to rejoin the group at the table. The unopened bottle of Scotch was left as a centrepiece, with an agreement to save it for the next time they all got together.

Nobody seemed surprised that Jon didn't leave the party with the rest.

At the door, Skim hung back a little.

"Maybe not the time to say it, Mercy, but..." He kept his voice low. "Hope we might be able to help each other out again, sometime. I know you're smart and all that. But I hear things that are outside your...lifestyle, like. Stuff you could maybe use in your job."

"Skim, I don't expect anything more from you. I already owe you more than—"

"Never mind that. Just offering."

"We're friends now, aren't we?" She put a hand on his arm on the way to the door. "I'd like to stay in touch whether you've got anything to tell me or not."

"Great." He walked to Luc's car, strutting a little.

Jon helped bring in the dishes and poured her more wine. They sat on the couch. She was quiet.

"Counting your blessings?" he asked.

"Sure. I'm alive, I have my job back, and the boss is eating out of my hand."

"And we got Chaz through the system with a minimum of paperwork. That's the blessing I'm counting." He was looking as relaxed as she'd ever seen him.

"I have to admit something, Jon. I really thought you were doing zero on Elspeth's assault case. Are you ever going to let me in on your clever investigating methods? "

"Not used to explaining after the fact. Brenda never wanted to know anything about the job."

"But I do."

He treated her to a warm smile. "I should have known. No secrets are safe from you." Then he laughed and moved a little closer on the couch. "Okay. Well, from the start I was more interested in the explosion and Danny. Remember that first argument we had? I said we figured Danny for a blackmailer looking for a chance? Well, when a blackmailer dies, 'accidental death' just doesn't sit right. I had a theory from the time I saw Chaz's first news report about the explosion."

"Why Chaz, though?"

"Those pictures in his report, taken from the top of the parkade. Danny could be seen from there once the smoke cleared. Then I found out Chaz's cameraman was sent off to get shots of the evacuation. So Chaz had the opportunity. And then when Skim showed up at the station and said he had an idea whose car took you away, we had enough to bring Chaz in. Without you going into that room, though, it would have been a long haul to nail him. You were amazing in there. But I'm not proud of putting you through it. I took advantage of your enthusiasm."

In his office he had held her until she stopped shaking, rocking her gently, whispering into her hair, "I'm sorry, Mercy. Mercy, I'm sorry. It's over. You're okay."

Now, here in the privacy of her little house, she wasn't thinking about what Jon had done, only about her own shabby manoeuvring in pursuit of a story to save her job, a side of her character she hoped he would never see. He reached and took her hand, turned it over and traced the lines on the palm.

"I see something in your future. Not far off, either. Tonight even?" Then he laughed. "Or should I wait for a sign, like the first time?"

Just as she was thinking that climbing into his lap might be a good start, the impulse was cut off by the ringing of his cellphone. He answered, but kept his eyes on her.

"How long ago? Serious? Well, you don't need me for that. Anyway, I've got an important personal situation to take care of tonight. No. But thanks for the offer." He was grinning at Mercy. "I think I can handle it."

Acknowledgements

An early draft of this story benefitted greatly from the feedback of novelist Susan Haley. And special thanks to former colleague Tom Murphy whose knowledge of the latest technical developments in television news gathering helped me decide to set this novel closer to the turn of the new millennium. Thanks also to my writerly friends Jackie, Vivien, Peggy, and Marcia for their unfailing encouragement. And I must also thank my dear pal Jane Schlosberg for asking regularly when I planned to send the manuscript out. But I'm especially grateful to my brilliant editor, Marianne Ward, who did a lot of the heavy lifting and whose talents are truly exceptional.